NEW GEPT

新制全民英檢
中級
聽力測驗必考題型

陳頎／著
國際語言中心委員會／監修

全書 MP3 一次下載

9789864541485.zip

「iOS 系統請升級至 iOS 13後再行下載，
此為大型檔案，建議使用 WIFI 連線下載，以免佔用流量，
並確認連線狀況，以利下載順暢。」

CONTENTS 目錄

CONTENTS 目錄

情境主題 ①1 On the Telephone （打電話）

Hint 常考句子

 情境解析

可能情境包括：借電話、講手機、打電話預約、打電話邀約、向查號台查電話等。

1 Hello. May I speak to George?
你好，我要找 George。

2 Where is the nearest public phone?
最近的公共電話在哪？

3 Do you have a cell phone?
你有手機嗎？

模擬試題

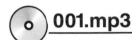 **001.mp3**

第一部分 看圖辨義

 作答說明 試題冊上有數幅圖畫，每一圖畫有 1~3 個描述該圖的題目，每題請聽光碟放音機播出題目以及四個英語敘述之後，選出與所看到的圖畫最相符的答案，每題只播出一遍。

Picture A Q1 ～ Q2

答案欄

Picture B Q3

答案欄

Dr. Li
☎ 2337-4341

John
☎ 2377-4134

Mr. Wang
☎ 3237-1443

Picture C Q4 ～ Q5

答案欄

out of order

第二部分 問答

 作答說明 每題請聽光碟放音機播出一英語問句或直述句後，從試題冊上 A、B、C、D 四個回答或回應中，選出一個最適合者作答。每題只播出一遍。

 Q 1

(A) Yes, sir. May I help you, too?

(B) I'd like to have an arrangement for my summer trip.

 答案欄

(C) Yes, who's calling please?

(D) Yes, I can do you a favor.

 Q 2

(A) Yes, I'd like the number of Jasmine.

(B) Yes, is that 222-5397?

(C) Show me your phone number directly.

 答案欄

(D) Sorry, I have little time.

 Q 3

(A) No, you are on another line.

(B) All right, let's do it now.

(C) Certainly, call me at five when I'm back.

 答案欄

(D) Of course, and hold on, please.

第三部分 簡短對話

作答說明 每題請聽光碟放音機播出一段對話及一個相關的問題之後，從試題冊上 A、B、C、D 四個選項中選出一個最適合者作答。每段對話及問題只播出一遍。

Conversation 1

Q 1

答案欄

(A) He is going to fix a car.

(B) They will have a meeting when he gets back.

(C) He needn't go to the meeting since it's been canceled.

(D) He has to buy a new car.

Conversation 2 新題型

Q 2

Company directory	
Department	Extension
Administration	601
Sales	501
Human Resources	520
Accounting	390

答案欄

(A) 601

(B) 501

(C) 520

(D) 390

第四部分 簡短談話 新題型

作答說明 每題請聽光碟放音機播出一段談話及一個相關的問題後，從試題冊上 A、B、C、D 四個選項中選出一個最適合者作答。每段談話及問題只播出一遍。

Short Talk 1

Q 1

(A) The customer can talk to the customer service.

(B) The customer can order something.

(C) The customer can get information about how to get their money back.

(D) The customer can have extra discounts.

Short Talk 2

Q 2

Telephone Etiquette Key Points
You should avoid :
1. Talk too loud
2. Talk with a full mouth
3. Talk too long in the public place
4. Talk some bad words

(A) Talk too loud.

(B) Talk with a full mouth

(C) Talk too long in the public place

(D) Talk some bad words.

答案解析

 第一部分 看圖辨義

 提示 **For questions number 1 and 2, please look at picture A.**
問題 1 跟問題 2 請看圖片 A。

Q1 　C　 Why can't Susan answer the phone?
為何 Susan 不能接電話。

(A) Because she is busy cooking. 因為她正忙著煮飯。
(B) Because the phone is out of order. 因為這個電話壞了。
(C) Because she is taking a shower. 因為她正在淋浴。
(D) Because it's too late to pick up the phone.
因為她接電話接的太晚了。

Q2 　B　 What's the time? 現在幾點？

(A) It's ten past ten. 十點過十分。
(B) It's thirty-five past ten. 十點過三十五分。
(C) It's ten fifty-three. 十點五十三分。
(D) It's twenty-five to ten. 還有二十五分到十點。

提示 **For question number 3, please look at picture B.**
問題 3 請看圖片 B。

Q3 　C　 What's Mr. Wang's phone number?
王先生的電話是幾號？

(A) It's 2377-4134. 是 2377-4134。
(B) It's 3237-1434. 是 3237-1434。
(C) It's 3237-1443. 是 3237-1443。
(D) It's 2337-4341. 是 2337-4341。

提示 **For questions number 4 and 5, please look at picture C.**
問題 4 跟問題 5 請看圖片 C。

Q4 　A　 What description matches the picture C?
哪一個敘述符合圖片 C？

(A) Charles can't make a phone call because the public phone is broken.
Charles 不能打電話因為公共電話壞了。

(B) Charles can't make a phone call because he has no change.
Charles 不能打電話因為他沒有零錢。

(C) Charles can't make a phone call because he can't find any phone nearby.
Charles 不能打電話因為他在附近找不到電話。

(D) Charles doesn't want to make a phone call at all.
Charles 根本不想打電話。

Q5　　A　**What's Charles wearing today?**
Charles 今天穿什麼？

(A) He's wearing a shirt, pants and shoes.
他穿襯衫、長褲與鞋子。

(B) He's wearing shorts, a T-shirt and sneakers.
他穿短褲、T 恤與球鞋。

(C) He's wearing a dress, a skirt and sandals.
他穿洋裝、裙子與涼鞋。

(D) He's wearing a shirt, a tie and slacks.
他穿襯衫、繫著領帶與穿著長褲。

第二部分　問答

Q1　　B　**Hello, this is M4 travel agency, may I help you?** 這是 M4 旅行社，有什麼我可以幫忙的嗎？

(A) Yes, sir. May I help you, too?
是的，先生。我也可以幫你嗎？

(B) I'd like to have an arrangement for my summer trip.
我想要安排我的暑期旅遊。

(C) Yes, who's calling please? 是的，請問哪裡找？

(D) Yes, I can do you a favor. 是的，我可以幫你。

單字解釋 ▶ travel agency 旅行社
have an arrangement 是「安排」的意思。

試題分析 ▶ 本題問：這裡是 M4 旅行社，有什麼可以效勞的嗎。可知答案為選項 B：我想對我暑期的旅遊做安排。本題考的是電話常用語，may I help you? 通常是詢問是否有需要幫助，回答應與其相關。I'd like to...通常是最有可能的答案。

Q2 ___A___ **Directory Assistance. May I help you?**
查號台，我可以為你服務嗎？
(A) Yes, I'd like the number of Jasmine.
是的，我要 Jasmine 的電話。
(B) Yes, is that 222-5397?
是的，那是 222-5397 嗎？
(C) Show me your phone number directly.
直接告訴我你的電話。
(D) Sorry, I have little time. 抱歉，我沒有時間。

單字解釋 ▶ directory assistance 查號台
directly 此處指「直接」。

試題分析 ▶ 本題問：查號台，有什麼我可以協助的。可知答案為選項 (A) 我要 Jasmine 的電話號碼。

Q3 ___C___ **Sorry, got to go. May I call back later?**
抱歉，我必須走了。我可以待會回電嗎？
(A) No, you are on another line.
不，你在另一線（電話）上。
(B) All right, let's do it now.
好的，我們現在做吧。
(C) Certainly. Then call me at five when I'm back.
當然。那麼我 5 點回來時再來電。
(D) Of course, and hold on, please. 當然，請等一下。

單字解釋 ▶ got to go 要走了
certainly 當然

試題分析 ▶ 本題問：抱歉，我必須要走了，我可以待會再回電嗎，表示準備掛電話，並提示自己晚點再撥。可知答案為選項 (C) 當然，我 5 點回來時再回電給我。

Conversation 1

W: Hello?

M: Hello, May? This is Ted. Is Davy there?

W: No, he is out for fixing his car. Shall I have him call you when he comes back?

M: No, that's OK. I just want to tell him today's meeting has been cancelled.

W: OK, I'll tell him when he gets back.

中文翻譯

女：喂？

男：喂，是 May 嗎？我是 Ted。請問 Davy 在嗎？

女：不，他外出修車了。他回來時我要叫他回電給你嗎？

男：不，沒關係。我只是要告訴他今天的會議取消了。

女：好的，他回來時我會跟他說的。

Q1 ___C___ **What will the woman tell Davy?**

女子將會告訴 Davy 什麼？

(A) He is going to fix a car.

他將去修車。

(B) They will have a meeting when he gets back.

當他回來時他們將有一個會議。

(C) He needn't go to the meeting since it's been canceled.

他不需要參加會議因為會議已經取消。

(D) He has to buy a new car. 他必須要買一輛新車。

單字解釋 ▶ cancel **v** 取消

試題分析 ▶ 本題問：女子要告訴 Davy 什麼。從對話中男子提醒的 I... tell him [Davy] today's meeting ... cancelled. 可知答案為選項 (C) 他不需參加會議。

Conversation 2

Company directory

Department	Extension
Administration	601
Sales	501
Human Resources	520
Accounting	390

W: Operator, how may I help you?

M: Hi, This is Hank Smith. I am calling for your job opening. I am interested in your job offer, a junior accountant in the accounting department. And I have already sent my resume with two references as you request. I am wondering if you have gotten them.

W: You should contact our personnel manager. He is in charge of recruitments and interview work. Let me put you through to his extension.

中文翻譯

公司通訊錄

部門	分機
行政部門	601
銷售部門	501
人資部門	520
會計部門	390

女：總機，有什麼我可以效勞的嗎？

男：你好，我是 Hank Smith，我來電是要問你們職缺。我對你們的工作機會感興趣，也就是會計部門的會計人員一職。我已經照你們的要求寄上履歷與兩封推薦信。我在想你們是否有收到？

女：你應該要聯絡我們的人事部經理，是由他來負責招募以及面試的工作。我來幫你轉到他的分機號碼。

Q2 ___C___ **What extension will the man be connected to?** 男子會被轉到哪一支分機？

(A) 601. 601 分機。

(B) 501. 501 分機。

(C) 520. 520 分機。

(D) 390. 390 分機。

單字解釋 ▶ job opening / job offer **n** 工作機會　resume **n** 履歷表
reference **n** 推薦函　recruitment **n** 招募
extension **n** 分機　in charge of 負責
put sb. through to 轉接至…

試題分析 ▶ 本題問：男子會被轉到哪一支分機。在對話中聽到 You should contact our personnel manager. He is in charge of recruitments and interview work. 表示「你（男子）應該要聯絡人事部經理。而人事部經理(personnel manager)所工作的部門，就是人資部，因此答案選 C。

第四部分 簡短談話

Short Talk 1

Thanks for calling Office Helper hotline. We are here to serve you every day from 8:00AM to 5:30PM. To place an order, please press 1. To hear our refund policy, please press 2. To talk to our customer service, please stay on the line.

中文翻譯

謝謝您來電 Office Helper 熱線。我們每天早上八點到下午五點半為您服務。若要訂貨，請按一。要聽退款辦法，請按二。要洽詢客服人員，請在線上稍候。

Q1   **C**   **What happens if a customer presses 2?**

如果顧客按二會怎樣？

(A) The customer can talk to the customer service.

顧客可以和客服人員對談。

(B) The customer can order something.

顧客可以訂貨。

(C) The customer can get information about how to get their money back.

顧客可以得知如何把錢要回的資訊。

(D) The customer can have extra discounts.

顧客可享有額外折扣。

單字解釋 ▶ place an order 下訂　refund policy **n** 退款政策

customer service **n** 客服人員

試題分析 ▶ 本題問：若顧客按二會發生什麼情形。在談話中得知 To hear our refund policy, please press 2.，表示要聽退款辦法，請按二，也就是要把他們的錢要回，故答案要選 C。

Short Talk 2

Telephone Etiquette Key Points

You should avoid :
1. Talk too loud
2. Talk with a full mouth
3. Talk too long in the public place
4. Talk some bad words

These days, people are always talking on the phone. That's why telephone manners are even more important today. You can follow some tips to help you get a good impression from other people. First, your telephone voice should be natural calm and clear. Second, you should never eat, drink or chew gum while you are on the phone. Lastly, don't talk too loud or too long in the public place.

 中文翻譯

電話禮儀重點

你應該避免：
1. 講太大聲
2. 說話時滿嘴都是東西
3. 在公眾場合講話講太久
4. 說不雅的文字

現今，人們總是會講電話。這就是為何電話禮儀越來越重要的原因。你可以藉由遵照一些技巧來獲得他人的良好印象。首先，講電話的聲音要自然、平靜以及清晰。第二，當你在講電話時，絕對不可以吃東西、喝東西或嚼口香糖。最後，在公眾場合說話不宜太大聲與太久。

Q2 ___D___ **Which point in the listing is NOT mentioned in this talk?**

這段談話中，以上清單的哪一項沒有被提到？

(A) Talk too loud.

講太大聲。

(B) Talk with a full mouth.

說話時滿嘴都是東西。

(C) Talk too long in the public place.

在公眾場合講話講太久。

(D) Talk some bad words.

說不雅文字。

單字解釋 ▶ etiquette **n** 禮節　calm **adj** 平靜的
public place **n** 公眾場合

試題分析 ▶ 本題問：這段談話中，沒有提到以上清單中的哪一項。在談話中得知 First, your telephone voice should be natural calm and clear... never eat, drink or chew gum 以及 don't talk too loud or too long in the public place.，表示講電話時要自然、平靜、清晰，絕對不可以吃喝東西或嚼口香糖，以及在公眾場合說話不宜太大聲與太久。全文沒提到 bad words 不雅文字，故答案要選 D。

情境
主題 **02** # Visiting & Greeting
拜訪和問候

可能情境包括：拜訪親戚、與朋友見面、新同事互相介紹、拜訪客戶等。

1 Hi, it's been a long time. How have you been?　已經過好一段時間了，你最近好嗎？

2 Mr. Wang, let me introduce Mr. Chen to you.　王先生，讓我介紹陳先生給你認識。

3 I want to meet you next Sunday.
我想在下星期天與你見面。

模擬試題

 **002.mp3**

第一部分 **看圖辨義**

 試題冊上有數幅圖畫，每一圖畫有 1~3 個描述該圖的題目，每題請聽光碟放音機播出題目以及四個英語敘述之後，選出與所看到的圖畫最相符的答案，每題只播出一遍。

Picture A   Q1 ～ Q2

Mon.	visit Tin and his family
Tue.	visit Tina and her mother
Wed.	take a class
Thu.	
Fri.	
Sat.	visit Tommy
Sun.	free time

答案欄

Picture B   Q3

Nice to meet you

Dan   **Tina**   **Sue**

答案欄

Picture C   Q4 ～ Q5

Robert

答案欄

第二部分 **問答**

每題請聽光碟放音機播出一英語問句或直述句後，從試題冊上 A、B、C、D 四個回答或回應中，選出一個最適合者作答。每題 只播出一遍。

Q 1

(A) I'm going home.

(B) Very good. How about you?

答案欄

(C) I'm tall and handsome.

(D) I always go to school by bus.

Q 2

(A) Sure, let's go shopping.

(B) I don't think so. I have lots of homework, which hasn't been finished.

答案欄

(C) I'm not visiting your uncle, either.

(D) No one will visit the Chen family.

Q 3

(A) I made a table myself.

(B) I can't believe it. Someone stole my car.

答案欄

(C) I'm mad, so I don't want to do it.

(D) I heard that you were in the bad mood.

第三部分 簡短對話

作答說明 每題請聽光碟放音機播出一段對話及一個相關的問題之後，從試題冊上 A、B、C、D 四個選項中選出一個最適合者作答。每段對話及問題只播出一遍。

Conversation 1

Q1

(A) She feels very cold now.

(B) She is in the hospital.

(C) She is sick.

(D) She looks ugly.

答案欄

Conversation 2 新題型

Q2

House Rent From 2017 to 2020	
Year	Rent
2017	$35,000/month
2018	$40,000/month
2019	$45,000/month
2020	$55,000/month

(A) 35,000/month

(B) 40,000/month

(C) 45,000/month

(D) 55,000/month

答案欄

第四部分 簡短談話 新題型

 作答說明 每題請聽光碟放音機播出一段談話及一個相關的問題後，從試題冊上 A、B、C、D 四個選項中選出一個最適合者作答。每段談話及問題只播出一遍。

Short Talk 1

Q 1

 答案欄

(A) He wanted to introduce Mr. Jackson to other students.

(B) He wanted to greet his students.

(C) He wanted to sell some textbooks.

(D) He wanted to turn down some students.

Short Talk 2

Q 2

A	B	C	D
Kevin Kim **1963~2020** **Died** **peacefully** **At age 68**	**Wanted** **Experienced** **editor** **Good pay**	**Good deal** **A used car** **nice quality** **reasonable** **price**	**Good** **medicine** **for** **Heart Attack** **Save your life**

 答案欄

(A) A.

(B) B.

(C) C.

(D) D.

答案解析

第一部分 看圖辨義

 For questions number 1 and 2, please look at picture A.
問題 1 跟問題 2 請看圖片 A。

Q1 ___D___ **Who may be visited on Monday?**
誰在週一可能會被拜訪？

(A) Tommy may be visited. Tommy 可能被拜訪。
(B) Tina and Tim may be visited. Tina 與 Tim 可能被拜訪。
(C) The man may visit Tina and her mother on Monday.
男子可能在週一拜訪 Tina 與她的母親。
(D) The man may visit Tim and his family on Monday.
男子可能在週一拜訪 Tim 與她的家人。

Q2 ___D___ **Is the man going to do anything on Sunday?** 男子將在週日做什麼事嗎？

(A) Yes, he's going to visit Tina. 是的，他將去拜訪 Tina。
(B) No, he's going to take an English class.
不，他將去上英文課。
(C) Yes, he's going to meet his family.
是的，他將去拜訪他的家人。
(D) No, he's not going to do anything on Sunday.
不，他在週日將不做任何的事情。

 For question number 3, please look at picture B.
問題 3 請看圖片 B。

Q3 ___A___ **Which statement is correct?** 哪一個敘述是正確的？

(A) Tina is introducing Dan to Sue.
Tina 正介紹 Dan 給 Sue 認識。
(B) Dan is introducing Tina to Sue.
Dan 將介紹 Tina 給 Sue 認識。
(C) Sue is introducing Dan to Tina.
Sue 正介紹 Dan 給 Tina 認識。
(D) They are arguing with one another.
他們彼此正在爭執。

For questions number 4 and 5, please look at picture C.
問題 4 跟問題 5 請看圖片 C。

Q4 ___D___ **What did Robert do at 3:00 pm?**
Robert 在下午 3:00 做了什麼？

(A) He rang the bell and a woman opened the door.
他按了門鈴，一位女子開門。

(B) He made a phone call, but nobody was at home.
他打電話，但是沒有人在家。

(C) He talked with a woman. 他與一位女士說話。

(D) He rang the bell but nobody opened the door.
他按了門鈴但是沒有人應門。

Q5 ___B___ **Which description doesn't match the picture C?** 哪一個描述不符合圖片 C？

(A) There are some flowers in the yard. 有一些花在院子。

(B) The woman is home at 3:00 pm. 女子下午 3:00 在家。

(C) Robert wants to visit the woman. Robert 想要拜訪女子。

(D) There's a dog in the woman's house.
在女子家有一隻狗。

第二部分 問答

Q1 ___B___ **Jason, how's it going?** Jason，你好嗎？
(A) I'm going home. 我正要回家。
(B) Very good. How about you? 很好，那你呢？
(C) I'm tall and handsome. 我又高又帥。
(D) I always go to school by bus. 我總是搭公車上學。

單字解釋 ▶ How is it going? 你好嗎？　　　　handsome **adj** 英俊的

試題分析 ▶ 本題問：「Jason，你好嗎」。其中 how's it going 的意思，與 how are you? 及 How are you doing? 的用法是一樣的，故答案為選項 (B)。本題 how's it going? 常會使人誤解是問「交通工具」或「方式」的問句。選項 (C) 及選項 (D)都是故意讓人混淆的答案。

Q2 **B** **I'm visiting Uncle Chen this afternoon. Are you coming with me?**

我今天下午要去拜訪陳叔叔，你要跟我一起來嗎？

(A) Sure, let's go shopping. 當然，我們一起去購物吧！

(B) I don't think so. I have lots of homework, which hasn't been finished.

我不這麼想，我還有許多未完成的功課。

(C) I'm not visiting your uncle, either.

我也沒有要拜訪你的叔叔。

(D) No one will visit the Chen family.

沒有人將要拜訪陳家人。

單字解釋 ▶ uncle **n** 叔叔，伯伯

試題分析 ▶ 本題問：「我下午要去看陳叔叔，你要一起來嗎」。可知答案為選項 (B)。這裡 which 引導的子句用法為形容詞子句。

Q3 **B** **Jacob, what's the matter with you? You look very furious.** Jacob 你怎麼了？你看起來很生氣。

(A) I made a table myself. 我自己擺碗筷。

(B) I can't believe it. Somcone stole my car.

我不敢相信，有人偷了我的車！

(C) I'm mad, so I don't want to do it.

我十分生氣，所以我不想做這事。

(D) I hcard that you were in the bad mood.

我聽說你的心情不好。

單字解釋 ▶ matter **n** 事情   furious **adj** 發怒的

stole **v** 偷（現在式 steal）   in the bad mood 心情糟

試題分析 ▶ 本題問：「Jacob，你怎麼了，你看起來很生氣」。可知答案為選項 (B)。

第三部分 簡短對話

Conversation 1

W: Maria doesn't look good. Is she OK?
M: No, she has a terrible cold.
W: That's too bad.
M: I think she is OK. She's been to a doctor, and she took some medicine as well.

中文翻譯

女：Maria 看起來不好。她還好嗎？
男：不，她重感冒。
女：實在太糟了。
男：我想她還好。她已經去看過醫師了，而且她也吃了一些藥。

Q1 ___C___ **What happened to Maria?**

Maria 怎麼了？

(A) She feels very cold now.
她現在覺得很冷。

(B) She is in the hospital.
她現在在醫院

(C) She is sick.
她感冒了。

(D) She looks ugly.
她看起來很醜。

單字解釋 ▶ medicine 藥 n

試題分析 ▶ 本題問：Maria 怎麼了。可知答案為選項 (C)：她生病了。

Conversation 2

House Rent From 2017 to 2020	
Year	Rent
2017	$35,000/month
2018	$40,000/month
2019	$45,000/month
2020	$55,000/month

W: Bob!

M: Rita! I can't believe it's you! We haven't seen each other for quite a while. How have you been doing?

W: Same old, same old. How about you? Are you still having your own grocery store?

M: No, I haven't owned my own business since January 1st, 2019. I closed my store because of the constantly increasing rent.

W: Life is indeed more and more difficult. Are you in a hurry or something? Why not have some coffee in that cute café and have a nice chat?

M: Sure!

 中文翻譯

2017 年到 2020 年房租變化	
年份	房租金額
2017	$35,000/月
2018	$40,000/月
2019	$45,000/月
2020	$55,000/月

女：Bob！

男：Rita！我真不敢相信是你！我們有好一陣子沒見到彼此了。你最近好嗎？

女：老樣子，老樣子，那你呢？你還在開雜貨店嗎？

男：不，我從 2019 年 1 月 1 日起就不再經營雜貨店了。我關店的原因是不斷上漲的房租。

女：生活的確是越來越困難了。你現在要去忙什麼嗎，我們何不去那家可愛的咖啡廳喝點咖啡，來好好聊一下天。

男：好呀！

Q2　B　How much was Bob's last rent for his store?

Bob 最後一次付的店租是多少？

(A) 35,000/month.

　　一個月 3 萬 5 千元。

(B) 40,000/month.

　　一個月 4 萬元。

(C) 45,000/month.

　　一個月 4 萬 5 千元。

(D) 55,000/month.

　　一個月 5 萬 5 千元。

單字解釋 ▶　for quite a while 好長的一段時間　　same old 老樣子

grocery store **n** 雜貨店　　constantly **adv** 不斷地

in a hurry 匆忙

have a nice chat 好好聊一聊

試題分析 ▶　本題問：Bob 最後一次付的店租是多少。在對話中提到 No, I haven't owned my own business since January 1st, 2019.，表示 Bob 從 2019 年 1 月 1 日起就不再開雜貨店了。換句話說，2018 年的 12 月就是最後一筆的房租費用，一個月 4 萬元，因此答案選 B。

第四部分 簡短談話

Short Talk 1

Good morning, class. Welcome to this course—Introduction to Economics. I am Professor Jackson, and I am so happy to meet all of you, my dear students. OK, let's start for today's lesson. Please open your textbook and turn to page seven.

中文翻譯

同學早，歡迎來到這堂經濟學導論的課程。我是傑克森教授，我很高興來和所有親愛的同學們見面。好的，我們開始上今天的課程吧。請打開教科書，並翻到第七頁。

Q1 __B__ **Why did the professor give this talk?**

為何教授做這段談話？

(A) He wanted to introduce Mr. Jackson to other students. 他想要介紹傑克森先生給其他同學認識。

(B) He wanted to greet his students.
他想要問候他的學生。

(C) He wanted to sell some textbooks.
他想要賣一些教科書。

(D) He wanted to turn down some students.
他想要拒絕一些學生。

單字解釋 ▶ Economics **n** 經濟學　　　　professor **n** 教授
textbook **n** 教科書　　　　turn down **v** 拒絕

試題分析 ▶ 本題問：為何教授做這段的談話。在談話中提到 I am Professor Jackson, and I am so happy to meet all of you, my dear students. 表示自己是傑克森教授，很高興與自己的學生見面。也就是在問候他的學生們，故答案要選 B。

A	B	C	D
Kevin Kim 1963~2020 Died peacefully At age 68	Wanted Experienced editor Good pay	Good deal A used car nice quality reasonable price	Good medicine for Heart Attack Save your life

Hi, Sherry. I am sorry to hear that your husband passed away several days ago because of the heart attack. I can understand how depressed you are at this moment because you love each other so much. As your best friend, I'd like to do something to help you go through this difficult time. I want you to know I'm always by your side. Let me write an article for your husband since I work at the newspaper. I have experience and certainly know how to write it right.

中文翻譯

A	B	C	D
凱文‧金 1963~2020 安詳離世 享年六十八歲	徵才 有經驗的編輯 薪資佳	划算的交易 二手車 品質佳 價格合理	良藥 針對心臟病人士 拯救你的生命

哈囉，雪莉。我很難過聽說你的丈夫在幾天前因為心臟病而過世。我可以理解此時你是多麼的沮喪，因為你們是如此地相愛。身為你最好的朋友，我想做一些事情來幫助你度過這個難關。我想要你知道我永遠都在你身邊。讓我來幫你丈夫寫一篇文章，因為我本身在報社工作。我有經驗，也知道要如何正確地撰寫。

Q2 ___A___ **Look at the graphics. Which one would be written by Sherry's best friend?**

請看圖表，哪一項是雪莉最好朋友所寫的？

(A) A.
A 項。

(B) B.
B 項。

(C) C.
C 項。

(D) D.
D 項。

單字解釋 ▶ pass away 死去　　　　　　heart attack **n** 心臟病

試題分析 ▶ 本題問：圖表中哪一項是雪莉最好朋友所寫的。在談話的一開始提到 your husband passed away，以及最後一句 Let me write an article for your husband since I work at the newspaper.。由此可知雪莉的丈夫過世，而她的好友要幫她寫篇文章，故答案要選 A。

情境主題 (03) Eats & Drinks
（飲食）

Hint 常考句子

情境解析　可能情境包括：食物、喝飲料、與朋友聚餐等。

1 Do you want to go for a bite?
你想出去吃點東西嗎？

2 I like Chinese food so much.
我很喜歡中式料理。

3 I'll have a big dinner next Sunday.
我下星期天將吃大餐。

4 What is today's special?
今天的特餐是什麼？

5 For here or to go?
在這裡吃還是帶走？

6 Let's go Dutch, shall we?
我們分開付帳，如何？

7 Would you like some coffee or tea?
你要喝一些咖啡或茶嗎？

模擬試題

003.mp3

第一部分　看圖辨義

作答說明

試題冊上有數幅圖畫，每一圖畫有 1~3 個描述該圖的題目，每題
請聽光碟放音機播出題目以及四個英語敘述之後，選出與所看到
的圖畫最相符的答案，每題只播出一遍。

Picture A　Q1 ～ Q3

Picture B　Q4 ～ Q5

每題請聽光碟放音機播出一英語問句或直述句後，從試題冊上
A、B、C、D 四個回答或回應中，選出一個最適合者作答。每題
作答說明 只播出一遍。

 Q 1

(A) Yes, sir. May I help you?

(B) So am I.

 答案欄

(C) I couldn't agree with you.

(D) Yes, the restaurant is full of people.

 Q 2

(A) Yes, don't you like it, either?

(B) Thai food is my second choice.

 答案欄

(C) I haven't been to Thailand.

(D) I like Italian food so much.

 Q 3

(A) That's a good idea. I want to have a vacation.

(B) Sure. I am so hungry that I can eat a horse.

答案欄

(C) Let's go bowling together.

(D) Do you need to serve the guests?

第三部分 **簡短對話**

每題請聽光碟放音機播出一段對話及一個相關的問題之後，從試題冊上 A、B、C、D 四個選項中選出一個最適合者作答。每段對話及問題只播出一遍。

Conversation 1

(A) Drink a cup of milk tea.

(B) Drink a cup of coffee with sugar and milk.

(C) Drink a cup of coffee without sugar and milk.

(D) Drink a cup of lemonade.

答案欄

Conversation 2

Taiwan Snacks	
Beef Noodles Soup	$180
Stinky Tofu	$60
Pig Blood Cake	$45
Dumplings	$6 /per

(A) $105.

(B) $120.

(C) $ 240.

(D) $ 225.

答案欄

作答說明　每題請聽光碟放音機播出一段談話及一個相關的問題後，從試題冊上 A、B、C、D 四個選項中選出一個最適合者作答。每段談話及問題只播出一遍。

Short Talk 1

Q 1

(A) Cheese.

(B) Bacon.

(C) Ham.

(D) Peppers and onions.

答案欄

Short Talk 2

Q 2

Ingredients listing
You need :   Flour/Sugar/Honey/Baking soda   Raisins/Apples/Bananas/Oranges

(A) Flour.

(B) Apples.

(C) Bananas.

(D) Raisins.

答案欄

答案解析

第一部分 看圖辨義

 For questions number 1, 2 and 3, please look at picture A.
問題 1、2 跟問題 3 請看圖片 A。

Q1 ___A___ **Which floor is the fast food restaurant on?**
速食店在幾樓？

(A) The first floor. 1 樓。
(B) The second floor. 2 樓。
(C) The third floor. 3 樓。
(D) The fourth floor. 4 樓。

Q2 ___B___ **How many stories are there in this building?**
這棟大樓有幾層樓？

(A) 5. 五層。
(B) 4. 四層。
(C) 3. 三層。
(D) 2. 兩層。

Q3 ___C___ **Which description doesn't match the picture A?** 哪一個敘述不符合圖片 A？

(A) If you want to have Japanese food, you have to go to the second floor. 假如你想要吃日本料理，你必須去 2 樓。
(B) There's no Chinese food restaurant in this building. 這大樓沒有中式餐廳
(C) We can't eat steak in this building. 我們無法在這棟大樓裡吃牛排。
(D) French food restaurant is on the fourth floor. 法式料理是在 4 樓。

 For questions number 4 and 5, please look at picture B.
問題 4 跟問題 5 請看圖片 B。

Q4 ___B___ **What's James doing?**
James 正在做什麼？

(A) He is cooking a big dinner. 他正在煮一頓豐盛的晚餐。
(B) He is enjoying his dinnertime. 他正享受他的晚餐。
(C) He is working until midnight. 他工作直到午夜。
(D) He is talking on the phone right now.
他現在正在講電話。

Q5 ___D___ **What does James have for dinner?**
James 晚餐吃什麼？

(A) A hamburger, a cake and a soda. 漢堡、蛋糕與汽水。
(B) A sandwich, some lemonade and French fries.
三明治、一些檸檬水與薯條。
(C) French fries, a hamburger and some lemonade.
薯條、漢堡與一些檸檬水。
(D) A hamburger, French fries and a coke.
漢堡、薯條與可樂。

第二部分 問答

Q1 ___B___ **I can't eat anymore. I am full.**

我不能再吃了。我好飽。
(A) Yes, sir. May I help you?
是的，我可以幫你嗎？
(B) So am I. 我也是。
(C) I couldn't agree with you more.
我再同意不過了。
(D) Yes, the restaurant is full of people.
是啊，這家餐廳擠滿了人。

單字解釋 ▶ full **adj** 飽的
I couldn't agree with you. 我再同意不過了。

試題分析 ▶ 本題說：我再也吃不下了，我已經飽了。可知適合的答案為選項 (B)，表示「我也是」，這是一種倒裝句的用法。而 (C) 選項 I couldn't agree with you more. 是「我再同意不過了」，而 (D) 則是說餐廳裡充滿了人，無法回應原句。

Q2 ___B___ **Do you like Thai food?**

你喜歡泰國菜嗎？

(A) Yes, don't you like it, either?

是的，你也不喜歡嗎？

(B) Thai food is my second choice.

泰國菜是我的第二選擇。

(C) I haven't been to Thailand.

我沒去過泰國。

(D) I like Italian food so much.

我非常喜歡義大利菜。

單字解釋 ▶ Thai 泰國的 `adj`

second choice 第二選擇

試題分析 ▶ 本題問：你喜歡吃泰國菜嗎。可知答案為選項 (B)：表示「泰國菜是我第二個喜歡的」。其中 (A) 應改成 Do you like it, too 才正確。而 (C) I haven't been to Thailand 表示從未去過泰國。

Q3 ___B___ **Let's go for a buffet this evening.**

我們今晚去吃到飽餐廳吧。

(A) That's a good idea. I want to have a vacation.

那是個好主意，我想去度假。

(B) Sure. I am so hungry that I can eat a horse.

當然，我已經餓到可以吃下一匹馬了（形容非常餓）。

(C) Let's go bowling together.

我們一起去打保齡球吧！

(D) Do you need to serve the guests?

你需要服務客人嗎？

單字解釋 ▶ buffet `n` （可吃到飽的）自助式餐廳

go bowling 打保齡球

guest `n` 客人

試題分析 ▶ 本題說：我們晚上去吃吃到飽吧，可知答案為選項 (B) 的「當然，我已經餓到可以吃下一匹馬了」，用一種誇飾法來表示自己很餓。

Conversation 1

W: Would you like something to drink? My treat.
M: Thanks. I need a cup of coffee.
W: Sounds great. With sugar and milk?
M: No, I always take it black. You should try it.

中文 翻 譯

女：你想喝些什麼？我請客。
男：謝謝。我需要一杯咖啡。
女：聽起來不錯。要加糖與牛奶嗎？
男：不，我總是喝黑咖啡。你應該試一試。

Q1 ___C___ **What does the man want the woman to try?**
男子要女子嘗試什麼？

(A) Drink a cup of milk tea.
喝一杯奶茶。

(B) Drink a cup of coffee with sugar and milk.
喝一杯有加糖與牛奶的咖啡。

(C) Drink a cup of coffee without sugar and milk.
喝一杯沒加糖與牛奶的咖啡。

(D) Drink a cup of lemonade.
喝一杯檸檬水。

單字解釋 ▶ My treat. 我請客。

試題分析 ▶ 本題問：男子要女子試什麼。從對話最後一句可知答案為選項
(C)：喝沒加糖、牛奶的咖啡。

Conversation 2

Taiwan Snacks

Beef Noodles Soup	$180
Stinky Tofu	$60
Pig Blood Cake	$45
Dumplings	$6 /per

W: Mike, let me introduce you to this place, Shin Lin night market!

M: I read about this place in some tourist's magazines. Taiwan is known for its numerous delicious food. Actually, what do you think I should try?

W: The safest choice is beef noodles soup. It is not so unusual for most foreigners.

M: Not me! I would like to try some special food.

W: In that case, I would recommend you some stinky tofu. Don't worry. It tastes better than it smells.

M: Okay. I want a dish of that, plus ten dumplings for my dinner. I am starving.

 中文翻譯

台灣小吃

牛肉麵	$180
臭豆腐	$60
豬血糕	$45
水餃	$6／1 顆

女：麥克，我來介紹你這個地方，士林夜市！

男：我在一些旅遊雜誌讀過這個地方。台灣以數不清的美食而聞名。到底你覺得我應該要嘗試什麼東西呢？

女：最安全的選擇是牛肉麵。這對大部分的外國人來說，比較不會那麼奇怪。

男：我可不算喔！我想要嘗試一些特殊的食物。

女：如果是這樣的話，我會建議你吃臭豆腐。別擔心，它嚐起來比聞起來好多了。

男：好的，那我要一盤，另加十個水餃當晚餐。我快餓死了。

Q2 ___B___ How much did Mike need to pay for his dinner?

麥克需要付多少晚餐錢？

(A) $105.

105 元。

(B) $120.

120 元。

(C) $ 240.

240 元。

(D) $ 225.

225 元。

單字解釋 ▶ numerous adj 很多的   unusual adj 不尋常的

starving adj 飢餓的

試題分析 ▶ 本題問：麥克需要付多少晚餐錢。

在對話一開始可知男子為麥克。女子說 I would recommend ~ stinky tofu，麥克回應 I want a dish of that, 並提到 plus ten dumplings for my dinner.，表示麥克要一盤臭豆腐，另加十個水餃當晚餐。一盤臭豆腐 60 元，十顆水餃 60 元，所以一共是 120 元，因此是要答案選 B。

第四部分 簡短對話

Short Talk 1

Let me tell you how to make a delicious omelet. First, break the eggs into a bowl. Chop an onion, cut up a pepper, slice the ham, and grate the cheese. Then, mix all of these ingredients. Next, heat the skillet and butter. Pour the mixture into the skillet and cook it for five to ten minutes. Finally, everything is done. Put the omelet on a plate and enjoy it.

中文 翻譯

讓我來告訴你如何做一個美味的歐姆蛋。首先，在碗裡打一顆蛋。切洋蔥，切青椒，將火腿切片，並將起士刨成絲。然後，將這些食材倒在一起攪拌。接下來，將平底鍋加熱並上牛油。倒入剛攪拌的食材入平底鍋，並煮五到十分鐘。最後就完成了。將歐姆蛋裝入盤中，並好好享用。

Q1 __B__ **What ingredient is NOT mentioned when making an omelet?**

製作歐姆蛋時，那一項食材沒有被提到？
(A) Cheese. 起士。
(B) Bacon. 培根。
(C) Ham. 火腿。
(D) Peppers and onions. 青椒與洋蔥。

單字解釋 ▶ omelet n 歐姆蛋　　　　　chop v 剁，切
grate v 刨（絲）　　　　　ingredient n 食材
skillet n 平底鍋

試題分析 ▶ 本題問：那一項食材在談話中沒有被提到。在談話中有聽到 Chop an onion, cut up a pepper, slice the ham, and grate the cheese.，可知有提到洋蔥、青椒、火腿、起士，但沒有提到培根，故答案要選 B。

Short Talk 2

Ingredients listing

You need :
Flour/Sugar/Honey/Baking soda
Raisins/Apples/Bananas/Oranges

When is your best friend's birthday? Are you going to bake something special for this special day? Charles the baker recommends this recipe for fruitcake. Everyone says it's out of this world! The first step is to put a few cups of flour in the mixing bowl. Then add a little sugar. Next, slice a few apples, cut up a few oranges, pour in a little honey, add a little baking soda, and mix in a few raisins. Finally, bake for about forty-five minutes. Your friend will definitely love it.

....

食材清單

你需要：
麵粉／糖／蜂蜜／烘焙蘇打粉
葡萄乾／蘋果／香蕉／柳橙

你最好的朋友何時生日呢？在這特別的日子裡，你打算烤一個特別的東西來當作禮物嗎？蛋糕師傅 Charles 推薦水果蛋糕做法的這份食譜。每個人都說這世界一流。第一個步驟是倒幾杯的麵粉到攪拌盆。然後加入一點糖。接著，將一些蘋果切片、切一些柳橙、加一些蜂蜜，再加一些烘培蘇打粉，然後加入一些葡萄乾。最後，放進烤箱烤約四十五分鐘。你的朋友絕對會愛死它。

Q2   **C**   **Look at the graphics. Which item in this ingredients listing is NOT mentioned in this talk?**

請看圖表，在這份食材清單中，哪一項在談話中沒有被提到？

(A) Flour.

　　麵粉。

(B) Apples.

　　蘋果。

(C) Bananas.

　　香蕉。

(D) Raisins.

　　葡萄乾。

單字解釋▶ recommend **v** 推薦　　　　mixing bowl **n** 攪拌盆

　　　　 slice **v** 切片　　　　　　 raisin **n** 葡萄乾

試題分析▶ 本題問：圖表的食材清單中，哪一項沒有被提到。從談話中的 put a few ~ flour、add a little sugar、slice a few apples、cut up a few oranges、pour in a little honey、add a little baking soda，以及 mix in a few raisins 可知，提到了「麵粉」「糖」「蘋果」「柳橙」「蜂蜜」「烘培蘇打粉」以及「葡萄乾」。

由此可知沒有提到的是香蕉，故答案要選 C。

Hint 常考句子

情境解析

可能情境包括：服飾、配件、買衣服、向服飾店店員詢問等。

1 Can I try it on?
我可以試穿嗎？

2 What's Linda wearing today?
Linda 今天穿什麼？

3 Nice bracelet. Where did you buy it?
好棒的手鐲。哪裡買的？

模擬試題

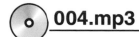
004.mp3

第一部分 **看圖辨義**

作答說明

試題冊上有數幅圖畫，每一圖畫有 1~3 個描述該圖的題目，每題請聽光碟放音機播出題目以及四個英語敘述之後，選出與所看到的圖畫最相符的答案，每題只播出一遍。

Picture A Q1

答案欄

Picture B Q2 ～ Q3

答案欄

Picture C Q4 ～ Q5

答案欄

第二部分　問答

每題請聽光碟放音機播出一英語問句或直述句後，從試題冊上
A、B、C、D 四個回答或回應中，選出一個最適合者作答。每題
只播出一遍。

Q 1

答案欄

(A) Yes, I have some coins.

(B) Now, I have contacts.

(C) As a matter of fact, I am used to wearing glasses.

(D) It's almost one year.

Q 2

答案欄

(A) Yes, I'll wear my blue sweater.

(B) OK. Blue shirts are in the drawer.

(C) Why? I prefer the yellow one.

(D) Today is Monday, so I have to go to school.

Q 3

答案欄

(A) Sorry, I have had the red one already.

(B) Oh, I can't wait to show my fit body.

(C) Red swimming suits are on sale.

(D) I would rather to buy a black suit.

第三部分　簡短對話

每題請聽光碟放音機播出一段對話及一個相關的問題之後，從試題冊上 A、B、C、D 四個選項中選出一個最適合者作答。每段對話及問題只播出一遍。

Conversation 1

(A) He has to give a speech in the conference.

(B) Because his boss is going to fire him.

(C) Because he is not sure if he should go to the conference.

(D) He has to attend a conference but he doesn't know what to wear.

Conversation 2

Q 2

> Are you hunting for fashion bargains?
> ### Beautiful dresses　FOR YOU
> ### Buy two, get the second one for free!
> Another 10% off if total payment is over $2,500
>
> All sales are final! Vouchers and gift certificates are acceptable.

(A) $5,400.

(B) $2,700.

(C) $5,000.

(D) $3,000.

第四部分　簡短談話 新題型

 每題請聽光碟放音機播出一段談話及一個相關的問題後，從試題冊上 A、B、C、D 四個選項中選出一個最適合者作答。每段對話及問題只播出一遍。

Short Talk 1

Q 1

(A) The zipper was broken.

(B) The lengths of the two arms are different.

(C) It had no special discount.

(D) Some buttons were lost.

Short Talk 2

Q 2

Evening Reception Dress Code
Women: elegant formal dress/evening bag/jewelry(optional)
Men: suit or tuxedo/black leather shoes/watch(optional)

(A) Formal dress with jewelry.

(B) Elegant dress with an evening bag.

(C) Tuxedo with a pair of sneakers.

(D) Suit with an expensive watch.

答案解析

 第一部分 看圖辨義

提示 **For question number 1, please look at picture A.**
問題 1 請看圖片 A。

Q1　D　What's Sarah going to do?
Sarah 將要做什麼？
(A) She is going to hike in the mountain. 她將要登山。
(B) She is going to swim at the beach. 她將要在海邊游泳。
(C) She is going to clean the swimming pool.
　　她將要清潔游泳池。
(D) She is going to learn how to swim. 她將要學游泳。

提示 **For questions number 2 and 3, please look at picture B.**
問題 2 跟問題 3 請看圖片 B。

 Q2　A　What time does Tim go home?
Tim 何時回家？
(A) Four o'clock on the dot. 4 點整。
(B) Exactly five o'clock. 5 點整。
(C) Half past four. 4 點 30 分。
(D) A quarter to five. 4 點 45 分（差 15 分 5 點）。

 Q3　C　What happened to Tim? Tim 發生了什麼事？
(A) Because he didn't take an umbrella, he took a cab
　　home. 因為他沒有帶傘，所以他搭了計程車回家。
(B) Because it was a rainy day, he felt a bit
　　uncomfortable. 因為是下雨天，他覺得有些不舒服。
(C) Because he didn't wear a raincoat, he got totally
　　wet. 他因為沒穿雨衣，所以全身淋濕了。
(D) Because he didn't get good grades, he had to leave
　　the school early.
　　因為他沒獲得好成績，所以他必須要提早離開學校。

For questions number 4 and 5, please look at picture C.
問題 4 跟問題 5 請看圖片 C。

Q4 ___A___ **Why is Kiki wearing sunglasses?**

為何 Kiki 戴太陽眼鏡？

(A) Since the sun is shining. 因為陽光很大。
(B) Since she got black eyes. 因為她眼睛瘀青。
(C) Since she didn't sleep at all last night.
     因為她昨晚完全沒睡。
(D) Since she wears shorts, too. 因為她也穿短褲。

Q5 ___D___ **Which statement matches the picture C?**

哪一項敘述符合圖 C？

(A) Kiki is wearing a necklace. Kiki 正戴著項鍊。
(B) Kiki is wearing a shirt. Kiki 正穿著襯衫。
(C) Kiki is wearing shorts. Kiki 正穿著短褲。
(D) Kiki is wearing sneakers. Kiki 正穿著球鞋。

第二部分 問答

Q1 ___B___ **You've changed a little bit. You used to wear glasses, didn't you?**

你有些改變。你以前戴眼鏡，不是嗎？

(A) Yes, I have some coins. 是的，我有一些硬幣。
(B) Now, I have contacts. 現在我戴隱形眼鏡。
(C) As a matter of fact, I am used to wearing glasses.
     事實上我習慣戴眼鏡。
(D) It's almost one year. 幾乎有一年了。

單字解釋 ▶ a little bit 一點　　　　contact **n** 隱形眼鏡
used to 過去經常…（比較：be used to 習慣於…）
as a matter of fact 事實上（= in fact）

試題分析 ▶ 本題說：你有些改變。你以前都戴眼鏡的不是嗎。答案為選項
(B) 我現在戴隱形眼鏡。本題考兩個重點，其一是 used to 的
意思，指「以前經常做～但現在不做了」。另一為「附加問
句」的用法，回答應與其相關。

Q2 ___C___ **John, wear your blue sweatshirt before going to school.** John，上學前穿上你的藍色運動衫。

(A) Yes, I'll wear my blue sweater.
是的，我將穿上藍色的毛衣。

(B) OK. Blue shirts are in the drawer.
好的，藍色襯衫在抽屜裡。

(C) Why? I prefer the yellow one.
為什麼？我比較喜歡黃色的。

(D) Today is Monday, so I have to go to school.
今天是星期一，所以我得上學。

單字解釋 ▶ wear **v** 穿著　　　　　sweatshirt **n** 運動衫
sweater **n** 毛衣　　　　drawer **n** 抽屜
prefer **v** 更喜歡

試題分析 ▶ 本題說：要求 John 在上學前穿上藍色運動衫。答案為選項 (C) 為什麼？我比較喜歡黃色的，表示 John 不想穿對方要求的顏色。本題考發音的相似度，如 sweater、shirt 與 sweatshirt 的相似性。

Q3 ___B___ **Take your red swimming suit. Our hotel has a spa.** 帶著你的紅色泳衣，我們的旅館有水療設施。

(A) Sorry, I have had the red one already.
抱歉，我已經有紅色的了。

(B) Oh, I can't wait to show my fit body.
喔，我等不及秀我的健美身材了。

(C) Red swimming suits are on sale.
紅色泳衣在特價。

(D) I would rather buy a black suit.
我寧可買黑色西裝。

單字解釋 ▶ swimming suit 泳衣　　　spa **n** 水療按摩
fit body 健美的身材　　　on sale 拍賣中
would rather 寧願…　　　black suit 黑色西裝

試題分析 ▶ 本題說：帶著你紅色的泳衣，我們的旅館有水療按摩。答案為選項 (B) 我等不及秀我的健美身材了。其他選項皆文不對題。

Conversation 1

M: I don't know what to wear today?
W: Why are you being so fussy about clothes today?
M: Actually, I will attend a conference today.
W: Well, a blue shirt with a black suit is fine.
M: I don't think I look good in it.

中文翻譯

男：我不知道今天要穿什麼。
女：你今天為何特別講究穿著？
男：其實我今天要參加會議。
女：喔，藍襯衫配黑西裝不錯。
男：我不認為我這樣穿會好看。

Q1 ___D___ **Why is the man worried?**

男子為什麼會擔心？

(A) He has to give a speech in the conference.
他必須在會議中演講。

(B) Because his boss is going to fire him.
因為他的老闆要開除他。

(C) Because he is not sure if he should go to the
conference. 因為他不確定他是否該參加會議。

(D) He has to attend a conference but he doesn't know
what to wear. 他得參加會議，但他卻不知道要穿什麼。

單字解釋 ▶ attend a conference 參加會議

試題分析 ▶ 本題問：為何男子很擔心。可知答案為選項 (D)：因為他要參
加會議卻不知要穿什麼才好。

Conversation 2

Are you hunting for fashion bargains?

Beautiful dresses FOR YOU

Buy two, get the second one for free!

Another 10% off if total payment is over $2,500
All sales are final! Vouchers and gift certificates are acceptable.

W: Darling, look at these beautiful dresses! They are having a big sale now. Buy one get one free. That's a real bargain!

M: But you have already had enough.

W: No, not enough. Okay, I've decided to buy six of them. Each of them is only $1000, not to mention some other discounts. These dresses can really make me more beautiful.

你正在找尋划算的時尚服飾精品嗎？

適合你的 美麗的洋裝

買一送一！

消費總金額超過 2,500 元另打九折。
貨品既出概不退貨！優惠券與禮券皆可使用。

女：親愛的，你看看這些美麗的洋裝。它們現在大特賣耶！買一送一，真是划算！

男：但是你的洋裝夠多了。

女：不夠的。好，我決定要買六件。每一件只要 1,000 元，更別說還有其他折扣。這些洋裝真的會讓我更美。

Q2   B   **How much will they pay for the purchases?**

他們買這些東西需要付多少錢？

(A) $5,400.

   5400 元。

(B) $2,700.

   2700 元。

(C) $2,500.

   2500 元。

(D) $3,000.

   3000 元。

單字解釋 ▶ bargain **n** 特價品，便宜貨　　voucher **n** 優惠券
gift certificate **n** 禮券

試題分析 ▶ 本題問：他們需要付多少錢。在對話中聽到 I've decided to buy six of them. Each of them is only $1000，表示決定買六件，且每一件 1,000 元。另外，對話中有提到 Buy one get one free，也就是買一送一，因此六件 3,000 元。從圖片中可知超過 2,500 元以上可再打九折，所以最後的總金額是 2,700 元，因此答案選 B。

第四部分 簡短談話

Short Talk 1

Yesterday I was shopping in the outlet, and I was so happy to buy some clothing with fifty percent off the regular price. However, my happiness didn't last very long. When I got home, I noticed that one arm of the jacket was longer than the other. What's worse, the zipper on the pants was broken. I told myself that I would be more careful when buying something on sale next time.

中文翻譯

昨天我在暢貨中心購物，很高興買到原價打對折的服裝。然而，我的高興沒有持續太久。當我到家時才發現這夾克的一隻袖長比另一隻要長，更糟糕的是，長褲上的拉鍊壞了。我告訴我自己，下回買這些特價品時，要更加小心。

Q1 __B__ **What is wrong with the jacket?** 夾克怎麼了？
(A) The zipper was broken. 拉鍊壞了。
(B) The lengths of its two arms are different.
    兩隻袖長的長度不一。
(C) It had no special discount. 它沒有折扣。
(D) Some buttons were lost. 一些鈕扣不見了。

單字解釋 ▶ outlet **n** 暢貨中心　　　　　happiness **n** 高興，幸福
　　　　　What's worse 更糟糕的是　　　last **v** 持續

試題分析 ▶ 本題問：夾克發生什麼事。在談話中聽到 When I got home, I noticed that one arm of the jacket was longer than the other. ，表示發現這夾克的一隻袖長比另一隻要長，也就是兩隻袖長的長度不一，故答案要選 B。

59

Short Talk 2

Evening Reception Dress Code

Women: elegant formal dress/evening bag/ jewelry(optional)

Men: suit or tuxedo/black leather shoes/ watch(optional)

May I have your attention folks? For this year's year-end reception, we have a dress code that we need everyone to follow. For female guests, please wear an elegant formal dress with an evening bag. For male guests, please wear a suit or a tuxedo. Thank you for your cooperation. We believe you all will have a wonderful night.

晚宴的服裝規定

女性：優雅的正式禮服／晚宴包／珠寶（非強制性）
男性：西裝或是燕尾服／黑皮鞋／手錶（非強制性）

我可以請各位注意嗎？今年年底的晚宴，我們會有服裝規定需要大家來遵守。針對女性貴賓，請穿著優雅正式禮服，並帶晚宴包。男性貴賓則穿著西裝或是燕尾服。謝謝各位的合作。我們相信你們都將有一個美好的夜晚。

Q2 __C__ **What kind of attire is NOT appropriate in the reception?**

哪一種服裝不適合在宴會中出現？

(A) Formal dress with jewelry.
正式禮服配珠寶。

(B) Elegant dress with an evening bag.
優雅禮服配晚宴包。

(C) Tuxedo with a pair of sneakers.
燕尾服搭配球鞋。

(D) Suit with an expensive watch.
西裝搭配昂貴手錶。

單字解釋 ▶ reception **n** 宴會　　　　　elegant **adj** 優雅的
optional **adj** 可以選擇的　　　tuxedo **n** 燕尾服

試題分析 ▶ 本題問：哪一種服裝不適合在宴會中出現。在談話中可知 For female guests ~ elegant formal dress with an evening bag. For male guests ~ a suit or a tuxedo.，表示女性貴賓穿著優雅正式禮服並帶晚宴包，男性貴賓穿西裝或是燕尾服。此外，對照圖表，還提到 jewelry、black leather shoes 以及 watch。由此可知，沒有提到的是 sneakers（球鞋），故答案要選 C。

Hint
常考句子

可能情境包括：詢問價格、要求折扣、詢問想購物的地點、與好友們一起逛街等。

情境解析

1 **Can you give me a discount?**
你可以給我打折嗎？

2 **I am a bargain hunter.**
我是個殺價高手。

3 **I like going window shopping so much.**
我很喜歡逛街。

模 擬 試 題  005.mp3

第一部分 看圖辨義

作答說明

試題冊上有數幅圖畫，每一圖畫有 1~3 個描述該圖的題目，每題請聽光碟放音機播出題目以及四個英語敘述之後，選出與所看到的圖畫最相符的答案，每題只播出一遍。

Picture A Q1 ～ Q2

答案欄

Picture B Q3 ～ Q4

答案欄

Picture C Q5

答案欄

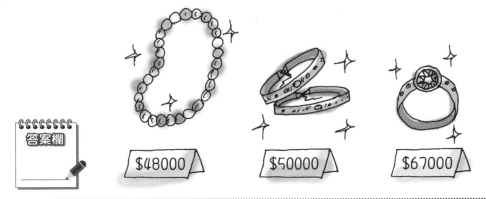

每題請聽光碟放音機播出一英語問句或直述句後，從試題冊上 A、B、C、D 四個回答或回應中，選出一個最適合者作答。每題只播出一遍。

(A) Yes, sir. May I help you?

(B) Will a medium do?

(C) Sure, let's go to the fitness center.

(D) Let's see. Oh, fitting room is over there.

(A) Yes, I need a pair of sport shoes.

(B) I don't usually watch sports.

(C) No, it's on the third floor.

(D) Let's see. Maybe we can buy a ticket to the ball game.

(A) Yes, here you are.

(B) I can't offer you a special service.

(C) Are you a bargain hunter? This is my last price.

(D) The price is the most expensive in the department store.

第三部分　簡短對話

 每題請聽光碟放音機播出一段對話及一個相關的問題之後，從試題冊上 A、B、C、D 四個選項中選出一個最適合者作答。每段對話及問題只播出一遍。

Conversation 1

(A) Toilet paper.

(B) Oil.

(C) Fruit.

(D) Shampoo.

Conversation 2

Model	Type	Suitable	Price
CC324	Desktop	Gaming	$20,000
GG563	Desktop	Basic users	$18,000
SS424	Laptop	Gaming	$25,000
BB589	Laptop	Basic users	$21,000

(A) CC324

(B) GG563

(C) SS424

(D) BB589

 答案欄

 答案欄

第四部分 **簡短談話** 新題型

 每題請聽光碟放音機播出一段談話及一個相關的問題後，從試題冊上 A、B、C、D 四個選項中選出一個最適合者作答。每段談話及問題只播出一遍。

Conversation 1

 Q 1

(A) Ship models.

(B) Second-hand rugs.

(C) Previously owned vehicles.

(D) Automatic doors.

Conversation 2

Q 2

Sports World End of Summer Sales!	
ITEMS:	
1. Tank tops	$1,500/one
2. Biking shorts	$1,500/pair
3. Gym bags	$1,500/one
4. Athletic shoes	$2,500/pair
5. Men's and women's swimsuits	$1,500/one
All items above are 20% off!	

(A) $3,200

(B) $3,000

(C) $2,400

(D) $1,500

答案解析

第一部分 看圖辨義

 For questions number 1 and 2, please look at picture A.
問題 1 跟問題 2 請看圖片 A。

Q1 ___B___ **How much does a belt cost?**

皮帶要多少錢？

(A) $590. 590 元。
(B) $120. 120 元。
(C) $280. 280 元。
(D) $390. 390 元。

Q2 ___C___ **Which descriptions match the picture A?**

哪個描述符合圖 A？

(A) Customers pay $590 for a coat.
　　顧客付 590 元買一件外套。
(B) Customers pay $120 for a shirt.
　　顧客付 120 元買一件襯衫。
(C) A shirt and a belt cost $400.
　　一件襯衫和一條皮帶要花費 400 元。
(D) It costs $390 to buy a belt. 買一條皮帶要花費 390 元。

 For questions number 3 and 4, please look at picture B.
問題 3 跟問題 4 請看圖片 B。

Q3 ___A___ **What's Vicky doing at present?**

現在 Vicky 正在做什麼？

(A) She is bargaining with the salesperson.
　　她正在跟店員殺價。
(B) She is trying on a new shirt. 她正在試穿一件新襯衫。
(C) She is buying a shirt. 她正在買襯衫。
(D) She is talking to someone on the phone.
　　她正在跟人講電話。

Q4   **B**   **Is Vicky paying $500 for a skirt?**

Vicky 花 500 元買裙子嗎？

(A)Yes, she is. But she forgot to bring her money.

是的，但是她忘記帶錢了。

(B) Yes, she is. And she is happy buying that skirt.

是的，她很高興買了那件裙子。

(C) No, she isn't. But she pays $590.

不，但她付 590 元。

(D) Yes, she is. But she pays $590. 是的，但她付 590 元。

提示   **For question number 5, please look at picture C.**

問題 5 請看圖片 C。

Q5   **A**   **Which one is the most expensive?**

哪一個最貴？

(A) The right one has the highest price. 右邊的最高價。

(B) The middle one is the most expensive. 中間的最貴。

(C) The right one has the best quality. 右邊的品質最好。

(D) The left one is the most expensive and beautiful.

左邊的最貴、最美。

第二部分 問答

Q1   **B**   **Can I try a different size? This one doesn't fit.** 我可以試其他尺寸嗎？這個不合身。

(A) Yes, sir. May I help you? 是的，我可以為你服務嗎？

(B) Will a medium do? M 號的可以嗎？

(C) Sure, let's go to the fitness center.

當然，我們去健身房吧。

(D) Let's see. Oh, fitting room is over there.

我想想。喔，更衣室在那裡。

單字解釋 ▶ different size 不一樣的尺寸   fit **V** 適合

fitness center 健身中心   fitting room 更衣室

試題分析 ▶ 本題問：我可否試其他尺寸。答案為選項 (B)。本題考的是試穿衣服，回答應提到 M 號與問話相關的內容。

Q2 ___C___ **I'm sorry. Is sportswear on this floor?**

抱歉，請問運動服裝是在這層樓嗎？

(A) Yes, I need a pair of sport shoes.

是的，我需要一雙運動鞋。

(B) I don't usually watch sports. 我通常不看運動比賽。

(C) No, it's on the third floor. 不是，它在三樓。

(D) Let's see. Maybe we can buy a ticket to the ball game. 讓我想一想。也許我們可以買票去看球賽。

單字解釋 ▶ sportswear **n** 體育服裝   a pair of 一雙…

sport shoes 運動鞋   watch sports 看球賽

試題分析 ▶ 本題問：運動服飾是否在這層樓。可知答案為選項 (C)：不，在三樓。

Q3 ___C___ **Could you give me a discount? I think it's too expensive.** 你可以給我折扣嗎？我認為它太貴了。

(A) Yes, here you are. 是的，在這裡。

(B) I can't offer you a special service.

我無法提供你特別的服務。

(C) Are you a bargain hunter? This is my last price.

你是殺價高手嗎？這已是我最後的底價了。

(D) The price is the most expensive in the department store. 這個價格是這間百貨公司裡最貴的。

單字解釋 ▶ discount **n** 折扣   offer **v** 提供

special service 特別服務   bargain hunter 殺價高手

last price 最後的價格   department store 百貨公司

試題分析 ▶ 本題問：是否可以給我折扣，這價格實在太貴了。答案為選項 (C)：你是殺價高手嗎？這已經是最後底價了。表示不給對方殺價的意思。

Conversation 1

M: I'm going to the store. Do you need anything?

W: Oh, we are out of toilet paper, and we're running low on shampoo. We also need some fruit and oil.

M: Well, I probably won't have enough money.

W: OK, so don't buy oil. I think we still have some.

中文翻譯

男：我要去商店。你要買什麼嗎？

女：喔，沒有衛生紙了，而且洗髮精也用完了。我們也需要一些水果與油。

男：我可能沒有足夠的錢。

女：好吧，那別買油。我想我們還有一些。

Q1 __B__ **Which of the four is the man not going to buy?** 這四樣東西中，何者男子將不會買？

(A) Toilet paper. 衛生紙。

(B) Oil. 油。

(C) Fruit. 水果。

(D) Shampoo. 洗髮精。

單字解釋 ▶ shampoo n 洗髮精

試題分析 ▶ 本題問：什麼東西男子將不會買。女子最後建議提到 OK, so don't buy oil.，可知答案為選項 B：油。

Conversation 2

Model	Type	Suitable	Price
CC324	Desktop	Gaming	$20,000
GG563	Desktop	Basic users	$18,000
SS424	Laptop	Gaming	$25,000
BB589	Laptop	Basic users	$21,000

M: May I help you?

W: Yes, my computer has crashed. It no longer works. I am looking for a notebook, but to tell the truth, I am short of money and on a budget.

M: I see. Will you be installing a lot of programs, like online games, on the computer?

W: In fact, I am not interested in gaming at all. I need it to do my paperwork and sometimes present some oral reports.

M: Let me show you our product list.

中文 翻 譯

機型	型態	適合於	價格
CC324	桌上型	遊戲	$20000
GG563	桌上型	基本使用	$18000
SS424	筆記型	遊戲	$25000
BB589	筆記型	基本使用	$21000

男：有什麼是我可以幫忙的嗎？

女：是的，我的電腦不會動，壞了。我在找一個筆記型電腦。但說實話，我錢不多，也有預算限制。

男：我了解。你會在電腦上安裝很多程式嗎，像是線上遊戲之類的？

女：事實上，我對遊戲一點興趣都沒有。我需要它來做一些文書處理，有時要用來做一些口頭報告。

男：我給你看看我們的產品清單。

Q2 __D__ **Which computer will the woman probably buy?**

女子可能會買哪一台電腦？

(A) CC324.

型號 CC324。

(B) GG563

型號 GG563。

(C) SS424

型號 SS424。

(D) BB589

型號 BB589。

單字解釋 ▶ short of 缺乏…　　　　　　　on a budget 有預算限制

install **v** 安裝　　　　　　　　　oral report 口頭報告

試題分析 ▶ 本題問：女子可能會買哪一台電腦。在對話中女子提到 I am looking for a notebook 表示女子在找筆記型電腦，又提到 I am not interested in gaming at all. 可知女子對遊戲一點興趣都沒有。所以是基本用途的筆記型電腦，因此是要答案選 D。notebook 的另一種講法是 laptop。

第四部分 簡短談話

Short Talk 1

Thinking of buying a car but can't afford a brand new one? There's no better time than now. Come in and look at our wide selection of used cars. All cars are reduced by 50%. Nothing in the store will last long at these prices, so hurry on down. Come to Johnson's Auto Plant, located on the corner of Maple and First.

中文翻譯

想著要買一部車，卻負擔不起新車嗎？沒有比現在這個時機更好了。進來看看我們多樣化選擇的二手車。所有車款皆打對折。在這樣的價格下，店內的這些車子不會陳列太久，很快就會有人買走，所以動作要快喔。歡迎蒞臨 Johnson 車廠。位於楓葉街與第一街的交叉路口處。

Q1 __C__ **What is being sold?** 在販售什麼？
(A) Ship models. 船的模型。
(B) Second-hand rugs. 二手地毯。
(C) Previously owned vehicles. 之前用過的車。
(D) Automatic doors. 自動門。

單字解釋 ▶ afford v 負擔　　　　used cars 二手車
plant n 工廠　　　　hurry on down 動作要快

試題分析 ▶ 本題問：在販售的東西。在談話中提到 Come in and look at our ... used cars... reduced by 50%.，可知說話者在賣二手車，價格打對折，故答案要選 (C)。

73

Sports World
End of Summer Sales!

ITEMS:

1. Tank tops	$1,500/one
2. Biking shorts	$1,500/pair
3. Gym bags	$1,500/one
4. Athletic shoes	$2,500/pair
5. Men's and women's swimsuits	$1,500/one

All items above are 20% off!

I am a real bargain hunter. I always shop when the stores have some sales. Yesterday I went to Sports World in Taipei. First, I looked at some sneakers, but I found nothing I liked. I want to learn how to swim, and I bought a men's swimsuit at a reasonable price. Also, I picked up a pair of biking shorts because I am taking up biking. Since I already have lots of gym bags, this time I skipped them. That was a good shopping day!

 中文翻譯

運動世界
夏末特賣

品項：

1.無袖上衣	$1500／一件
2.腳踏車短褲	$1500／一件
3.運動包	$1500／一個
4.運動球鞋	$2500／一雙
5.男性泳裝、女性泳裝	$1500／一件

以上所有品項享八折優惠！

我真的很會找便宜。我總是在商店有特賣時來購物。昨天我去了台北的運動世界。首先,我看了一些球鞋,但沒有找到我喜歡的。我想學游泳,於是我以合理的價格買了一件男性泳裝。而且,因為我喜歡上了騎腳踏車,我也挑了一件腳踏車運動短褲。因為我已經有了很多運動包,所以我這一次就忽略它們了。真是個美好的購物日!

Q2 ___C___ **How much did the man pay for his purchases?**

男子付了多少錢買他要買的東西?
(A) $ 3,200. 三千二百元。
(B) $ 3,000. 三千元。
(C) $ 2,400. 兩千四百元。
(D) $ 1,500. 一千五百元。

單字解釋 ▶ bargain hunter 專買便宜商品的人　　athletic adj 運動的
sneakers n 球鞋　　　　　　　　　reasonable adj 合理的
gym bag 運動包

試題分析 ▶ 本題問:男子付了多少錢。在談話中提到 I want to learn how to swim... I bought a men's swimsuit at a reasonable price. ,又提到 I picked up a pair of biking shorts because I am taking up biking. ,可知男子買了一件男性泳裝和腳踏車運動短褲。由此可知,他一共買了兩個品項:泳裝1500 元、腳踏車運動褲 1500 元,這樣共 3000 元。不過圖表中寫到所有品項都八折,所以總金額為 2400 元,故答案要選(C)。

Hint

常 考 句 子

情境解析 可能情境包括：要求或抱怨飯店服務、不知如何使用飯店設備、要求換房、要求 morning call。

---

1 **Can you give me a wake-up call?**
可以給我 morning call 嗎？
（註：morning call 為日式英文的誤用。）

2 **Can you change a room for me?**
可否換一個房間給我？

3 **I don't know how to use the TV set.**
我不知道如何使用這台電視。

模擬試題

 006.mp3

第一部分 **看圖辨義**

作答說明 試題冊上有數幅圖畫，每一圖畫有 1~3 個描述該圖的題目，每題請聽光碟放音機播出題目以及四個英語敘述之後，選出與所看到的圖畫最相符的答案，每題只播出一遍。

Picture A Q1 ～ Q2

答案欄

Picture B Q3 ～ Q4

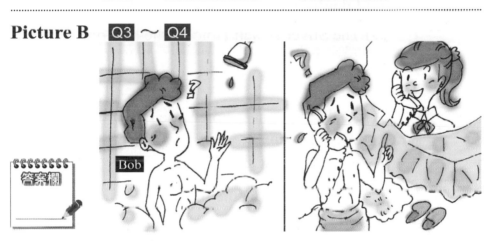

答案欄

Bob

Picture C Q5

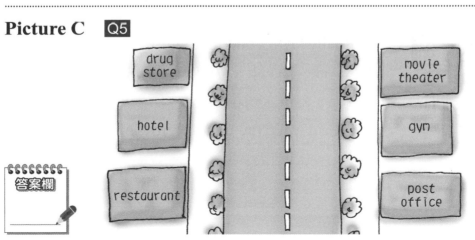

答案欄

drug store

hotel

restaurant

movie theater

gym

post office

情境
主題
06 The Hotels（飯店）

模擬
試題

每題請聽光碟放音機播出一英語問句或直述句後，從試題冊上 A、B、C、D 四個回答或回應中，選出一個最適合者作答。每題只播出一遍。

(A) Really? Tell me about your trip plan.

(B) Me, too. What does yours have?

(C) I don't feel like surfing on the Net.

(D) The Silver Beach Hotel is the best one.

(A) Really? Business hotels are only for businessmen.

(B) Because I am short of money.

(C) The bathroom is the top one.

(D) All right, let's book a room for two nights.

(A) Really? Are you kidding?

(B) A wake-up call at 7:00. No problem.

(C) You should sleep longer.

(D) Please wake me up tomorrow morning.

第三部分 簡短對話

作答說明 每題請聽光碟放音機播出一段對話及一個相關的問題之後，從試題冊上 A、B、C、D 四個選項中選出一個最適合者作答。每段對話及問題只播出一遍。

Conversation 1

Q 1

答案欄

(A) Because they can buy them in the hotel.

(B) Because the hotel they are living in provides towels.

(C) Because they have no time to wash them.

(D) Because they don't need them.

Conversation 2 新題型

Q 2

> ## DAMDI HOTEL CONFIRMATION FORM
>
> Guest: Mariam Thomas
> Telephone: 0956-856-898
> Reservation Date: July 1st
> Check-in Time: July 8th (after 3:00 PM)
> Check-out Time: July 9th (before 12:00 PM)
> ● Non-smoking Room　○ Smoking Room
> ● Single Room　　　○ Double Room
> ○ Triple Room　　　○ Family Room

答案欄

(A) Single room

(B) Double room

(C) Triple room

(D) Family room

第四部分 簡短談話 _{新題型}

Short Talk 1

 Q 1

(A) A beach.

(B) A log cabin.

 (C) A swimming pool.

(D) A tennis court.

Short Talk 2

 Q 2

Most important aspects of a "Good Hotel"

PERCENTAGE OF ASPECTS THAT CUSTOMERS CARE ABOUT

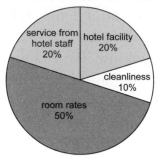

service from hotel staff 20%

hotel facility 20%

cleanliness 10%

room rates 50%

(A) Hotel facility.

 (B) Cleanliness.

(C) Room rates.

(D) Service from hotel staff.

答案解析

第一部分 看圖辨義

For questions number 1 and 2, please look at picture A.
問題 1 跟問題 2 請看圖片 A。

Q1 ___D___ **What did Kelly do before she walked into the room?** 在 Kelly 走進房間前她做了什麼？

(A) She had a phone call. 她打了一通電話。
(B) She talked with a client. 她與客戶說話。
(C) She chatted with her boyfriend. 她與男友聊天。
(D) She talked with a receptionist. 她與接待員說話。

Q2 ___D___ **Which room did Kelly walk into?**

Kelly 走進幾號房？

(A) Room 201. 201 號房。
(B) Room 200. 200 號房。
(C) Room 120. 120 號房。
(D) Room 210. 210 號房。

For questions number 3 and 4, please look at picture B.
問題 3 跟問題 4 請看圖片 B。

Q3 ___B___ **What's wrong with the bathroom?**

浴室出了什麼問題？

(A) The toilet is broken. 馬桶壞了。
(B) It's short of water. 沒水了。
(C) The lock is broken. 鎖壞了。
(D) It's short of gas and the mirror is not clean.
　　沒瓦斯了，而且鏡子不乾淨。

Q4 ___C___ **What is Bob going to do?** Bob 打算做什麼？

(A) He's going to fix the sink. 他打算修水槽。
(B) He's going to blame the receptionist.
　　他打算責怪接待員。

(C) He's going to tell the desk clerk the problem.
他打算告知櫃台人員這問題。

(D) He's going to ignore it.
他打算忽略它。

For question number 5, please look at picture C.
問題 5 請看圖片 C。

Q5　　B　　**Where is the hotel?** 旅館在哪？

(A) It's next to the post office. 在郵局旁邊。
(B) It's opposite the gym. 在運動場對面。
(C) It's across from the drugstore. 在藥局對面。
(D) It's between the movie theater and the restaurant.
在電影院與餐廳之間。

第二部分 問答

Q1　　B　　**I look on the Internet today, and I found a good hotel.** 我今天上網查看了一下，發現了一間好飯店。

(A) Really? Tell me about your trip plan.
真的？告訴我你的旅遊計畫。

(B) Me, too. What does yours have?
我也是，你的有什麼？

(C) I don't feel like surfing on the Net.
我不喜歡上網。

(D) The Silver Beach Café is the best one.
「銀色沙灘咖啡廳」是最棒的。

單字解釋 ▶　look on **V** 查閱　　　　　　trip plan 旅遊計畫
feel like 想要　　　　　　　surf **V** 上網
on the Net 網路

試題分析 ▶　本題說：我今天上網查看，發現了一個好飯店。答案為選項
(B)：「我也是，你的有什麼？」本題考的是以「直述句」說
明目的，回答應與其相關。

Q2　　D　　**It's a business hotel. The bathroom has a bathtub, but no shower.**

這是一家商務旅館。浴室有一個浴缸，但沒有淋浴設備。

(A) Really? Business hotels are only for businessmen.

真的嗎？商務旅館只提供給生意人。

(B) Because I am short of money. 因為我缺錢。

(C) The bathroom is the top one. 浴室是最佳的。

(D) All right, let's book a room for two nights.

好的，我們訂兩晚的房間吧。

單字解釋▶ business hotel 商務旅館　　　　　bathtub **n** 浴缸

short of 短缺 …　　　　　　　　　book **v** 預訂

試題分析▶ 本題說：這是一家商務旅館。有一間浴室，浴室裡有一個浴缸但沒有淋浴設備。答案為選項 (D)：好吧，我們訂兩晚的房間。

Q3　　B　　**Give me a wake-up call at 7:00 tomorrow morning.** 明早 7 點請給我 morning call 。

(A) Really? Are you kidding? 真的嗎？你在開玩笑嗎？

(B) A wake-up call at 7:00. No problem.

明早 7 點的 morning call，沒問題。

(C) You should sleep longer. 你應該睡久一點。

(D) Please wake me up tomorrow morning.

明天早上請叫醒我。

單字解釋▶ wake-up call 晨喚電話　　　　　longer **adv** 更久一些

試題分析▶ 本題說：明早 7 點請給我 morning call。答案為選項(B)：明早 7 點的 morning call，沒問題。

（註：morning call 為日式英文，在日本、韓國、台灣及中國大陸多半可以了解什麼是 morning call，但 wake-up call 才是正確的英文說法。）

Conversation 1

W: Peter, our hotel has a spa and a swimming pool. Take your swimming suit.

M: Right. Then, of course, I need to take my white bathrobe and towel.

W: I don't think you need to bring towels because you can ask them in the hotel.

中文翻譯

女：Peter ，我們的旅館有 spa 和游泳池，帶著你的泳衣。

男：好，那麼，當然我需要帶我的白色浴袍與毛巾。

女：我不認為你需要帶毛巾，因為你可以跟飯店要。

Q1 ___B___ **Why does the woman ask the man not to bring towels?** 女子為何不要男子帶毛巾？

(A) Because they can buy them in the hotel.
因為他們可以在飯店買。

(B) Because the hotel they are living in provides towels.
因為他們住的飯店有提供了。

(C) Because they have no time to wash them.
因為他們沒有時間洗。

(D) Because they don't need them.
因為他們不需要。

單字解釋 ▶ bathrobe **n** 浴袍

試題分析 ▶ 本題問：女子為何不要男子帶毛巾。答案為選項 (B)：因為飯店已經有提供了。

Conversation 2

Damdi Hotel Confirmation form

Guest: Mariam Thomas
Telephone: 0956-856-898
Reservation Date: July 1st
Check-in Time: July 8th (after 3:00 PM)
Check-out Time: July 9th (before 12:00 PM)
● Non-smoking Room   ○ Smoking Room
● Single Room   ○ Double Room
○ Triple Room   ○ Family Room

W: Excuse me, I have a room reservation for tonight.

M: Yes, madam, what is your name please?

W: Mariam Thomas.

M: Let's see.., yes, you have a non-smoking single room reservation for tonight. Is that right?

W: Yes and No. Actually, I asked for a double room. We are two.

M: I am terribly sorry. Our double rooms and triple rooms are fully booked. But I can arrange a much bigger room for you. And as an apology, I will provide complimentary breakfasts for you two.

W: Oh, that's music to my ears.

中文翻譯

丹迪飯店確認單

房客：Mariam Thomas
電話號碼: 0956-856-898
預訂日期：七月一日
入住時間：七月八日（下午三點之後）
退房時間：七月九日（中午十二點前）
●非吸菸房 ○吸菸房
●單人房   ○雙人房
○三人房   ○家庭房

女：不好意思，我有預約今晚的房間。

男：是的，女士，您的大名是？

女：Mariam Thomas。

男：讓我查一下，有的，你預訂了今晚的一間非吸菸的單人房。是吧？

女：不完全對。事實上，我要的是雙人房。我們是兩位。

男：真的很抱歉。我們的雙人房與三人房已經完全訂滿了。但我可以安排一個更大一點的房間給你。為了向您致歉，我將提供免費的早餐給兩位使用。

女：喔，那聽起來令我滿意。

Q2　　D　Which room will Mariam probably stay in ?

Mariam 可能會入住哪種房間？

(A) Single room.

　　單人房。

(B) Double room.

　　雙人房。

(C) Triple room.

　　三人房。

(D) Family room.

　　家庭房。

單字解釋 ▶　triple room 三人房　　　　　fully booked 完全訂滿

　　　　　　　apology n 道歉　　　　　　complimentary adj 免費的

試題分析 ▶　本題問：Mariam 可能入住哪種房間。在對話中可知女子是 Mariam，接著聽到 Actually, I asked for a double room.，表示女子要的是雙人房。接著男子說 Our double rooms and triple rooms are fully booked. 表示雙人房與三人房都訂滿了，便建議幫女子換更大一點的房型（arrange a much bigger room），從圖表上來看，再大一點的房型為 Family Room。因此要選 D。

第四部分 簡短談話

Short Talk 1

Want to have a vacation and relax a little bit? We offer some packages just like you want! Stay at a resort hotel, and enjoy our two swimming pools, two tennis courts and a private sandy beach. You will love our luxury accommodations and economical prices. Call today to book your tour, and you are ready for your beautiful vacation.

中文翻譯

想要有一個假期來放鬆一下嗎？我們提供一些你想要的套裝行程。住在度假村，並好好享用我們的兩個游泳池、兩個網球場與一個私人的沙灘吧。你會愛上我們的豪華住宿與經濟實惠的價格。今天就打電話來訂你的旅程，準備好你的美好假期吧！

Q1   **B**   **What can NOT be found in the resort hotel?**
哪一項在此渡假村中找不到？
(A) A beach. 海灘。
(B) A log cabin. 小木屋。
(C) A swimming pool. 游泳池。
(D) A tennis court. 網球場。

 單字解釋 ▶ package **n** 套裝   resort hotel 度假村
private **adj** 私人的   accommodation **n** 住宿

試題分析 ▶ 本題問：哪一項在此渡假村中找不到。在談話中提到 Stay at a resort hotel ~ swimming pools ~ tennis courts ~ a private sandy beach.，可知會有游泳池、網球場、私人沙灘，沒提到小木屋。故答案要選 (B)。

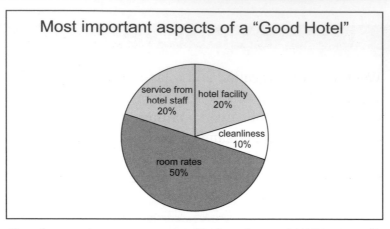

Most important aspects of a "Good Hotel"

Good morning, everyone. Today I would like to talk about how to run a successful hotel. First, I will start with some small details, for example, how to provide high quality service. Then, I'll talk about some other tips, like providing various hotel facilities and maintaining clean surroundings. Finally, I will go over the most important thing that customers care about when they choose an ideal hotel. Are you ready for today's lecture?

中文翻譯

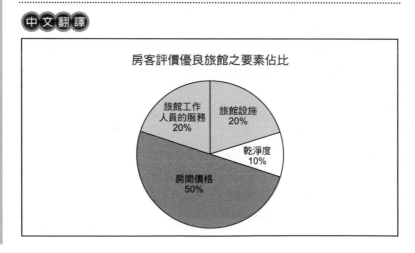

房客評價優良旅館之要素佔比

大家早。今天要跟各位談談如何經營一間成功的旅館。首先，我想以一些細節開始，例如像是如何提供高品質的服務。然後，我再說一些其他的祕訣，像是提供多樣化的旅館設施以及維護旅館環境的清潔度。最後我會談談顧客選擇一間理想旅館時，他們最關心的部分。各位準備好今天的課程了嗎？

Q2 ___C___ **What is the last item for the speaker to talk about?**

說話者最後要談的項目是什麼？

(A) Hotel facility.
旅館設施。
(B) Cleanliness.
乾淨度。
(C) Room rates.
房間價格。
(D) Service from hotel staff.
旅館工作人員的服務。

單字解釋▶ hotel facility 旅館設施　　　　cleanliness **n** 乾淨度
room rates 房間價格　　　　various **adj** 多樣的
surroundings **n** 周圍環境　　ideal **adj** 理想的

試題分析▶ 本題問：說話者最後要談的項目。在談話中的 Finally, I will go over the most important thing that customers care about when they choose an ideal hotel.可知，提到說話者最後會談到顧客選旅館時最關心的部分。從圖表中可知，占比最多的是50%的 room rates（房間價格），故答案要選 (C)。

情境解析 可能情境包括：計畫旅行、飛機上、旅途中、迷路
等。

1 Do you plan to go aboard?
你有計畫出國嗎？

2 How nice the trip is.
多麼棒的一趟旅遊。

3 I fly to L. A. next month.
我下個月將飛往洛杉磯。

模擬試題

 007.mp3

第一部分 看圖辨義

 試題冊上有數幅圖畫，每一圖畫有 1~3 個描述該圖的題目，每題
請聽光碟放音機播出題目以及四個英語敘述之後，選出與所看到
的圖畫最相符的答案，每題只播出一遍。

Picture A Q1 ～ Q2

答案欄

Picture B Q3

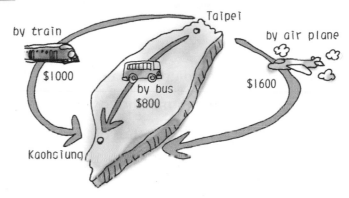

答案欄

Picture C Q4 ～ Q5

答案欄

第二部分 問答

 每題請聽光碟放音機播出一英語問句或直述句後，從試題冊上 A、B、C、D 四個回答或回應中，選出一個最適合者作答。每題只播出一遍。

 Q 1

(A) Sorry, I haven't got your passport.

(B) You have passed it, have you?

 答案欄

(C) Didn't you put it in your purse?

(D) Yes, I'll find the passport tomorrow.

 Q 2

(A) Sorry, there's no empty seat.

(B) Sure, tell me about your travel plans.

(C) I don't like to travel to Germany.

答案欄

(D) No, our agent is in London.

 Q 3

(A) Sorry, you can't go traveling without me.

(B) OK, I'm going to study English hard.

(C) I don't like to travel to France.

 答案欄

(D) I still have no ideas now.

第三部分 簡短對話

 每題請聽光碟放音機播出一段對話及一個相關的問題之後，從試題冊上 A、B、C、D 四個選項中選出一個最適合者作答。每段對話及問題只播出一遍。

Conversation 1

 Q 1

(A) At the train station.

(B) At the airport.

(C) Police station.

(D) MRT station.

Conversation 2

Q 2

Time	Destination	Platform
7:00 PM	Victoria Park	2
7:20 PM	Green Valley	3
7:30 PM	Stream Park	4
8:00 PM	White Valley	1

(A) 7:00 PM

(B) 7:10 PM

(C) 7:20 PM

(D) 7:30 PM

第四部分 簡短談話 新題型

每題請聽光碟放音機播出一段談話及一個相關的問題後，從試題冊上 A、B、C、D 四個選項中選出一個最適合者作答。每段談話及問題只播出一遍。

Short Talk 1

Q 1

(A) Line up at the gate.

(B) Carry their own bags.

(C) Show their boarding pass.

(D) Go to the counter immediately.

Short Talk 2

Q 2

Day	Date	Destination
Day 1	8/15 Fri.	Dan-shui's Fisherman's Wharf
Day 2	8/16 Sat.	Sun Moon Lake
Day 3	8/17 Sun.	Taroko National Park
Day 4	8/18 Mon.	Back home

(A) 8/15.

(B) 8/16.

(C) 8/17.

(D) 8/18.

答案解析

第一部分 看圖辨義

 For questions number 1 and 2, please look at picture A.
問題 1 跟問題 2 請看圖片 A。

Q1 ___D___ **What kind of advertisement is it?**

這是什麼樣的廣告？

(A) It's about studying overseas. 有關海外留學。
(B) It's about selling motors. 有關賣車。
(C) It's about selling computers. 有關賣電腦。
(D) It's about a tour. 有關旅行。

Q2 ___A___ **Which statement is NOT true?** 哪項敘述不是真的？

(A) It costs $38,000 for a 4-day trip in Japan.
　　日本四天三夜的旅行要花費 38,000 元。

(B) It costs $42,000 for a 5-day trip in Korea.
　　韓國五天四夜的旅行要花費 42,000 元。
(C) It costs $38,000 for a 6-day trip in China.
　　中國六天五夜的旅行要花費 38,000 元。
(D) The trip to Korea is the most expensive.
　　到韓國的旅遊行程最貴。

....

 For question number 3, please look at picture B.
問題 3 請看圖片 B。

Q3 ___B___ **I have only $900 with me. What's the most probable way for me to go?**

我只有 900 元。我最有可能採用哪種交通方式前往？

(A) Take a train. 搭火車。
(B) Take a bus. 搭公車。
(C) Take the subway. 搭地鐵。
(D) Take a plane. 搭飛機。

提示 For questions number 4 and 5, please look at picture C.
問題 4 跟問題 5 請看圖片 C。

Q4 __C__ **Where are Jeff and Tina?**

Jeff 與 Tina 在哪裡？

(A) They are in the emergency. 他們在急診室。

(B) They are in the office building. 他們在辦公大樓。

(C) They are in the customs. 他們在海關。

(D) They are customers in the shop. 他們是商店裡的顧客。

Q5 __D__ **Which description is right?** 哪個敘述是對的？

(A) Jeff is holding a handbag. Jeff 正拿著一個手提袋。

(B) Jeff is drinking a coke. Jeff 正在喝可樂。

(C) Tina and Jeff both have a cup of drinking.
Tina 與 Jeff 都有一杯飲料。

(D) Tina and Jeff both have passports in their hands.
Tina 與 Jeff 手中都拿著護照。

第二部分 問答

Q1 __C__ **Oh, my goodness! I just can't find my passport.** 喔，我的老天呀！我就是找不到我的護照！

(A) Sorry, I haven't got your passport.
抱歉，我沒有拿你的護照。

(B) You have passed it, haven't you?
你有經過它，不是嗎？

(C) Didn't you put it in your purse?
你沒放在你的皮包裡嗎？

(D) Yes, I'll find the passport tomorrow.
是的，我明天會找到護照。

單字解釋 ▶ my goodness 我的老天　　　　passport **n** 護照
purse **n** 皮包

試題分析 ▶ 本題說：我找不到我的護照。可知最適合的答案為選項(C)：
你難道沒放在你的皮包裡嗎。

Q2 __B__ **Can you give me some information about your agency's Germany tours?**

你能否給我一些關於你們旅行社的德國旅遊資訊?

(A) Sorry, there's no empty seat.

抱歉,沒有空位。

(B) Sure, tell me about your travel plans.

沒問題,告訴我你的旅遊計畫。

(C) I don't like to travel to Germany.

我不喜歡去德國旅行。

(D) No, our agent is in London.

不,我們的業務員在倫敦。

單字解釋 ▶ agency **n** 旅行社

Germany tour 德國的旅遊

試題分析 ▶ 本題問:可否給我德國旅遊的相關資訊。可知最適合的答案為選項(B):沒問題,告訴我你的旅行計畫。

Q3 __D__ **What's your travel plans next year?**

你明年的旅遊計畫是什麼?

(A) Sorry, you can't go traveling without me.

抱歉,沒有我你不能去旅行。

(B) OK, I'm going to study English hard.

好,我會努力學英文。

(C) I don't like to travel to France.

我不喜歡去法國旅遊。

(D) I still have no ideas now.

我還沒有什麼想法。

單字解釋 ▶ travel plan 旅行計畫

試題分析 ▶ 本題問:你明年的旅遊計畫是什麼。可知答案為選項 (D):我尚未有想法。

Conversation 1

W: Is this where I check in for Flight No. 251?
M: Yes, would you like to check in now?
W: Yep, here's my ticket and passport.
M: Do you have any luggage that you'd like to check?
W: Just one.
M: Here's your boarding pass. Have a nice flight.

中文翻譯

女：251 次班機在這裡辦理登機嗎？
男：是的，妳現在要辦理登機嗎？
女：是的，這是我的機票與護照。
男：妳有任何行李要拖運嗎？
女：只有一個。
男：這是妳的登機證。祝妳有一趟美好的旅程。

Q1 ___B___ **Where does the conversation take place?**
這個對話在哪裡發生？
(A) At the train station.
在火車站。
(B) At the airport.
在機場。
(C) Police station.
警察局。
(D) MRT station.
捷運站。

單字解釋 ▶ passport n 護照   luggage n 行李
試題分析 ▶ 本題問：對話發生的地點。從 Flight、ticket、passport、luggage 可知答案為選項 (B)：機場。

Conversation 2

Time	Destination	Platform
7:00 PM	Victoria Park	2
7:20 PM	Green Valley	3
7:30 PM	Stream Park	4
8:00 PM	White Valley	1

W: David, I'm here at Platform two now. Where are you?

M: I am at Platform four. The information board says the train to Stream Park departs in thirty minutes.

W: No, Dave. We are going to Victoria Park, not Stream Park. You always do that to me. Drive me crazy. Quickly come to Platform two now!

中文翻譯

時間	目的地	月台
晚上 7 點	維多莉亞公園	2
晚上 7 點 20 分	綠谷	3
晚上 7 點 30 分	小溪公園	4
晚上 8 點	白色山谷	1

女：大衛，我現在在第二月台了，你人在哪裡？

男：我在第四月台。火車資訊告示牌說，到小溪公園的車，三十分鐘後發車。

女：不是的，大衛。我們是要去維多莉亞公園，不是小溪公園。你總是對我做這樣的事情，快把我給逼瘋了。快到第二月台來。

Q2 __A__ **What time does the conversation take place?**

對話發生在幾點？
(A) 7:00 PM
　　晚上七點
(B) 7:10 PM
　　晚上七點十分
(C) 7:20 PM
　　晚上七點二十分
(D) 7:30 PM
　　晚上七點三十分

單字解釋 ▶ destination **n** 目的地
information board 資訊告示牌
depart **V** 啟程

試題分析 ▶ 本題問：對話的時間是發生在幾點。在對話中提到 The information board says the train to Stream Park departs in thirty minutes.，可知火車資訊告示牌說，到小溪公園的車，三十分鐘後發車，而圖表中往小溪公園的火車的出發時間是七點三十分啟程，所以現在是七點鐘，故答案選(A)。

第四部分 簡短談話

Short Talk 1

Flight 274 is now ready for boarding. All passengers please stand in line at the gate. If your carry-on bags are too large, please check them at the counter. Let me remind you that it is a non-smoking plane. Thanks for your cooperation.

中文翻譯

274 號班機的乘客請準備登機。所有乘客請在登機門前排隊，假如您的手提行李過大，請交至櫃檯託運。容我提醒大家，這是非吸菸的班機。感謝您的合作。

Q1 __A__ **What are the passengers asked to do?**

乘客被要求做什麼？

(A) Line up at the gate.

在登機門前排隊。

(B) Carry their own bags.

拿自己的行李。

(C) Show their boarding pass.

出示登機證。

(D) Go to the counter immediately.

立即至櫃檯處。

單字解釋 ▶ boarding **n** 登機　　　　　carry-on bag **n** 手提行李
cooperation **n** 合作

試題分析 ▶ 本題問：乘客被要求做什麼。在談話中提到 Flight ~ ready for boarding. All passengers please stand in line at the gate.，可知說話者請班機的乘客準備登機，並在登機門前排隊。故答案要選 (A)。

Short Talk 2

Day	Date	Destination
Day 1	8/15 Fri.	Dan-shui's Fisherman's Wharf
Day 2	8/16 Sat.	Sun Moon Lake
Day 3	8/17 Sun.	Taroko National Park
Day 4	8/18 Mon.	Back home

Good morning, ladies and gentlemen. I am your tour guide, Mimi. Let me tell you what we are going to visit in this beautiful island, Taiwan. Today our first stop is Dan-shui's Fisherman's Wharf. We'll stay there all day and enjoy some seafood at the same time. Tomorrow, we are going to take a train to Sun Moon Lake. It's a wonderful place to watch beautiful scenes. The day after tomorrow, we are going to Taroko National Park, which is well known for its spectacular mountains and canyons. I hope everyone enjoys your time in Taiwan.

中文翻譯

第幾天	日期	目的地
第一天	八月十五日週五	淡水漁人碼頭
第二天	八月十六日週六	日月潭
第三天	八月十七日週日	太魯閣國家公園
第四天	八月十八日週一	回家

早安，各位女士先生們。我是各位的導遊，米米。容我來告訴各位，我們在這座美麗的島嶼台灣，將會看到的事物。今天我們的第一站是淡水的漁人碼頭。我們將在這裡待一整天，同時享用美味的海產。明天我們將要搭火車去日月潭。這是一處可以看見美景的絕佳地點。後天，我們將會去太魯閣國家公園，這個地方以其壯觀的山脈與峽谷而聞名。我希望大家都可以好好享受在台灣的時光。

Q2 ____A____ **On what date does the speaker talk?**

說話者在講這段談話時的日期為何？

(A) 8/15.

八月十五日。

(B) 8/16.

八月十六日。

(C) 8/17.

八月十七日。

(D) 8/18.

八月十八日。

單字解釋 ▶ destination **n** 目的地　　　　wharf **n** 碼頭

spectacular **adj** 壯觀的

試題分析 ▶ 本題問：說話者在講這段談話時的日期是哪一天。在談話中，導遊談到 Today our first stop is Dan-shui's Fisherman's Wharf.，從 Today（今天）和 Dan-shui's Fisherman's Wharf（淡水漁人碼頭），以及對照圖表中的時間可知，日期是八月十五日，故答案要選 (A)。

情境主題 ⓽08 The Movies
（電影）

常考句子 Hint

情境解析 可能情境包括：討論電影劇情、喜歡的電影種類、相約看電影、電影放映時刻表等。

1 What kind of movies do you like?
你喜歡什麼種類的電影？

2 I hate to see a horror movie.
我討厭看恐怖電影。

3 Let's see a movie this afternoon.
我們今天下午去看場電影吧。

模擬試題

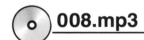 008.mp3

第一部分 看圖辨義

 作答說明 試題冊上有數幅圖畫，每一圖畫有 1~3 個描述該圖的題目，每題請聽光碟放音機播出題目以及四個英語敘述之後，選出與所看到的圖畫最相符的答案，每題只播出一遍。

104

Picture A Q1 ～ Q2

答案欄

Picture B Q3

答案欄

Picture C Q4 ～ Q5

答案欄

每題請聽光碟放音機播出一英語問句或直述句後，從試題冊上 A、B、C、D 四個回答或回應中，選出一個最適合者作答。每題只播出一遍。

Q 1

答案欄

(A) No, thanks. I have to study for tomorrow's test.

(B) Yes, the movie is so terrible.

(C) Yes, I would like to go for a play.

(D) Do you want to go with me?

Q 2

答案欄

(A) I don't like this movie.

(B) Is detective good for you?

(C) I like thriller.

(D) My friends all like comedy.

Q 3

答案欄

(A) I would rather have a DVD home.

(B) So, you like to rent a DVD home.

(C) I have a DVD player.

(D) OK, let's have a DVD home.

第三部分 簡短對話

Conversation 1

(A) The man doesn't want to see a movie.

(B) The movie begins at 7:00.

答案欄

(C) The woman wants to see a movie.

(D) The movie begins at 7:30.

Conversation 2 新題型

Viking Movie Cinema		
Cinema A	Love is blind	Comedy
Cinema B	Who's the murderer?	Thriller
Cinema C	Star War	Science Fiction
Cinema D	You light up my life	Romance

(A) Love is blind.

答案欄

(B) Who's the murderer.

(C) Star War.

(D) You light up my life.

第四部分　簡短談話 新題型

每題請聽光碟放音機播出一段談話及一個相關的問題後，從試題冊上 A、B、C、D 四個選項中選出一個最適合者作答。每段談話及問題只播出一遍。

Short Talk 1

Q 1

(A) Attires.
(B) Jewelry.
(C) New films.
(D) Awards.

答案欄

Short Talk 2

Q 2

4th French Film Festival shows		
Day 1	Friday	Family Comedy
Day 2	Saturday	Thriller
Day 3	Sunday	Science Fiction
Day 4	Monday	Romantic drama
Day 5	Tuesday	Animated Cartoon
Day 6	Wednesday	Action Movie
Day 7	Thursday	Horror Movie

(A) There are seven different styles of movies playing.
(B) If you want to watch four of the movies, you have to spend $1400.
(C) You can get a brochure by calling 055-555-895.
(D) The festival takes place once a year.

答案欄

答案解析

第一部分 看圖辨義

 For questions number 1 and 2, please look at picture A.
問題 1 跟問題 2 請看圖片 A。

Q1 __A__ **How much time do Andy and his friend have in case they want to see the first play?** Andy 與他的朋友若要看第一場戲還有多少時間？

(A) They still have 65 minutes. 他們還有 65 分鐘。
(B) They still have 2 hours and 35 minutes.
他們還有 2 小時 35 分鐘。
(C) They don't have much time. 他們沒有很多時間。
(D) They have much time to see a movie.
他們有很多時間看電影。

Q2 __C__ **What time is the last play?** 最後一場戲是幾點？
(A) It's 8:13. 是 8 點 13 分。
(B) It's at half before 8. 是 7 點半。
(C) It's 30 minutes after 8. 是 8 點半。
(D) They don't have the last play.
它們沒有最後一場戲。

 For question number 3, please look at picture B.
問題 3 請看圖片 B。

Q3 __A__ **Why is Ben so mad?** 為何 Ben 如此生氣？

(A) Because someone's phone is ringing and it's annoying. 因為某人的電話一直在響，這很煩人。
(B) Because someone is eating popcorn.
因為某人在吃爆米花。
(C) Because someone is sitting on Ben's seat and doesn't want to give it back to Ben.
因為某人坐在 Ben 的位子上而不肯讓座。

(D) Because someone stole his money, and Ben has no money to pay for the movie tickets.

因為某人偷了 Ben 的錢，導致他沒錢買電影票。

提示 For questions number 4 and 5, please look at picture C.

問題 4 跟問題 5 請看圖片 C。

Q4 __A__ **Can Chris choose a war movie in this movie theater?** Chris 可以在這家電影院選擇戰爭片嗎？

(A) No, he can't. But he can choose a romance.

不，他不能。但他能選愛情片。

(B) No, he can't. And he can't choose a cartoon, either.

不，他不能。而且他也不能選擇卡通片。

(C) No, he can't. But he can choose an adventure movie. 不，他不能。但他可以選一齣冒險片。

(D) Yes, he can. And it's his favorite kind.

是的，他可以。而且那是他最愛的種類。

Q5 __A__ **What description matches the picture C?**

哪一項敘述符合圖 C？

(A) There's a thriller named "Who's the Murderer".

有一部叫「誰是兇手」的驚悚片。

(B) In the end, Chris decided to see a romance.

最後 Chris 決定看愛情片。

(C) There are 5 kinds of movies in the cinema.

這家電影院裡有 5 種電影。

(D) The cinema has 4 different kinds of movies. They are romance, thriller, adventure and cartoon.

這家電影院有四種不同的電影。它們是愛情片、驚悚片、冒險片與卡通片。

第二部分 問答

Q1 __A__ **There's a terrific movie downtown. Would you like to see it?**

在市區有一部很棒的電影。你要去看嗎？

(A) No, thanks. I have to study for tomorrow's test.
不了，謝謝。我必須準備明天的考試。
(B) Yes, the movie is so terrible. 是的，這部電影很糟。
(C) Yes, I would like to go for a play. 是，我想去看舞台劇。
(D) Do you want to go with me? 你想和我去嗎？

單字解釋 ▶ terrific adj 很棒的　　　terrible adj 很糟的

試題分析 ▶ 本題問：在市中心有一個很棒的電影，問對方要不要去看。可知答案為選項 (A)：不，謝謝。我必須要準備明天的考試。

Q2 　C　 What kind of movie do you like?
你喜歡哪一種電影？
(A) I don't like this movie. 我不喜歡這部電影。
(B) Is detective good for you? 你喜歡偵探片嗎？
(C) I like thriller. 我喜歡驚悚片。
(D) My friends all like comedy. 我的朋友都喜歡喜劇片。

單字解釋 ▶ detective n 偵探片　　　thriller n 驚悚片
comedy n 喜劇片

試題分析 ▶ 本題問：你喜歡哪種電影。可知答案為選項 (C)：我喜歡驚悚片。

Q3 　A　 I prefer going to the cinema to renting a DVD home. 我比較喜歡去電影院而不想租 DVD 回家看。
(A) I would rather have a DVD home.
我寧願租 DVD 回家看。
(B) So, you like to rent a DVD home.
所以，你喜歡租 DVD 回家看。
(C) I have a DVD player. 我有一台 DVD 播放機。
(D) OK, let's have a DVD home. 好，我們租 DVD 回家看吧。

單字解釋 ▶ go to the cinema 去看電影
rent a DVD home 租 DVD 回家看
DVD player DVD 錄放影機

試題分析 ▶ 本題說：我比較喜歡去電影院而不想租 DVD 回家看。答案為選項(A) 我寧願租 DVD 回家看。

Conversation 1

W: There's a very terrific movie at the Lido tonight.
M: What is it?
W: "Ghost". Do you want to go?
M: See you there at 7:00.
W: Terrific.

中文翻譯

女：今晚在 Lido 戲院有一部很棒的電影。
男：是什麼？
女：「第六感生死戀」。你想去看嗎？
男：7 點整在戲院見。
女：太棒了。

Q1 ___C___ **Which statement is true?**

哪一個敘述是真的？

(A) The man doesn't want to see a movie.
男子不想看電影。

(B) The movie begins at 7:00.
這部電影 7 點開演。

(C) The woman wants to see a movie.
女子想看電影。

(D) The movie begins at 7:30.
這部電影 7 點半開演。

單字解釋 ▶ terrific adj 很棒的

試題分析 ▶ 本題問：哪一個敘述是真的。從女子的邀約（今晚在 Lido 戲院有一部很棒的電影，你想去看嗎？），以及男子的赴約（7 點整在戲院見）可知答案為選項 (C)：女子想看電影。對話中並未提到電影的放映時間，所以 (B) 和 (D) 不正確。

Conversation 2

Viking Movie Cinema		
Cinema A	Love is blind	Comedy
Cinema B	Who's the murderer?	Thriller
Cinema C	Star War	Science Fiction
Cinema D	You light up my life	Romance

W: You are late again, Pete. I've been standing in front of the cinema waiting for you.

M: I am sorry honey, this traffic is...

W: Okay, okay, better late than never.

M: What kind of movies do you want to see? Something romantic? Love story?

W: Not really, in fact, I want something to make me laugh aloud. Then, I can feel better after waiting here so long.

維京電影院		
放映廳 A	愛是盲目的	喜劇
放映廳 B	誰是謀殺者	驚悚劇
放映廳 C	星際大戰	科幻劇
放映廳 D	你點亮我的生命	愛情劇

女：Pete 你又遲到了。我一直站在戲院前等你。

男：親愛的真是抱歉，這交通…

女：好好好，遲到總比不到好。

男：你想看什麼類型的電影？羅曼蒂克的？有關愛情故事的？

女：不要。事實上，我想看能讓我大笑的。這樣我的心情會好一些，尤其是在等這麼久之後。

Q2 _A_ **What movie will they probably watch?**

他們可能會看哪部片？

(A) Love is blind.

愛是盲目的。

(B) Who's the murderer.

誰是兇手。

(C) Star War.

星際大戰。

(D) You light up my life.

你照亮我的生命

單字解釋 ▶ murderer **n** 謀殺者　　　　　　romantic **adj** 羅曼蒂克的

試題分析 ▶ 本題問：對話者可能會看哪部片。在對話中提到 I want something to make me laugh aloud. 表示想看能讓自己大笑的電影，也就是喜劇片，故答案選 (A)。

第四部分 簡短談話

Short Talk 1

I love to watch the movie awards shows every year. The biggest movie stars in Hollywood arrive on the red carpet before the show. There are interviews with the most famous celebrities. They talk about their lives and their latest movies. Female stars always wear lots of shiny jewelry. I like to vote for the prettiest and ugliest dresses in that year. So interesting!

中文翻譯

我每年都喜歡看電影的頒獎節目。好萊塢的巨星們都在節目開始前抵達紅毯，會有一些針對這些名人的訪談。他們都會聊聊他們的生活與最新的電影。女明星都會戴很多的閃亮珠寶。我喜歡針對當年度的服裝票選出最美與最醜的服裝。這很有趣！

Q1 ___A___ **What does the speaker vote for?**

說話者喜歡針對什麼投票？

(A) Attires. 服飾。
(B) Jewelry. 珠寶。
(C) New films. 新片。
(D) Awards. 獎項。

單字解釋 ▶ awards show **n** 頒獎節目   red carpet **n** 紅毯
celebrity **n** 名人

試題分析 ▶ 本題問：說話者喜歡針對什麼投票。在談話中提到 I like to vote for the prettiest and ugliest dresses in that year.，可知說話者喜歡針對最美與最醜的服裝進行票選。選項中的 attire 即服飾的意思，故答案要選(A)。

4th French Film Festival shows

Day 1	Friday	Family Comedy
Day 2	Saturday	Thriller
Day 3	Sunday	Science Fiction
Day 4	Monday	Romantic drama
Day 5	Tuesday	Animated Cartoon
Day 6	Wednesday	Action Movie
Day 7	Thursday	Horror Movie

The fourth annual French Film Festival starts tomorrow, Friday December 9th. From Friday to Sunday, there are seven films playing, including family comedies and romantic dramas. Admission to each film is $350. You can buy tickets in advance at Patrick Art Theatre or by calling 055-555-895. Please act quickly because some shows are already sold out. For more information, you can get a brochure at the theatre when it opens.

第四屆法國電影節節目

第一天	週五	家庭喜劇
第二天	週六	驚悚片
第三天	週日	科幻片
第四天	週一	愛情文藝片
第五天	週二	動畫
第六天	週三	動作片
第七天	週四	恐怖片

第四屆法國年度電影節，明天 12 月 9 日開始囉！從週五開始到週日，有七部電影將上映，包括家庭喜劇與愛情文藝片。每一部片的門票費是 350 元。您可以預先在派翠克藝術戲院買票，或是打電話 055-555-895。請趕快行動，因為一些場次已經銷售一空。若想要進一步的資訊，您可以在戲院營業時來索取手冊。

Q2 ___C___ **Which statement is NOT correct?**

下列敘述何者為非？

(A) There are seven different styles of movies playing.

有七種不同型態的電影上映。

(B) If you want to watch four of the movies, you have to spend $1400.

假如你想看其中四部片，你必須花費 1,400 元。

(C) You can get a brochure by calling 055-555-895.

你可以撥打 055-555-895 來索取手冊。

(D) The festival takes place once a year.

這個節日一年辦一次。

（單字解釋）annual **adj** 年度的　　　　　in advance 預先
brochure **n** 手冊

（試題分析）本題問：這些敘述中何者不正確。在談話中可以得知 there are seven films playing, including family comedies and romantic dramas.，表示有七部電影會上映，因此 (A) 正確。從 Admission to each film is $350. 也可知 (B) 正確。從一開始的 fourth annual French Film Festival 的 annual（年度的）可知 (D) 正確。談話中只提到買票的話可以撥打 055-555-895。故答案要選(C)。

Hint

常
考
句
子

情境解析 可能情境包括：計畫派對、參加某人派對、讚美或抱怨派對、派對影響鄰居安寧等。

1 How was Charles's party last night?
昨晚 Charles 的派對如何？

2 Did Joe invite you to his party?
Joe 有邀請你去他的派對嗎？

3 The party is too lousy.
這個派對真糟。

4 We will have a big party in November.
十一月我們將有一個大型的舞會。

5 Do you know where Mary's birthday party will be held?
你知道瑪麗的生日舞會會在哪裡舉行嗎？

6 You should have come! The party was fantastic!
你應該要來的！這個派對簡直就是太棒了？

7 Will you come to my party?
你會來我的宴會嗎？

模擬試題

🔘 **009.mp3** ────●

第一部分 看圖辨義

試題冊上有數幅圖畫，每一圖畫有 1~3 個描述該圖的題目，每題請聽光碟放音機播出題目以及四個英語敘述之後，選出與所看到的圖畫最相符的答案，每題只播出一遍。

Picture A Q1 ～ Q2

答案欄

Picture B Q3 ～ Q5

答案欄

第二部分　問答

每題請聽光碟放音機播出一英語問句或直述句後，從試題冊上 A、B、C、D 四個回答或回應中，選出一個最適合者作答。每題只播出一遍。

Q 1

(A) She enjoyed playing the musical instrument so much.

(B) I guess so. She had a good time last night.

(C) I am sorry that I don't like the party.

(D) No, I didn't enjoy myself at all.

Q 2

(A) Yes, I wasn't.

(B) Yes, she was.

(C) No, I wasn't.

(D) Alice is my best friend.

Q 3

(A) Sure, I held the party for Tim.

(B) No, I didn't know that.

(C) Really? You got the invitation?

(D) Anyone else?

第三部分 簡短對話

作答說明 每題請聽光碟放音機播出一段對話及一個相關的問題之後，從試題冊上 A、B、C、D 四個選項中選出一個最適合者作答。每段對話及問題只播出一遍。

Conversation 1

Q 1

答案欄

(A) They are talking about going to a cinema.

(B) They are talking about preparing for a birthday party.

(C) They are talking about the party held yesterday.

(D) They are talking about going to a party tonight.

Conversation 2

Q 2

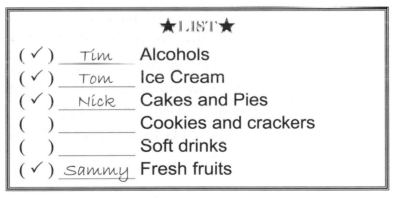

★LIST★

(✓) __Tim__ Alcohols
(✓) __Tom__ Ice Cream
(✓) __Nick__ Cakes and Pies
( ) _____ Cookies and crackers
( ) _____ Soft drinks
(✓) __Sammy__ Fresh fruits

答案欄

(A) Alcohols or cookies

(B) Cookies or pies

(C) Fruits or ice cream

(D) Crackers or soft drinks

第四部分 簡短談話 新題型

作答說明 每題請聽光碟放音機播出一段談話及一個相關的問題後,從試題冊上 A、B、C、D 四個選項中選出一個最適合者作答。每段談話及問題只播出一遍。

Short Talk 1

 Q 1

(A) Manager and staff.

(B) Teacher and student.

(C) Parent and child.

(D) Wife and husband.

 答案欄

Short Talk 2

 Q 2

Things to do for tonight's party

(1) Decorate around the house
(2) Go to the supermarket to buy some food
(3) Go to a record store to buy some music
(4) Call friends to make sure if they will come tonight

(A) Decorate around the house

(B) Go to the supermarket to buy some food

(C) Go to a record store to buy some music

(D) Call friends to make sure if they will come tonight

 答案欄

答案解析

第一部分 看圖辨義

提示 **For questions number 1 and 2, please look at picture A.**
問題 1 跟問題 2 請看圖片 A。

Q1 __A__ **What's the time?**

現在幾點？
(A) It's 11:00. 11 點。
(B) It's 3:00. 3 點。
(C) It's 7:00. 7 點。
(D) It's 11:30. 11 點半。

Q2 __C__ **Why were Tim's neighbors angry?**

為何 Tim 的鄰居們生氣？
(A) Because Tim didn't invite them to the party.
　　因為 Tim 沒有邀請他們參加派對。
(B) Because they couldn't eat a big cake.
　　因為他們不能吃大蛋糕。
(C) Because the music was too loud. 因為音樂太吵了。
(D) Because the party was not big enough.
　　因為這個派對不夠大。

提示 **For questions number 3, 4 and 5, please look at picture B.**
問題 3、4 跟問題 5 請看圖片 B。

Q3 __D__ **What's this?**

這是什麼？
(A) It's a grade report. 是一張成績單。
(B) It's a public notice. 是一個公告。
(C) It's an advertisement. 是一個廣告。
(D) It's an invitation. 是一張邀請函。

Q4   **D**   **Where is the party?** 這場派對是在哪裡？

(A) In a garage. 在車庫裡。
(B) In a cinema. 在戲院裡。
(C) In a private house. 在私人住宅裡。
(D) In a hotel. 在飯店裡。

Q5   **C**   **Which statement is right?** 哪個敘述是對的？

(A) For men, if they want to enter this party, they must wear socks. 如果男士們想參與這個派對，他們必須穿短襪。
(B) For women, if they want to enter this party, they can wear sandals.
如果女士們想參與這個派對，她們可以穿涼鞋。
(C) People who wear jeans and sandals can't enter the party.
穿牛仔褲與涼鞋者不能參加這個派對。
(D) The party begins at 10:20. 派對 10 點 20 分開始。

第二部分 問答

Q1   **B**   **Did Tina enjoy herself at the party last night?** Tina 昨晚在派對玩得愉快嗎？

(A) She enjoyed playing the musical instrument so much. 她很喜歡彈樂器。
(B) I guess so. She had a good time last night.
我想是的，她昨晚玩得很愉快。
(C) I am sorry that I don't like the party.
我很遺憾我不喜歡那個派對。
(D) No, I didn't enjoy myself at all.
不，我一點也不開心。

單字解釋 ▶ enjoy oneself 玩得愉快   musical instrument 樂器
have a good time 玩得愉快   not. . . at all 一點也不

試題分析 ▶ 本題問：Tina 昨晚在派對玩得愉快嗎。可知答案為選項 (B)：
我想是的，她玩得很愉快。

Q2 __C__ **Weren't you at Alice's party last night?**

你昨晚沒在 Alice 的派對上嗎？

(A) Yes, I wasn't.

是的，我沒有。

(B) Yes, she was.

是的，她有。

(C) No, I wasn't.

不，我沒有。

(D) Alice is my best friend.

Alice 是我最好的朋友。

單字解釋 ▶ best friend 最好的朋友

試題分析 ▶ 本題問：你昨晚沒在 Alice 的派對上嗎。可知答案為選項
(C)：不，我沒有。請特別注意否定疑問句的回答方式跟肯定
疑問句的回答方式相同。

Q3 __B__ **Did Tim invite you to his party?**

Tim 有邀請你去他的派對嗎？

(A) Sure, I held the party for Tim.

當然，我為 Tim 舉辦了派對。

(B) No, I didn't know that.

不，我不知道那件事。

(C) Really? You got the invitation?

真的嗎？你收到邀請函了？

(D) Anyone else?

還有其他人嗎？

單字解釋 ▶ invite V 邀請

hold V 舉辦（過去式為 held）

invitation n 邀請函

試題分析 ▶ 本題問：Tim 有邀請你去她的派對嗎。可知答案為選項 (B)：
我不知此事。

Conversation 1

W: Did you go to Davy's party last night?

M: I wish I hadn't gone there. It was too lousy.

W: Really? I heard that he has prepared for a long time.

M: Maybe. But, in fact, it was the worst party that I had ever gone to.

中文翻譯

女：你昨晚去了 Davy 的派對嗎？

男：我真希望我沒去，那實在太糟糕了。

女：真的嗎？我聽說他準備很久了。

男：也許吧，但事實上，那是我參加過最糟的派對。

Q1 ___C___ **What are the speakers talking about?**

說話者在談論什麼？

(A) They are talking about going to a cinema.
他們正在討論去電影院。

(B) They are talking about preparing for a birthday party. 他們正在討論準備一場生日派對。

(C) They are talking about the party held yesterday.
他們在討論昨天舉辦的派對。

(D) They are talking about going to a party tonight.
他們正在討論今晚去一場派對。

單字解釋 ▶ lousy adj 糟糕的

試題分析 ▶ 本題問：說話者在談論什麼。從 party last night 可知答案為選項 (C)：他們在討論昨天舉辦的派對。

Conversation 2

★LIST★

(✓) ___Tim___ Alcohols
(✓) ___Tom___ Ice Cream
(✓) ___Nick___ Cakes and Pies
( ) _____ Cookies and crackers
( ) _____ Soft drinks
(✓) __Sammy__ Fresh fruits

W: I am in the good mood today.

M: Really? Any good news?

W: Well, I got my English test sheet back this morning. I didn't fail it as I expected before.

M: That's great. I am planning to have a party tonight at my home. This semester is over, and I want to celebrate it. Wanna come?

W: Sure! You know I love parties. Should I bring something to the party?

M: Just check our list. Bring the things that haven't been checked by anyone.

中文翻譯

清單

(✓) ___Tim___ 酒
(✓) ___Tom___ 冰淇淋
(✓) ___Nick___ 蛋糕與派
( ) _____ 餅乾
( ) _____ 汽水
(✓) __Sammy__ 新鮮水果

女：我今天心情好。

男：真的嗎？有何好消息？

女：今天早上我拿回了我的英文考卷。我並沒有如我當初預期的被當掉。

男：那太好了。我計畫今晚在我家開派對，我想來慶祝學期結束。你想來嗎？

女：當然！你知道我喜歡派對的。我要帶什麼來派對呢？

男：就檢視一下我們的清單。帶還沒有人打勾的東西來。

Q2 ___D___ **What might the woman bring to the party?**

女子可能會帶什麼到派對？

(A) Alcohols or cookies.

酒或餅乾。

(B) Cookies or pies.

餅乾或派。

(C) Fruits or ice cream.

水果或冰淇淋

(D) Crackers or soft drinks.

餅乾或汽水

單字解釋 ▶ celebrate **v** 慶祝　　　　　　semester **n** 學期

cracker **n** 脆餅乾

試題分析 ▶ 本題問：女子可能會帶什麼到派對。在對話中的最後一句聽到 Just check our list. Bring the things that haven't been checked by anyone. 表示檢視清單，並帶還沒有人打勾的品項來。從表格可知，尚未打勾的是餅乾與汽水，故答案選 (D)。

第四部分 簡短談話

Short Talk 1

Good evening, everybody, and welcome to the birthday party for Ben. As his supervisor, I am happy to have this party for him. He is a nice coworker. OK, let's enjoy the party! And happy birthday to Ben.

中文翻譯

大家晚安，歡迎各位來到 Ben 的生日派對。身為他的主管，我非常高興替他安排這場派對。他是一位很好的同事。好的，讓我們好好享受這場派對吧！並祝福 Ben 生日快樂。

Q1 ___A___ **What probably is the relationship between the speaker and Ben?**

說話者與 Ben 的關係可能為何？

(A) Manager and staff. 經理與員工。
(B) Teacher and student. 老師與學生。
(C) Parent and child. 家長與小孩。
(D) Wife and husband. 太太與先生。

單字解釋 ▶ supervisor n 主管　　coworker n 同事

試題分析 ▶ 本題問：說話者與 Ben 的關係為何。在談話中聽到 As his supervisor, I am happy to have this party for him. He is a nice coworker. 身為他的主管，我非常高興替他安排這場派對。他是一位很好的同事。因此是上司與部屬的關係，故答案要選 (A)。

Short Talk 2

Things to do for tonight's party

(1) Decorate around the house
(2) Go to the supermarket to buy some food
(3) Go to a record store to buy some music
(4) Call friends to make sure if they will come tonight

Allison is pretty busy today because she is going to throw a party tonight. She has done something she has to do today, but there are many other things she hasn't done yet. She has gone to the supermarket to buy some food, and she's also prepared some awesome party music. She has made several phone calls to make sure whether the people she has invited will come or not, but she still hasn't made her house special with some ornaments.

今晚派對的待辦事項

(1) 裝飾家裡四周
(2) 去超市買食物
(3) 到唱片行買一些音樂
(4) 打電話給朋友確定他們今晚是否出席

Allison 今天很忙,因為今晚她要辦一場派對。她已經做完一些她今天必須做的事,但還有許多她尚未完成的事情。她已經去了超市買了食物,她也已經準備了一些很棒的派對音樂。她撥了幾通電話來確定她邀請的人是否會來,但她還沒有用一些裝飾品來裝飾她家,好讓這個家看起來特別。

Q2 ___A___ **What else does Allison need to do besides the things she's done?**

除了已經完成的事之外，Allison 還需要做什麼？

(A) Decorate around the house.

　　裝飾家的四周。

(B) Go to the supermarket to buy some food.

　　去超市買食物。

(C) Go to a record store to buy some music.

　　去唱片行買些音樂。

(D) Call friends to make sure if they will come tonight.

　　打電話給朋友確定他們今晚是否會來。

單字解釋 ▶ decorate **V** 裝飾　　　　ornament **n** 裝飾品

試題分析 ▶ 本題問：除了已經完成的事外，Allison 還需要做什麼事。在談話中提到 She has gone to the supermarket to buy some food、prepared some ~ music，以及 phone calls to make sure whether the people ~ come or not，可知已完成的事是：去超市買了食物、準備好音樂、打電話確定邀請的人是否會來。此外也提到 but she still hasn't made her house special with some ornaments.，表示家裡還沒有裝飾。故答案要選 (A)。

Invitation
（邀請）

 可能情境包括：邀請參加派對、寄邀請函、邀請參加結婚典禮或畢業典禮、邀請他人到家中作客等。

1 Did you get my wedding invitation card? 你收到我的結婚喜帖了嗎？

2 Do you have free time this evening?
你今晚有空嗎？

3 You won't have time to go out with me, will you? 你不會有時間和我出去的，你有嗎？

4 Will you come to my party tonight?
你今晚會出席我的派對嗎？

5 Let's go for a drink!
一起去喝一杯吧！

6 Please come over and have dinner with us sometimes.
請您有時來我家作客，吃頓晚餐吧。

7 Haven't you invited John to the party?
你還沒邀請 John 來派對嗎？

模擬試題

010.mp3

(010.mp3)

第一部分　看圖辨義

作答說明　試題冊上有數幅圖畫，每一圖畫有 1~3 個描述該圖的題目，每題請聽光碟放音機播出題目以及四個英語敘述之後，選出與所看到的圖畫最相符的答案，每題只播出一遍。

Picture A　Q1 ～ Q2

Mary's Birthday Party
Time: 8. 20. at 7:00pm.
Place: Mary's home

答案欄

Picture B　Q3 ～ Q4

答案欄

Steak House

每題請聽光碟放音機播出一英語問句或直述句後,從試題冊上
A、B、C、D 四個回答或回應中,選出一個最適合者作答。每題
只播出一遍。

Q 1

(A) I go to church every Sunday.

(B) I got a fine ticket yesterday.

(C) Really? The graduation ceremony will be held in a small church.

(D) I'll probably send a red envelope instead of attending the wedding party.

Q 2

(A) I went to a baseball game with you.

(B) The ticket for the baseball game is not free.

(C) Great. Volleyball is my favorite.

(D) I can't wait it.

Q 3

(A) Why not get an invitation from him?

(B) Believe me! You will have a lot of fun there!

(C) Really? I will give you an invitation.

(D) Let's go for a BBQ party.

第三部分 簡短對話

作答說明 每題請聽光碟放音機播出一段對話及一個相關的問題之後，從試題冊上 A、B、C、D 四個選項中選出一個最適合者作答。每段對話及問題只播出一遍。

Conversation 1

Q 1

答案欄

(A) Fast food.

(B) Steak.

(C) Korean food.

(D) Hotpot cuisine.

Conversation 2 新題型

Q 2

POP Music Queens		
Singer	Song	Release Year
Taylor	Cardigan	2020
Katy	Roar	2016
Gaga	Bad romance	2015
Britney	Baby one more time	1999

答案欄

(A) Taylor.

(B) Katy.

(C) Gaga.

(D) Britney.

第四部分 **簡短談話** 新題型

 作答說明 每題請聽光碟放音機播出一段談話及一個相關的問題後，從試題冊上 A、B、C、D 四個選項中選出一個最適合者作答。每段談話及問題只播出一遍。

Short Talk 1

Q 1

(A) In 5 minutes.

(B) In 15 minutes.

(C) In 25 minutes.

(D) On May 17th.

 答案欄

....

Short Talk 2

Q 2

> ### BRIAN AND JENNY'S WEDDING INVITATION
>
> We are going to have a wedding ceremony and reception, and we sincerely invite you to be our preferred guests. Please reply if you can attend before March 1st.

(A) Between December and January.

 答案欄

(B) Between January and February.

(C) Between February and March.

(D) Between March and April.

....

答案解析

第一部分 看圖辨義

For questions number 1 and 2, please look at picture A.
問題 1 跟問題 2 請看圖片 A。

Q1 ___A___ **Whose party is it?**
這是誰的派對？

(A) It's Mary's. 是 Mary 的。
(B) It's Mike's. 是 Mike 的。
(C) It's Dennis's. 是 Dennis 的。
(D) It's Harry's. 是 Harry 的。

Q2 ___C___ **What date is this party on?**
這個派對的日期是哪一天？

(A) It's August 30th. 8 月 30 日。
(B) It's September 20th. 9 月 20 日。
(C) It's August 20th. 8 月 20 日。
(D) It's March 3rd. 3 月 3 日。

For questions number 3 and 4, please look at picture B.
問題 3 跟問題 4 請看圖片 B。

Q3 ___A___ **Why is Den making a phone call ?**
為何 Den 打電話？

(A) Because he wants to invite his classmates for a reunion. 因為他要邀請他的同學參加同學會。
(B) Because he wants to make sure if everyone can come to a party. 因為他想確定是否每個人都會參加派對。
(C) Because he wants to hand his paper in tomorrow and he needs some help.
因為他想在明天交報告，而他需要一些幫助。
(D) Because he wants to gossip with his best friends and classmates. 因為他想跟最好的朋友和同學聊八卦。

Q4 __C__ **Which description matches the picture B?**

哪一項敘述符合圖 B？

(A) Den asks his classmates to a steakhouse before he goes to bed. Den 在上床睡覺前邀請他的同學去牛排館。

(B) Den asks his classmates to a party because it has lots of fun. Den 邀請他的同學去派對，因為很好玩。

(C) Den asks his classmates to a steakhouse when he calls them. Den 在打電話時邀請同學們去牛排館。

(D) Den decides to invite all of his classmates to a steakhouse, but no one wants to go there.

Den 決定邀請他所有的同學去牛排館，但沒有一個人想去那裡。

第二部分 問答

Q1 __D__ **Did you get the invitation from Mary? Her wedding party will be held next Saturday in a small church.**

你收到 Mary 的邀請函了嗎？她的婚禮將在下週六於一個小教堂舉行。

(A) I go to church every Sunday. 我每週日去教堂。

(B) I got a fine ticket yesterday. 我昨天被開罰單。

(C) Really? The graduation ceremony will be held in a small church. 真的嗎？畢業典禮將在一個小教堂舉行。

(D) I'll probably send a red envelope instead of attending the wedding party.

我可能會包紅包而不去參加婚禮。

單字解釋 ▶

invitation **n** 邀請函	wedding party 喜宴
church **n** 教堂	fine ticket 罰單
graduation ceremony 畢業典禮	probably **adv** 可能
red envelope 紅包	instead of 而非…

試題分析 ▶ 本題問：是否收到 Mary 的邀請函，她下週六舉辦婚禮。答案為選項(D)：我可能會包紅包，而不參加婚禮。其他選項皆不適合。

Q2 ___D___ **Are you free tomorrow night? Let's go to a baseball game.** 明晚你有空嗎？我們去看棒球賽吧。

(A) I went to a baseball game with you.
我和你去看了棒球賽。
(B) The ticket for the baseball game is not free.
棒球賽的票不是免費的。
(C) Great. Volleyball is my favorite.
太棒了。排球是我的最愛。
(D) I can't wait it. 我等不及去看。

單字解釋 ▶ go to a baseball game 去看棒球賽　ticket **n** 門票
volleyball **n** 排球
試題分析 ▶ 本題問：明晚是否有空，一起去看棒球賽吧。可知答案為選項
(D)：我等不及去看。

Q3 ___B___ **I haven't decided to go to his party or not even though I got his invitation.**
即使收到了他的邀請函，我還沒決定是否要參加他的派對。
(A) Why not get an invitation from him?
為何不向他拿邀請函？
(B) Believe me! You will have a lot of fun there!
相信我！你會在那裡遇到很多有趣的事。
(C) Really? I will give you an invitation.
真的嗎？我會給你邀請函。
(D) Let's go for a BBQ party.
我們辦一場烤肉派對吧。

單字解釋 ▶ invitation **n** 邀請函
試題分析 ▶ 本題說：即使我收到他的邀請函，我仍沒決定是否要參加他的
派對。答案為選項 (B)。

第三部分 簡短對話

Conversation 1

W: Harry was talking about going out to eat on Sunday. Maybe we'll go to one of those hotpot places.

M: I have a better idea. Let's go for Korean food. I know a terrific restaurant.

W: Fine with me. But, I am not sure if Harry is OK.

M: Let me suggest it to Harry. I think that'd be fine with him, too.

....

中文翻譯

女：Harry 正在討論星期天出去吃飯。也許我們會去其中一間火鍋店。

男：我有一個更好的主意。我們去吃韓式料理吧。我知道一家很棒的餐廳。

女：我覺得很好。但是我不確定 Harry 是否可以。

男：讓我來跟 Harry 建議看看。我想那對他來說應該也沒問題。

Q1 ___C___ **What will the speakers probably eat on Sunday?** 說話者星期天可能會吃什麼？

(A) Fast food.
　　速食。

(B) Steak.
　　牛排。

(C) Korean food.
　　韓式料理。

(D) Hotpot cuisine.
　　火鍋料理。

單字解釋 ▶ hotpot place 火鍋店　　　　　suggest Ⅴ 建議

試題分析 ▶ 本題問：說話者星期天可能會吃什麼。可知答案為選項 (C)：韓式料理。

主題
⑩
Invitation（邀請）

答案
解析

Conversation 2

POP Music Queens

Singer	Song	Time for released
Taylor	Cardigan	2020
Katy	Roar	2016
Gaga	Bad romance	2015
Britney	Baby one more time	1999

W: Our school wants to invite one of these four pop music queens for the year-end school party. Do you think who the most talented is?

M: Neck and Neck. But I think you should invite someone who has the latest song.

W: Maybe you are right. People like new songs.

中文翻譯

流行音樂天后

歌手	歌曲	發行年份
泰勒	羊毛衫	2020
凱蒂	獅吼	2016
卡卡	壞羅曼史	2015
布蘭妮	寶貝再一次	1999

女：我們學校想要邀請這四位流行音樂天后中的其中一位來參加年底的學校派對。你認為誰最有才？

男：平分秋色。但我想你們應該要邀請有最新歌曲的人來。

女：也許你是對的。大家都喜歡新歌。

Q2   __A__   **Who will be the most likely invited to the school party?**

誰最有可能被邀請到學校派對？

(A) Taylor.

泰勒。

(B) Katy.

凱蒂。

(C) Gaga.

卡卡。

(D) Britney.

布蘭妮。

單字解釋 ▶   talented **adj** 有天份的   latest **adj** 最新的

neck and neck 並駕齊驅；勢均力敵（慣用語）

試題分析 ▶   本題問：誰最有可能被邀請到學校派對，在對話中聽到 But I think you should invite someone who has the latest song. 以及 People like new songs.，表示建議邀請有最新歌曲的人，因為大家都喜歡新歌。從圖表可得知最新歌曲是 2020 年 Taylor 的 Cardigan，故答案要選 (A)。

第四部分 簡短談話

Short Talk 1

Attention, customers. In 15 minutes, author Susan Martin is going to introduce her new book, *Five steps to be a rich man*. We invite you to this wonderful speech. All interested please proceed to Room 25 now. Also, we would like to remind you again that we will be closed on May 17th. Have a nice day!

中文翻譯

顧客們請注意。十五分鐘後，作者 Susan Martin 將要介紹她的新書《五個步驟變成有錢人》。我們邀請各位來聽這場極棒的演講。所有有興趣的人現在請前往會議室 25 室。同時，我們要再次提醒各位，本店五月十七日不營業。祝福大家有美好的一天。

Q1 ___B___ **When can people listen to a speech?**

聽眾何時可以聽演講？
(A) In 5 minutes. 5 分鐘後。
(B) In 15 minutes. 15 分鐘後。
(C) In 25 minutes. 25 分鐘後。
(D) On May 17th. 五月十七日。

單字解釋 ▶ proceed to 前往

試題分析 ▶ 本題問：聽眾何時可以聽演講。在談話中提到 In 15 minutes, author Susan Martin ~ introduce her new book, Five steps to be a rich man.，表示十五分鐘後，作者將介紹她的新書，因此再過十五分鐘就可以聽到演講，故答案要選 (B)。

Brian and Jenny's Wedding Invitation

We are going to have a wedding ceremony and reception, and we sincerely invite you to be our preferred guests. Please reply if you can attend before March 1st.

Brian and I announced our engagement just not long ago, and now we are going to get married! In early December, we reserved the ceremony site and a place for the reception. Later the same month, I had to order the wedding dresses for myself and my bridesmaids. Planning the guest list also took a lot of time. In January, we ordered the invitations. In early February, we sent them to make sure how many people would come. As soon as we know the results, we will start to arrange our guests' gifts.

中文翻譯

Brian 與 Jenny 的婚禮邀請函

我們要舉行婚禮與宴客了,我們真心地邀請您來當我們的首選佳賓。請在三月一日前回覆您是否可以參加。

就在不久前,Brian 與我宣布了我們訂婚的事,而現在我們要結婚囉!在十二月初,我們預訂了典禮場地與宴會處。同月份的稍晚,我下訂了我自己的和我伴娘的婚紗。擬定貴賓清單也花了很多時間。一月份時,我們訂好了喜帖邀請函。在二月初,我們把喜帖寄出,以便確定有多少人會參加。一旦知道結果,我們將準備貴賓的禮品。

Q2 ___C___ **When does the talk happen?**

這段談話發生在何時？

(A) Between December and January.

在十二月與一月之間。

(B) Between January and February.

在一月與二月之間。

(C) Between February and March.

在二月與三月之間。

(D) Between March and April.

在三月與四月之間。

單字解釋 ▶ engagement **n** 訂婚   ceremony site 典禮場地

bridesmaid **n** 伴娘   preferred guest 首選佳賓

試題分析 ▶ 本題問：這段談話發生的時間。在談話中提到 In early February, we sent them[invitations] to make sure how many people would come.，可知在二月初時，說話者寄出喜帖，而邀請函上註明要貴賓於三月一日前回覆。由此可知談話是在二月與三月之間進行的，故答案要選(C)。

情境解析

可能情境包括：掛號看診、跟朋友約見面、男女朋友約會、聚餐、跟指導教授約見面談論文等。

1 I'd like to make an appointment with Dr. Lee. 我想預約看李醫師的診。

2 I've had an appointment with Mr. Lin.
我已經跟林先生有約了。

3 I want to meet you tomorrow.
我明天想跟你見面。

4 What time did you say?
你剛剛說幾點？

5 My schedule is full tomorrow, so don't fit any extra things in.
我明天的行程滿檔，所以別再安排任何額外的事進來。

6 Are you dating with Peter?
你正在跟彼得交往嗎？

7 We should fix a date for the next meeting.
我們應該為下一次會議訂個日期。

模擬試題

 011.mp3

第一部分 看圖辨義

 作答說明

試題冊上有數幅圖畫，每一圖畫有 1~3 個描述該圖的題目，每題請聽光碟放音機播出題目以及四個英語敘述之後，選出與所看到的圖畫最相符的答案，每題只播出一遍。

Picture A Q1 ～ Q2

答案欄

Picture B Q3 ～ Q4

答案欄

每題請聽光碟放音機播出一英語問句或直述句後，從試題冊上
A、B、C、D 四個回答或回應中，選出一個最適合者作答。每題
只播出一遍。

Q 1

答案欄

(A) Of course. My teeth hurt

(B) I'd like to make a reservation, too

(C) Yes, I went there yesterday.

(D) This is my first date with a girl.

Q 2

答案欄

(A) Please have a seat and wait a second.

(B) So you are an interviewer.

(C) Do you want an interview with me?

(D) Do not be nervous. I'll teach you.

Q 3

答案欄

(A) Have a cold drink, please.

(B) Give me your health insurance card.

(C) I got a doctorate degree last year.

(D) How much money do you want?

第三部分　簡短對話

 作答說明　每題請聽光碟放音機播出一段對話及一個相關的問題之後，從試題冊上 A、B、C、D 四個選項中選出一個最適合者作答。每段對話及問題只播出一遍。

Conversation 1

Q 1

 答案欄

(A) At a company
(B) On the campus
(C) In the hospital
(D) In the hotel.

Conversation 2 新題型

Q 2

Tim's Schedule		
MON.	10:00 AM	Meeting with office manager
TUE.	20:00 PM	John's wedding ceremony
WED.	13:00 PM	Lunch w/ Tammy Kim
THURS.	11:00 AM	Dentist
FRI.	21:00 PM	Office Party

 答案欄

(A) On Monday.
(B) On Tuesday.
(C) On Wednesday.
(D) On Friday.

每題請聽光碟放音機播出一段談話及一個相關的問題後,從試題冊上 A、B、C、D 四個選項中選出一個最適合者作答。每段談話及問題只播出一遍。

Short Talk 1

Q 1

(A) At the front of school at 9:00 in the morning.

(B) At the auditorium at 9:00 in the morning.

(C) At the front of school at 4:15 in the afternoon.

(D) At the auditorium at 4:15 in the afternoon.

Short Talk 2

Q 2

First Date Advice
(1) Be respectful to the girl's parents.
(2) Drive safely and slowly.
(3) Take the girl home before 10:00 PM.
(4) Don't dress too sloppily.

(A) Be respectful to the girl's parents

(B) Drive safely and slowly

(C) Take the girl home before 10:00 PM

(D) Don't dress too sloppily.

答案解析

第一部分 看圖辨義

| 提示 | **For questions number 1 and 2, please look at picture A.**
問題 1 跟問題 2 請看圖片 A。 |

Q1 　A　 Which description is correct?
哪一個敘述是正確的？

(A) Tony has a date with his girlfriend, but she is terribly late. Tony 與他的女友約會，但是她遲到很久。
(B) Tony makes an appointment with his girlfriend at 3:30 pm. Tony 與他的女友約下午 3 點半見面。
(C) Tony has a bunch of flowers for his mother.
　　Tony 有一束花要給他媽媽。
(D) Tony is waiting for his sister and classmate.
　　Tony 在等他的妹妹與同學。

Q2 　D　 Where is Tony exactly?
Tony 究竟在哪裡？

(A) He is at home in bed. 他在家中床上。
(B) He is in a department store. 他在百貨公司。
(C) He is in the garage. 他在車庫。
(D) He is at a café. 他在咖啡廳。

| 提示 | **For questions number 3 and 4, please look at picture B.**
問題 3 跟問題 4 請看圖片 B。 |

Q3 　D　 Which description is correct?
哪一個說明是正確的？

(A) Tammy and Gray are walking in the parking lot.
　　Tammy 與 Gray 正在停車場裡走路。
(B) There are two cats under the tree.
　　在樹下有兩隻貓。

(C) There isn't a bench on the path.

小徑上沒有長椅。

(D) Two birds are singing in the tree.

兩隻鳥在樹上唱歌。

Q4　__C__　**Is there a bench nearby?**

附近有長椅嗎？

(A) Yes, there is one under the tree.

有，樹下有一個。

(B) No, there isn't.

不，沒有。

(C) Yes, there is one on the path.

有，小徑上有一個。

(D) There is one above the garden.

花園上方有一個。

第二部分 問答

Q1　__A__　**Have you made an appointment with the dentist?**

你已經跟牙醫掛號了嗎？

(A) Of course. My teeth hurt.

當然。我的牙齒痛死了。

(B) I'd like to make a reservation, too.

我也想預約。

(C) Yes, I went there yesterday.

是的，我昨天去了那裡。

(D) This is my first date with a girl.

這是我第一次與女生約會。

單字解釋 ▶ make a reservation 預約　　make an appointment 約定會面
date **n** 約會　　dentist **n** 牙醫

試題分析 ▶ 本題問：你是否已經跟牙醫約看診了。可知答案為選項 (A)：
當然，我牙齒痛死了。

152

Q2 __A__ **I am here for an interview. I've got an appointment with the marketing manager.**

我是來面試的。我與行銷經理有約。

(A) Please have a seat and wait a second.

請坐，稍等一下。

(B) So you are an interviewer.

所以你是主持面試的人。

(C) Do you want an interview with me?

你想要與我面談嗎？

(D) Do not be nervous. I'll teach you.

不要緊張。我會教你。

單字解釋▶ interview **n** 面談　　　　make an appointment 約定會面
marketing manager 行銷經理 interviewer **n** 面試官
nervous **adj** 緊張的

試題分析▶ 本題說：我是來面試的，與行銷經理有約。答案為選項 (A)：
請坐並稍等一下。

Q3 __B__ **I have an appointment with Dr. Wang. I have a cold.** 我和王醫師有約診。我感冒了。

(A) Have a cold drink, please. 請喝杯冷飲。

(B) Give me your health insurance card.

給我你的健保卡。

(C) I got a doctorate degree last year.

我去年獲得了博士學位。

(D) How much money do you want?

你想要多少錢？

單字解釋▶ heath insurance card 健保卡
doctorate degree 博士學位

試題分析▶ 本題說：我和王醫師有約看診，並提到自己感冒。表示說話者
應該是在診所，可知答案為櫃台人員所說的選項(B)：給我你
的健保卡。(A) 利用選項中的 cold 試圖混淆考生。

Conversation 1

W: I am here for an interview. I've got an appointment with the marketing manager.

M: Please have a seat and fill out the form. And I'll have him talk to you in a few minutes.

中文翻譯

女：我是來面試的。我與行銷經理有約。
男：請坐，請把這張表格填好。稍後我會請他來與妳談。

Q1 ___A___ **What is the probable place for this conversation?** 這個對話的可能發生地點是在哪裡？

(A) At a company.
在一家公司。
(B) On the campus.
在校園。
(C) In the hospital.
在醫院。
(D) In the hotel.
在旅館。

單字解釋▶ interview **n** 面談
marketing manager 行銷經理

試題分析▶ 本題問：這段對話的可能發生地點是何處。從 interview 和 marketing manager 可知答案為選項(A)：在一家公司。

Conversation 2

Tim's Schedule		
MON.	10:00 AM	Meeting with office manager
TUE.	20:00 PM	John's wedding ceremony
WED.	13:00 PM	Lunch w/ Tammy Kim
THURS.	11:00 AM	Dentist
FRI.	21:00 PM	Office Party

W: Hello, Tim? This is Tammy.

M: Hi, Tammy, what's up?

W: Listen, I am calling to cancel our lunch on Wednesday because I just found out I have to pick up my daughter at the airport on that day.

M: That's no problem. So, are you going to John's wedding? Last time you said you couldn't come, didn't you?

W: I am afraid I can't make it. I will be out of town.

M: Oh, at least we can meet at the office party, right? Talk to you then.

W: See you soon.

 中文翻譯

Tim 的行程表		
週一	早上 10 點	與辦公室經理會談
週二	晚上 8 點	John 的婚禮
週三	下午 1 點	與 Tammy Kim 共進午餐
週四	早上 11 點	牙醫
週五	晚上 9 點	辦公室派對

女：哈囉！是 Tim 嗎？我是 Tammy。
男：嗨！Tammy，怎麼啦？
女：聽好囉，我打來是要取消我們週三的午餐，因為我剛才才發現，我那天要去機場接女兒。
男：沒問題。所以，你會去 John 的婚禮嗎？上次你說你不能去，對嗎？
女：我恐怕無法趕到。我會在外縣市。
男：喔，至少我們會在辦公室派對見面，對吧？到時再聊。
女：到時見。

Q2 ___D___ **When might the speakers see each other?**

說話者們可能何時見面？
(A) On Monday. 在週一。
(B) On Tuesday. 在週二。
(C) On Wednesday. 在週三。
(D) On Friday. 在週五。

單字解釋 ▶ wedding **n** 婚禮

試題分析 ▶ 本題問：說話者可能見面的時間。在對話中一開始有提到 cancel our lunch on Wednesday 以及 John's wedding ~ I am afraid I can't make it，女子皆表示無法前往，因此說話者們這兩個場合應無法見面。最後聽到 at least we can meet at the office party right? Talk to you then. 表示說話者確認彼此會在辦公室派對見面，並提到到時再聊，且女子也回說到時候見，可以得知最快見面的時間是週五的辦公室派對，故答案要選 (D)。

第四部分 簡短談話

Short Talk 1

Following please make sure when your appointment is. All members of the basketball team are reminded that the bus to the game will leave at 9:00 this morning. Please wait for the bus at the front of school. BE ON TIME! For members of the writing club, you will all meet at the auditorium at 4:15 this afternoon. DO NOT FORGET IT!

中文翻譯

以下請務必確認自己的約定時間。提醒籃球隊的所有球員，前往比賽的巴士將在今早 9 點出發。請在校園前面等候巴士。「務必要準時」。至於寫作社社員，你們將在今天下午 4 點 15 分於禮堂見面。請別忘了。

Q1　D　**Where and when will the writing club meet?**

寫作社社員將於何時、何地見面？

(A) At the front of school at 9:00 in the morning.
早上 9 點在學校前。

(B) At the auditorium at 9:00 in the morning.
早上 9 點在禮堂。

(C) At the front of school at 4:15 in the afternoon.
下午 4 點 15 分在學校前。

(D) At the auditorium at 4:15 in the afternoon.
下午 4 點 15 分在禮堂。

單字解釋 ▶ appointment **n** 會面，約定　　auditorium **n** 禮堂

試題分析 ▶ 本題問：寫作社社員會在幾點、在哪裡碰面。在談話中聽到 the writing club...will all meet at the auditorium at 4:15 this afternoon. DO NOT FORGET IT，可知寫作社社員會在下午 4 點 15 分於禮堂碰面。故答案要選 (D)。

Short Talk 2

First Date Advice

(1) Be respectful to the girl's parents.
(2) Drive safely and slowly.
(3) Take the girl home before 10:00 PM.
(4) Don't dress too sloppily.

Eric went out on his first date yesterday evening. Before he left the house, he asked his parents if they had any advice. They told him to be polite when he met the girl's parents. They also told him not to drive too fast. And they told him not to bring his date home later than 10:00 PM. He wrote down all pieces of advice from his parents, and then put on his ripped clothing and dusty sneakers going out happily.

第一次約會的建議

(1) 要對女生的父母禮貌。
(2) 小心駕駛,並開慢點。
(3) 晚上 10 點前送女生回家。
(4) 穿著打扮不要太邋遢。

Eric 昨晚參加了他人生第一次的約會。在他離開家之前,他問了他的父母,是否能給他什麼建議。他們告訴他説,遇到女生的父母時要有禮貌。他們也告訴他説,車不要開太快。而且他們也告訴他,送女生回家的時間不要晚於晚上 10 點。他寫下父母所給的這些建議,並穿上了他上頭有破洞的衣服與上頭有塵土的球鞋,並高高興興地外出了。

Q2 __D__ **Which piece of advIce did Eric disobey apparently?**

哪一項建議 Eric 明顯沒有遵守？

(A) Be respectful to the girl's parents.

要對女生的父母禮貌。

(B) Drive safely and slowly. 小心駕駛，並開慢點。

(C) Take the girl home before 10:00 PM.

晚上 10 點前送女生回家。

(D) Don't dress too sloppily. 別穿得太邋遢。

單字解釋 ▶ respectful **adj** 有禮貌的，尊敬的　　sloppily **adv** 邋遢地

ripped **adj** 裂開的　　dusty **adj** 有塵土的

試題分析 ▶ 本題問：Eric 沒有遵守哪一項建議。在談話的最後可以得知，He ~ put on his ripped clothing and dusty sneakers going out happily，表示他穿上了上頭有破洞的衣服與上頭有塵土的球鞋，接著就出門了。由此可知，他沒有遵照不要穿得太邋遢的建議，故答案要選 (D)。

Hint 常 考 句 子

可能情境包括：上大學、入學考試、考試成績好或壞、老師家庭訪問、主銷選課等。

1 What's your major in college?
你在大學的主修是什麼？

2 How long have you been learning English? 你學英文多久了？

3 How long ago did you learn Spanish?
你多久前學西班牙文的？

4 What was the subject of your graduation thesis?
你畢業論文的題目是什麼？

5 I finished my bachelor's degree at Taiwan University.
我在台灣大學完成我的學士學位。

6 What if I fail my exam?
如果我沒考過的話怎麼辦？

7 He does very well in Physics.
他物理念得不錯。

模擬試題

第一部分　看圖辨義

試題冊上有數幅圖畫，每一圖畫有 1~3 個描述該圖的題目，每題請聽光碟放音機播出題目以及四個英語敘述之後，選出與所看到的圖畫最相符的答案，每題只播出一遍。

Picture A　Q1 ～ Q2

答案欄

Picture B　Q3 ～ Q4

答案欄

第二部分 問答

 作答說明 每題請聽光碟放音機播出一英語問句或直述句後，從試題冊上 A、B、C、D 四個回答或回應中，選出一個最適合者作答。每題 只播出一遍。

 Q 1

(A) Well, I'll ask my academic advisor.

(B) I'd like to achieve my goal in future.

(C) Without doubt. I want to have history as my major.

(D) Frankly speaking, business in school is going down.

 答案欄

 Q 2

(A) O-Oh, I totally forgot this thing.

(B) Give me yesterday's newspaper.

(C) Finally, I turned right, and found the house.

(D) Frankly speaking, I am too tired to write a composition.

 答案欄

 Q 3

(A) No, but I can speak Spanish.

(B) I think I couldn't speak English when I was 5.

(C) I don't like to speak English.

(D) I can translate from English into Chinese.

第三部分　簡短對話

 每題請聽光碟放音機播出一段對話及一個相關的問題之後，從試題冊上 A、B、C、D 四個選項中選出一個最適合者作答。每段對話及問題只播出一遍。

Conversation 1

Q 1

(A) The professor uses totally English in class.

(B) The speakers are high school students.

(C) The woman is worried about her "sociology".

(D) The professor doesn't give students too much homework.

Conversation 2

Q 2

Speaker	Topic	Time
Rebecca	Writing	10:00-12:00
Carol	Oral Speaking	13:00-15:00
Elize	Grammar	15:00-17:00
Jack	Pronunciation	19:00-21:00

English Speeches! Join any one of them!

(A) Carol will give a speech about grammar.

(B) Rebecca has strange accents.

(C) Juan will attend Jack's speech.

(D) Elise likes to criticize people who are learning English.

第四部分 簡短談話 新題型

作答說明 每題請聽光碟放音機播出一段談話及一個相關的問題後，從試題冊上 A、B、C、D 四個選項中選出一個最適合者作答。每段談話及問題只播出一遍。

Short Talk 1

Q1
(A) Employers.
(B) English teachers.
(C) Students who want to learn English.
(D) Trainers.

答案欄

Short Talk 2

Q2

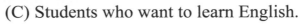

Class Information for New Session (January ~ March)		
Class	**Teacher**	**Time**
Pronunciation	Yvonne	Mon.&Wed. 10:00-12:00
Grammar	Olivia	Mon.&Wed. 13:00-15:00
Basic Conversation	Gina	Wed.&Fri. 15:00-17:00
Advanced Conversation	Peter	Sat.& Sun. 10:00-12:00

(A) Grammar class meets twice a week.
(B) Gina teaches Basic English conversation class.
(C) The language center Victor works in has good reputation.
(D) The new session is from January to February.

答案欄

答案解析

第一部分 看圖辨義

 For questions number 1 and 2, please look at picture A.
問題 1 跟問題 2 請看圖片 A。

Q1 __B__ **What is the teacher doing now?**
老師正在做什麼？

(A) She is laughing with students. 她正在和學生一起笑。
(B) She is angry and shouting. 她正在生氣與大聲講話。
(C) She is teaching hard. 她正在努力教學。
(D) She is crying out. 她正在哭喊。

Q2 __C__ **Which description is incorrect?**
哪一個敘述是不正確的？

(A) There is a student sleeping in the classroom.
一個學生在教室裡睡覺。
(B) The teacher is holding an eraser. 老師正拿著一個板擦。
(C) All students in class are very hardworking.
班上所有學生都很認真學習。
(D) The teacher is very unhappy now.
老師現在非常不高興。

 For questions number 3 and 4, please look at picture B.
問題 3 跟問題 4 請看圖片 B。

Q3 __C__ **What is the teacher probably teaching now?** 老師可能正在教什麼？

(A) English. 英文。
(B) History. 歷史。
(C) Math. 數學。
(D) Geography. 地理。

Q4 ___D___ What does the woman probably say?

女子可能在說什麼？

(A) OK. Everybody, let's stand up and have a dance.

好，各位，我們站起來跳舞吧。

(B) Do you all understand the grammar?

你們都了解這個文法嗎？

(C) I am so tired. I just went shopping for food.

我好累。我剛去採買食品。

(D) Can you tell me if you all understand me?

你們能否告訴我，你們是不是都懂了呢？

第二部分 問答

Q1 ___A___ Do you plan to major in business in college? 你計畫在大學裡主修商業嗎？

(A) Well, I'll ask my academic advisor.

嗯…我將問問我的指導員。

(B) I'd like to achieve my goal in future.

我想在未來達成我的目標。

(C) Without doubt. I want to have history as my major.

不用懷疑。我要以歷史作為我的主修。

(D) Frankly speaking, business in school is going down.

坦白說，學校的業務在下降中。

單字解釋 ▶ plan to **v** 計畫　　　　major **v** 主修
academic advisor （在大學輔導學業方面問題的）指導員
achieve **v** 達到　　　　goal **n** 目標
without doubt 不用懷疑　　frankly speaking 坦白說
go down 下降

試題分析 ▶ 本題問：你大學是否計畫主修商業。可知答案為選項 (A)：我
將問問我的指導員。

Q2   **A**   **We're supposed to turn in our final papers by Monday.** 我們週一前應該要交期末報告。

(A) O-Oh, I totally forgot this thing.

糟了，我完全忘了這檔事。

(B) Give me yesterday's newspaper. 給我昨天的報紙。

(C) Finally, I turned right, and found the house.

最後我右轉，然後找到了房子。

(D) Frankly speaking, she is too tired to write a composition. 坦白說，她太累了，以致於無法寫作。

單字解釋 ▶ be supposed to 應該…　　　　turn in 繳交

final paper 期末報告　　　　too...to... 太…以至於不能…

composition **n** 作文

試題分析 ▶ 本題說：我們週一前要交期末報告。從選項中可知答案為

(A)：糟了，我完全忘了這檔事。

Q3   **A**   **Can you speak English, sir?** 先生，你會說英文嗎？

(A) No, but I can speak Spanish. 不，但我會說西班牙文。

(B) I think I couldn't speak English when I was 5.

我想我 5 歲時不會說英文。

(C) I don't like to speak English. 我不喜歡說英文。

(D) I can translate from English into Chinese.

我可以英翻中。

單字解釋 ▶ Spanish **n** 西班牙文；**adj** 西班牙的

試題分析 ▶ 本題問：先生，你會說英文嗎。可知答案為選項 (A)：不，但

我會說西班牙文。

Conversation 1

W: Oh, I wish this sociology textbook weren't so difficult. I can't believe all this new English vocabulary.

M: Take it easy. The professor will explain everything in Chinese.

W: OK.

M: But that's not so OK. The professor always assigns lots of homework.

W: What a busy college life!

中文翻譯

女：喔，我希望這本社會學課本不會太難。我不敢相信全都是新的英文單字。

男：放輕鬆。教授會用中文解釋每個內容。

女：好吧。

男：但也沒那麼好。教授總是給我們很多作業。

女：真是忙碌的大學生活呀！

Q1 ___C___ **Which statement is true?** 哪一個敘述是真的？

(A) The professor only uses English in class.
   教授在課堂上只用英文教學。

(B) The speakers are high school students.
   說話者們是高中生。

(C) The woman is worried about her "sociology".
   女子擔心她的社會學。

(D) The professor doesn't give students too much homework. 這個教授不會給學生太多的作業。

單字解釋 ▶ sociology **n** 社會學　　　professor **n** 教授

試題分析 ▶ 本題問：哪一項敘述是正確的。

從 this sociology textbook、college 以及 professor 可知說話者是大學生，從 will explain everything in Chinese 以及 The professor always assigns lots of homework.可知他們的教授會用中文授課，且會出很多作業。由此可知答案為選項 (C)：女子擔心她的社會學。

Conversation 2

English Speeches! Join any one of them!

Speaker	Topic	Time
Rebecca	Writing	10:00-12:00
Carol	Oral Speaking	13:00-15:00
Elize	Grammar	15:00-17:00
Jack	Pronunciation	19:00-21:00

W: I am so excited about this year's English learning speeches. I think I will attend these four.

M: I don't have that much time. I think I'll just attend one of them.

W: Well, which one do you want to go to, Juan?

M: I'm interested in pronunciation topic. Sometimes people say I have a strange accent. I am so depressed.

W: Don't take people's criticisms to heart. You should look on the bright side and always keep your chin up.

英文演講！快來參加任何一場吧！		
講者	主題	時間
Rebecca	寫作	10:00-12:00
Carol	口說	13:00-15:00
Elize	文法	15:00-17:00
Jack	發音	19:00-21:00

女：我對於今年的英語學習演講感到十分有興趣。我想我會參加這四場。

男：我沒那麼多時間。我想我會參與其中一場。

女：那麼 Juan，你想參加哪一場呢？

男：我對發音的主題有興趣。有時大家會說我有奇怪的口音。我很沮喪。

女：別把別人的批評放在心上。你應該要往好的方面想，要有自信。

Q2 ___C___ **According to the conversation and graphic, which statement is true?**

根據對話與圖表，哪一個敘述為真？

(A) Carol will give a speech about grammar.
Carol 會做有關文法的演講。

(B) Rebecca has strange accents. Rebecca 有奇怪的口音。

(C) Juan will attend Jack's speech.
Juan 將參加 Jack 的演講。

(D) Elise likes to criticize people who are learning English. Elise 喜歡批評正在學英文的人。

單字解釋 ▶ pronunciation n 發音　　　　accent n 口音
criticism n 批評
look on the bright side 往好的方面想
keep your chin up 要有自信（字面意義：下巴抬高）

試題分析 ▶ 本題問：哪一個敘述為真。從對話中可知，Juan 是對話中的男子。男子（Juan）提到 I'm interested in pronunciation topic. Sometimes people say I have strange accents.，表示 Juan 對於發音的主題有興趣。從圖表可得知，Jack 是發音主題的演說者，故答案要選 (C)。

第四部分 簡短談話

Short Talk 1

Is your language school looking to hire experienced English teachers? Do you want to hire teachers who have been trained with the latest methodology? Look no more. Graduates of the International Village Teacher Training Institute are highly trained teachers able to teach your students very well. Call and hire one today!

中文翻譯

您的語文中心想雇用有經驗的英文老師嗎？您想要雇用經過最新教學法訓練的老師嗎？您不用再找了。國際村教師訓練機構的畢業生都是經過高度訓練的老師，能夠將您的學生教到好。今天就來電，並雇用一位老師吧！

Q1 ___A___ **Who is this advertisement directed to?**

廣告所要針對的對象是誰？

(A) Employers. 雇主。

(B) English teachers. 英文老師。

(C) Students who want to learn English.

想要學英文的學生。

(D) Trainers. 講師。

單字解釋 ▶ methodology **n** 教學法　　　　graduate **n** 畢業生

institute **n** 機構

試題分析 ▶ 本題問：廣告所要針對的對象是誰。在談話中聽到 Is your language school looking to hire experienced English teachers，可知聽者是語文中心單位，接著說 Do you want to hire teachers ~ trained with the latest methodology，向聽者提到是否想要雇用有經過最新教學法訓練的老師。而最後也聽到 Call and hire one today，表示請聽者來電雇用一位老師，言下之意聽者是雇主，故答案要選 (A)。

Short Talk 2

Class Information for New Session (January ~ March)		
Class	**Teacher**	**Time**
Pronunciation	Yvonne	Mon.&Wed.10:00-12:00
Grammar	Olivia	Mon.&Wed.13:00-15:00
Basic Conversation	Gina	Wed.&Fri.15:00-17:00
Advanced Conversation	Peter	Sat.& Sun.10:00-12:00

Welcome to our language center. I am your director, Victor. As you all know, our language center has a good reputation and confidence in promoting your English ability from bottom to top. This session, we'll offer you some useful classes, including pronunciation class, grammar class, different levels of conversation classes, etc. Please check the class information and decide which one is the most suitable for you. Thank you very much.

新學期的課程資訊（一月到三月）		
課程	老師	時間
發音班	Yvonne	週一與週三 10:00-12:00
文法班	Olivia	週一與週三 13:00-15:00
基礎會話班	Gina	週三與週五 15:00-17:00
高級會話班	Peter	週六與週日 10:00-12:00

歡迎來到我們的語言中心。我是你們的主任 Victor。就如您所知，我們的語言中心有好的名聲以及信心來提升各位從初階到高階的英文實力。本學期，我們將提供給各位有用的課程，包含發音班、文法班、不同程度的會話課程等等。請看一下我們的課程資訊，再決定哪個課程最適合您。非常感謝您。

Q2 ___D___ **Which of the statements is NOT true?**

哪一項敘述不是真的？

(A) Grammar class meets twice a week.

文法班一週上兩次課。

(B) Gina teaches Basic English conversation class.

Gina 教導基礎英文會話課。

(C) The language center Victor works in has good reputation. Victor 工作的語言中心有良好的名聲。

(D) The new session is from January to February.

新的學期從一月到二月。

單字解釋 ▶   reputation **n** 名聲   session **n** 學期

                    pronunciation **n** 發音   suitable **adj** 適合的

試題分析 ▶   本題問：哪一項敘述不是真的。從圖表中的 Grammar 以及其對照的 Mon.&Wed. 可知，(A)正確。從 Gina 所對照的 Basic Conversation 也可知(B)正確。另外從 Welcome to our language center. I am your director, Victor. 也可知，說話者 Victor 是在此語言中心工作，而從 our language center has good reputation 可知(C)正確。而從圖表中的 January ~ March 可知，新學期是從一月到三月，故答案要選(D)。

常考句子 Hint

可能情境包括：詢問天氣、颱風、帶雨衣雨傘、天氣預測等。

1 What a nice sunny day!
好棒的晴天呀！

2 It's raining cats and dogs.
正在下傾盆大雨。

3 The weather forecast says we're going to have a rainy day today.
天氣預報說今天會是雨天。

4 What's the temperature?
現在幾度？

5 I wonder how long this nasty weather will keep up.
我想知道這樣惡劣的天氣會持續多久。

6 What's the weather like?
天氣怎麼樣？

7 It's getting warmer and warmer.
天氣愈來愈暖和了。

模擬試題

 013.mp3

第一部分　看圖辨義

作答說明

試題冊上有數幅圖畫，每一圖畫有 1~3 個描述該圖的題目，每題請聽光碟放音機播出題目以及四個英語敘述之後，選出與所看到的圖畫最相符的答案，每題只播出一遍。

Picture A　Q1 ～ Q2

Taipei 30℃～38℃

Japan 28℃～32℃

答案欄

New York 24℃～30℃

Picture B　Q3 ～ Q4

答案欄

每題請聽光碟放音機播出一英語問句或直述句後,從試題冊上 A、B、C、D 四個回答或回應中,選出一個最適合者作答。每題只播出一遍。

Q 1

答案欄

(A) Yes, I have a coin.

(B) No worries. I don't feel cold.

(C) Ok, I'll take off my coat.

(D) Yes, have a cold drink.

Q 2

答案欄

(A) Why not have a cold drink and hide yourself in a cool room?

(B) Summer is also my favorite season.

(C) No doubt. I am going swimming this afternoon.

(D) Yes, the hot pot is hotter and hotter.

Q 3

答案欄

(A) Yes. It's raining cats and dogs. Don't you have a raincoat?

(B) We will have a wet weekend.

(C) You are always under the weather.

(D) Yes, you are completely right.

第三部分　**簡短對話**

作答說明　每題請聽光碟放音機播出一段對話及一個相關的問題之後，從試題冊上 A、B、C、D 四個選項中選出一個最適合者作答。每段對話及問題只播出一遍。

Conversation 1

 Q 1

(A) Wear more clothes due to the cold weather.

(B) Try on some new clothes.

 答案欄

(C) Donate old clothes.

(D) Discuss if the scarf is trendy.

Conversation 2 新題型

Q 2

> **Tainan's Weather:** June 29th, Friday
> **Temperature:** 39°C / Sunny day
> **Precipitation（Rainfall）:** 0%
> **Wind:** Breeze
> **Excessive Heat Warning**

(A) The speakers are both in Tainan.

 答案欄

(B) The wind today is not strong.

(C) It may rain later in the evening.

(D) The man thinks global warming is big trouble.

第四部分 簡短談話 新題型

 作答說明 每題請聽光碟放音機播出一段談話及一個相關的問題後，從試題冊上 A、B、C、D 四個選項中選出一個最適合者作答。每段談話及問題只播出一遍。

Short Talk 1

 Q 1

(A) To talk about traffic rules.
(B) To announce that schools and public officials are closed.
(C) To advise residents to conserve water.
(D) To ask residents to donate money to the victims of last night's flood.

答案欄

Short Talk 2

Q 2

Historical weather disasters in USA		
Disaster	**When**	**Where**
Hurricane	1992	Homestead, Florida
Tornado	1998	Oklahoma, Oklahoma
Heat Wave	1998	Houston, Texas
Snowstorm	2001	Buffalo, New York

(A) In 2001, a terrible snowstorm hit Buffalo.
(B) In 1998, heat waves hit Houston, Texas.
(C) In 1992, Homestead was destroyed by a terrible hurricane.
(D) This talk explained why some weather disasters happened in the USA.

 答案欄

答案解析

第一部分 看圖辨義

 For questions number 1 and 2, please look at picture A.
問題 1 跟問題 2 請看圖片 A。

Q1 __C__ **What's the forecast for tomorrow's weather in Japan?** 日本明天的天氣預測是如何？
(A) It's a sunny day. 有太陽。
(B) It's a rainy day. 雨天。
(C) It's a cloudy day. 多雲。
(D) It's a snowy day. 下雪天。

Q2 __D__ **What's the forecast of weather temperature in New York?** 紐約的氣溫預測是如何？
(A) It's 28-30 degrees. 28 至 30 度。
(B) It's 24-38 degrees. 24 至 38 度。
(C) It's 30-34 degrees. 30 至 34 度。
(D) It's 24-30 degrees. 24 至 30 度。

- -

For questions number 3 and 4, please look at picture B.
問題 3 跟問題 4 請看圖片 B。

Q3 __C__ **Which country's map is it?** 這是哪一個國家的地圖？
(A) It's the U.K. 英國。
(B) It's France. 法國。
(C) It's the U.S.A. 美國。
(D) It's the Mainland China. 中國。

Q4 __C__ **Which place in this map is the hottest?**
地圖上哪一個地方最熱？
(A) Los Angeles. 洛杉磯。
(B) New York. 紐約。
(C) Chicago. 芝加哥。
(D) Mexico City. 墨西哥市。

第二部分 問答

Q1 ___B___ **It's getting cold. Put on your coat.**

天氣變冷了。穿上你的外套吧！

(A) Yes, I have a coin. 是，我有一枚硬幣。

(B) No worries. I don't feel cold. 別擔心。我不覺得冷。

(C) Ok, I'll take off my coat. 好，我會脫下我的外套。

(D) Yes, have a cold drink. 是，來杯冷飲。

單字解釋 ▶ coat **n** 外套　　　　　　　　no worries 不用擔心

put on 穿上（比較：take off 脫掉） cold drink 冷飲

coin **n** 硬幣

試題分析 ▶ 本題說：天氣變冷了，請聽者穿上外套。可知答案為選項
(B)：別擔心，我不覺得冷。

Q2 ___A___ **It's getting hotter and hotter. I hate summer.**

天氣是愈來愈熱了。我討厭夏天。

(A) Why not have a cold drink and hide yourself in a cool room? 為何不來杯冷飲，並躲在涼快的房間裡？

(B) Summer is also my favorite season.
夏季也是我最愛的季節。

(C) No doubt. I am going swimming this afternoon.
沒問題，我今天下午將去游泳。

(D) Yes, the hot pot is hotter and hotter.
是，火鍋愈來愈熱了。

單字解釋 ▶ hate **v** 討厭　　　　　　　hide yourself 把你自己藏起來

favorite **adj** 最愛的　　　　　hot pot 火鍋

試題分析 ▶ 本題說：天氣是愈來愈熱了，我討厭夏天。可知答案為選項 (A)：
「為何不來杯冷飲，並躲在涼快的房間裡」。hotter and hotter
的用法是一種「比較級重複」的句型，強調「愈來愈…」。

Q3 __A__ **Oh, my shirt and pants are completely wet.**

喔，我的襯衫與長褲都溼透了。

(A)Yes. It's raining cats and dogs. Don't you have a raincoat?

是呀，雨下得很大。你沒有雨衣嗎？

(B) We will have a wet weekend.

我們將有一個潮濕的週末。

(C) You are always under the weather.

你總是不舒服。

(D) Yes, you are completely right.

是，你完全正確。

單字解釋 ▶ completely adv 完全地

rains cats and dogs 下大雨（美式俚語）

raincoat n 雨衣

under the weather 感到不舒服

試題分析 ▶ 本題說：我的襯衫與長褲都溼透了。可知答案為選項 (A)：是呀，雨下得很大。你沒有雨衣嗎。under the weather 指「感到不舒服」。

Conversation 1

W: It's getting cold. Put on your coat.
M: Yes. Mother. And I'll also wear my scarf.
W: Good.

....

中文翻譯

女：變冷了。把外套穿上。
男：好的，媽。我也會把圍巾戴上。
女：好。

Q1 ___A___ **What are they talking about?** 他們在談什麼？

(A) Wear more clothes due to the cold weather.
　　因為天氣冷，要多穿衣服。

(B) Try on some new clothes. 試穿一些新衣服。

(C) Donate old clothes. 捐出舊衣服。

(D) Discuss if the scarf is trendy. 討論一下這圍巾是否流行。

單字解釋 ▶ coat n 外套
put on 穿上（比較：take off 脫掉）

試題分析 ▶ 本題問：說話者們在談什麼。可知答案為選項 (A)：因為天氣冷要多穿衣服。

Conversation 2

Tainan's Weather: June 29th , Friday
Temperature: 39°C / Sunny day
Precipitation（Rainfall）: 0%
Wind: Breeze
Excessive Heat Warning

W: Hot! Hot! Hot! Have you heard the weather forecast for here, Tainan? We have another excessive heat warning.

M: Gee, I think global warming is a serious problem. Taiwan is just like a burnt yam.

W: Well, when you go out, don't forget to apply some sunblock and wear a pair of sunglasses.

中文翻譯

台南的天氣：6 月 29 號，星期五
氣溫：39℃／有太陽
降雨機率：0%
風勢：微風
過熱警告

女：熱熱熱！你有聽說台南這裡的氣象預測吧？我們又有另一個過熱警報了。

男：天啊！我想全球暖化是個嚴重的問題。台灣就像是一個烤焦的番薯。

女：嗯，你要外出時，別忘了塗抹防曬油，以及戴上一副太陽眼鏡。

Q2 **C** **According to the conversation and graphic, which statement is NOT true?**

根據對話與圖表，哪一項敘述不是真的？

(A) The speakers are both in Tainan.

說話者們現在都在台南。

(B) The wind today is not strong. 今天風勢不強。

(C) It may rain later in the evening. 傍晚稍晚時可能會下雨。

(D) The man thinks global warming is big trouble.

男子覺得地球暖化是大問題。

單字解釋▶ precipitation **n** 降雨　　　　breeze **n** 微風
sunblock **n** 防曬油

試題分析▶ 本題問：選項中哪一項敘述不正確。從 weather forecast for here, Tainan 中的「Tainan 和 here」可知，說話者現在在台南，從圖表中的 Wind: Breeze 以及男子所提到的 global warming is a serious problem 可知，(A)、(B)、(D)都正確。在表格中看到 precipitation 為 0%，表示不會下雨，故答案要選 (C)。

第四部分 簡短談話

Short Talk 1

All schools and public offices will be closed today due to last's night heavy rain. Some areas are flooded, so all residents are advised to stay home. Listen to the evening weather reports to find out tomorrow's school and public office schedule.

中文翻譯

由於昨晚的大雨，所有的學校與公家機關今天均停止上班上課。有些地區淹大水，所以建議所有居民都先待在家中。請收聽晚間的氣象報告，來掌握明日學校與公家機關上班上課的情況。

Q1 **B** **What is the purpose of this announcement?**

這則公告的目的為何？

(A) To talk about traffic rules 談論交通法規。
(B) To announce that schools and public offices are closed. 宣布學校與公家機關停班停課。
(C) To advise residents to conserve water. 建議居民儲水。
(D) To ask residents to donate money to the victims of last night's flood. 要求居民捐錢給昨晚淹大水的受災戶。

單字解釋 ▶ resident n 居民　public office n 公家機關
advise v 建議　conserve water 儲水

試題分析 ▶ 本題問：這則公告的目的。在談話中提到 All schools and public offices will be closed today due to ~ heavy rain.，可知由於昨晚的大雨，所有的學校與公家機關今天均停止上班上課。故答案要選 (B)。

185

Short Talk 2

Historical weather disasters in USA

Disaster	When	Where
Hurricane	1992	Homestead, Florida
Tornado	1998	Oklahoma, Oklahoma
Heat Wave	1998	Houston, Texas
Snowstorm	2001	Buffalo, New York

Let me tell you some historical natural weather disasters in the USA. In 1992, hurricane Andrew destroyed the whole town of Homestead, Florida. It was the most expensive hurricane in US history. In 1988, heat waves hit Houston, Texas. Totally forty days with temperature over 48℃ caused more than130 deaths. At the same time, tornadoes hit Oklahoma and caused 43 deaths. In 2001, a terrible snowstorm hit Buffalo, New York. Totally 82 inches of snow fell in one snowstorm.

 中文翻譯

美國歷史上的天災

災害	時間	地點
颶風	1992 年	霍姆斯特德，弗羅里達州
龍捲風	1998 年	奧克拉荷馬，奧克拉荷馬州
熱浪	1998 年	休士頓，德克薩斯州
暴風雪	2001 年	水牛城，紐約州

讓我來告訴你一些史上在美國發生的自然災害。在 1992 年，安德魯颶風摧毀了弗羅里達州的霍姆斯特德整個城鎮，它是美國史上最花錢的颶風。在 1998 年，熱浪襲擊德克薩斯州的休士頓。整整四十天其氣溫都超過攝氏 48 度，造成了 130 人死亡。同時，龍捲風侵襲奧克拉荷馬州，造成了 43 死。在 2001 年，可怕的暴風雪襲擊紐約州的水牛城，僅僅一場的暴風雪就降下了共 82 吋高的雪量。

Q2 ___D___ **Which of the statements is NOT true?**

哪一項敘述不是真的？

(A) In 2001, a terrible snowstorm hit Buffalo.

在 2001 年，可怕的暴風雪襲擊水牛城。

(B) In 1998, heat waves hit Houston, Texas.

在 1998 年，熱浪襲擊德克薩斯州的休士頓。

(C) In 1992, Homestead was destroyed by a terrible hurricane.

在 1992 年，霍姆斯特德整座城鎮被可怕的颶風摧毀。

(D) This talk explained why some weather disasters happened in the USA.

這段談話解釋了一些自然災害發生在美國的原因。

單字解釋 ▶ weather disaster 天災　　　hurricane **n** 颶風
tornado **n** 龍捲風

試題分析 ▶ 本題問：哪一項敘述不是真的。對照圖表與談話，(A)、(B)、(C)皆正確，但從談話中無法得知自然災害發生在美國的原因，在談話中並未說明原因，故答案要選(D)。

情境解析 可能情境包括：請求接送、幫忙提重物、幫忙做家事等。

1 Can you give me a ride?
你可否載我一程？

2 The box is too heavy. Can you do me a favor? 這個箱子太重了。你可否幫我搬？

3 You couldn't do me a favor, could you? 你不能幫我忙，能嗎？

4 Don't worry. I'll do it for you.
別擔心。我會為你做這件事。

5 I'll give him a hand with his homework.
我會幫忙他做回家作業。

6 May is a very helpful person.
May 是一個熱心助人的人。

7 We can turn to him for help.
我們可以求助於他。

模擬試題

 014.mp3

第一部分 看圖辨義

作答說明

試題冊上有數幅圖畫，每一圖畫有 1~3 個描述該圖的題目，每題
請聽光碟放音機播出題目以及四個英語敘述之後，選出與所看到
的圖畫最相符的答案，每題只播出一遍。

Picture A Q1 ～ Q2

答案欄

Picture B Q3 ～ Q4

答案欄

第二部分 問答

作答說明 每題請聽光碟放音機播出一英語問句或直述句後，從試題冊上 A、B、C、D 四個回答或回應中，選出一個最適合者作答。每題 只播出一遍。

Q 1

(A) Yes, a policeman is directing traffic on the corner.

(B) There's a post office in the neighborhood.

(C) I saw you last night.

(D) You are not kidding me, are you?

Q 2

(A) No, but I can speak Spanish.

(B) I think I couldn't use the computer when I was 5.

(C) Yes, that's pretty easy.

(D) The computer is so expensive.

Q 3

(A) Sure, but I can't find a public phone.

(B) Do you have a cell phone?

(C) Do you see the phone booth over there?

(D) I'm serving in a public school.

第三部分 簡短對話

 作答說明 每題請聽光碟放音機播出一段對話及一個相關的問題之後，從試題冊上 A、B、C、D 四個選項中選出一個最適合者作答。每段對話及問題只播出一遍。

Conversation 1

 Q 1

 答案欄

(A) At a diner.
(B) In a shopping mall.
(C) In a drugstore.
(D) In the barbershop.

Conversation 2 新題型

Q 2

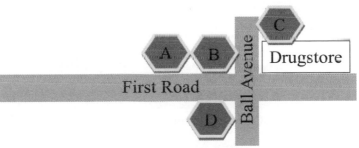

 答案欄

(A) A.
(B) B.
(C) C.
(D) D.

第四部分 簡短談話 新題型

Short Talk 1

Q 1

(A) To avoid being asked for assistance.

(B) To keep away from some bad things, like robberies.

(C) To get some information about the unfamiliar city.

(D) To buy some cameras in a shop with big discounts.

Short Talk 2

Q 2

Help Lines

Topic	Counselor	Phone Number
Child rearing	Benjamin	2564-8952
Money Management	Jessica	2658-5142
Time arrangement	Monica	2569-5875
Relationship problem	Peggy	2425-3619

(A) 2564-8952.

(B) 2658-5142.

(C) 2569-5875.

(D) 2425-3619.

答案解析

第一部分 看圖辨義

提示
For questions number 1 and 2, please look at picture A.
問題 1 跟問題 2 請看圖片 A。

Q1 ___C___ **According to the picture, where is the place?** 根據這張圖，這個地方是哪裡？
(A) In the post office. 郵局裡。
(B) In an attic. 閣樓裡。
(C) On a flight of stairs. 樓梯間。
(D) In an elevator. 電梯裡。

Q2 ___C___ **What does the woman probably say to the man?**

女子可能對男子說什麼？
(A) Can you get out of my house?
　　 你可否離開我的房子？
(B) Why on earth don't you give me some ideas?
　　 你究竟為何不給我一些想法？
(C) Can you do me a favor? I can't carry them myself.
　　 你可否幫我忙？我自己拿不動。
(D) Oh, boy. There he goes again.
　　 喔，天呀。他又來了。

提示
For questions number 3 and 4, please look at picture B.
問題 3 跟問題 4 請看圖片 B。

Q3 ___C___ **According to the picture, what happened here?**

根據這張圖，這裡發生什麼事了？

(A) Someone was robbed in the street.
　　 有人在街上被搶了。
(B) Someone got arrested in the street.
　　 有人在街上被捕了。

(C) Someone was injured in the street.

有人在街上受傷了。

(D) Someone was blamed in the street.

有人在街上被責備了。

Q4 __C__ **What did the woman probably say?**

女子可能說了什麼？

(A) Help! I am dying.

救命呀！我快死了。

(B) Somebody help my son! He is too young to cross the street.

誰來救救我的兒子呀！他太小不能過馬路。

(C) Goodness, somebody call 119.

老天，誰可以打 119。

(D) Is there an emergency here?

這裡有緊急事故嗎？

第二部分 問答

Q1 __A__ **Excuse me, did you see the police nearby?**

不好意思，你在附近有看到警察嗎？

(A) Yes, a policeman is directing traffic on the corner.

有，有個警察正在轉角指揮交通。

(B) There's a post office in the neighborhood.

附近有一間郵局。

(C) I saw you last night.

我昨晚有看到你。

(D) You are not kidding me, are you?

你不是在開我玩笑吧，是嗎？

單字解釋 ▶ police **n** 警察   nearby **adv** 在附近
　　　　　 direct traffic 指揮交通   corner **n** 角落，轉角

試題分析 ▶ 本題問：聽者是否有在附近看到警察。可知答案為選項 (A)：
　　　　　 有個警察正在轉角指揮交通。

Q2 ___C___ **Can you operate the computer, sir?**

先生,你會操作電腦嗎?

(A) No, but I can speak Spanish. 不,但我會說西班牙文。

(B) I think I couldn't use the computer when I was 5.

我想我 5 歲時還不會用電腦。

(C) Yes, that's pretty easy.

會,那太簡單了。

(D) The computer is so expensive.

這台電腦很貴。

單字解釋▶ operate **v** 操作

expensive **adj** 昂貴的

試題分析▶ 本題問:聽者是否會操作電腦。可知答案為選項 (C):會,
(操作電腦)太簡單了。

Q3 ___C___ **Where can I find a public phone?**

我在哪裡可以找到公共電話?

(A) Sure, but I can't find a public phone.

當然,但是我找不到公共電話。

(B) Do you have a cell phone? 你有手機嗎?

(C) Do you see the phone booth over there?

你有看到那裡的電話亭嗎?

(D) I'm serving in a public school. 我在公立學校服務。

單字解釋▶ public phone 公共電話　　cell phone 手機

phone booth 電話亭　　serve **v** 服務

public school 公立學校

試題分析▶ 本題問:在哪裡可找到公共電話。可知答案為選項 (C),反
問:你有看到那裡的電話亭嗎。本題考的是以常考的「Wh-問
句」來出題。(A) 回答 Sure,但後面卻又說找不到,因此語意
不通。此外,考生必須了解 phone booth 的意思是「電話
亭」,這與問題相關。

第三部分 簡短對話

Conversation 1

W: Excuse me, would you mind if I sit by the window?
M: Not at all.
W: Would you please pass me the salt? The soup is too plain.

中文翻譯

女：不好意思，你介意我坐在窗邊嗎？
男：一點也不。
女：可否請你把鹽遞給我？這碗湯沒味道。

Q1 __A__ **Where are the speakers?** 說話者們在哪裡？
(A) At a diner.
　　　在小餐館。
(B) In a shopping mall.
　　　在購物中心。
(C) In a drugstore.
　　　在藥局。
(D) In the barbershop.
　　　在理髮廳。

單字解釋 ▶ salt **n** 鹽巴
試題分析 ▶ 本題問：說話者所在的場所。可知答案為選項 (A)：在小餐館。

Conversation 2

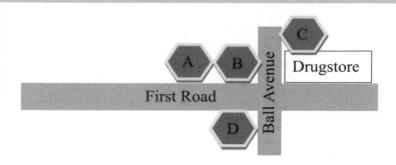

M: 119.

W: My friend just had a car accident. She is bleeding now. I think she's broken her leg. Can you send an ambulance quickly?

M: Can I have your name and phone number, please?

W: Gina Wang, and my number is 0965-859-862.

M: Where are you now?

W: We are at the corner of Ball Avenue and First Road. Kitty-corner to a drugstore.

M: Ms. Wang, please stay calm. We'll send an ambulance right away.

中文翻譯

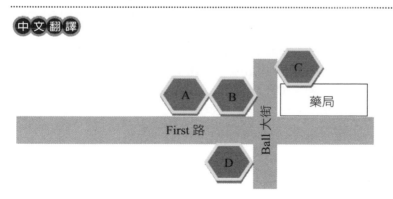

男：這裡是一一九，您好。

女：我朋友剛發生車禍。她現在在流血。我想她的腳斷了。可以快派一輛救護車來嗎？

男：可以給我您的名字與電話號碼嗎？

女：Gina Wang。我的電話是 0965-859-862。

男：你們現在人在哪？

女：我們在 Ball 大街與 First 路的交叉口處。在藥局的斜對角。

男：Wang 女士，請保持冷靜。我們現在就會派一輛救護車過去。

Q2 ___D___ **Where is the emergency?** 這緊急事故在哪裡？

(A) A.

位置 A。

(B) B.

位置 B。

(C) C.

位置 C。

(D) D.

位置 D。

單字解釋 ▶ car accident **n** 車禍　　　　bleed **v** 流血

ambulance **n** 救護車　　　kitty-corner to 在⋯的斜對角處

試題分析 ▶ 本題問：事故發生的地點。在對話中提到 We are at the corner of Ball Avenue and First Road.，可知是在圖片中兩條路的交叉路口的位置，接著又說 kitty-corner to a drugstore.，表示是在藥局的斜對角。所以答案選 (D)。若沒學過 kitty-corner，也可以用刪去法。由於是在圖片中兩條路的交叉路口的位置，所以 (A)、(C)可以淘汰。(B)的位置應該要用 across from a drugstore或 opposite to a drugstore 來表示，所以(B)也不正確。

第四部分 簡短談話

Short Talk 1

Exploring a new city can be fun and full of adventures, but getting lost in an unfamiliar city can be scary. If you lose your way, try to ask for directions or help. However, try not to look like a lost tourist. Wearing a camera around your neck and worriedly studying a map on the cell phone will make you an easy target of robbers. Therefore, you should think about who you should ask. Asking for help in a shop or a restaurant, or even a police officer will be better.

中文翻譯

探索一個新的城市可能很好玩又充滿冒險，但在一個不熟悉的城市中迷路，也可能很嚇人。假如你迷路了，就試著問路或尋求協助。然而，盡量不要看起來像是個迷路的觀光客一般。相機掛在脖子上，著急地研究著手機上的地圖，將容易地讓你成為搶劫犯下手的目標。因此，你該好好想想你該向誰問路。在商店或是餐廳中尋求協助，或是找警察都會比較好。

Q1   **B**   **Why does the speaker say "Try not to look like a lost tourist"?**

為何說話者說「盡量不要看起來像是個迷路的觀光客一般」？

(A) To avoid being asked for assistance.

為了避免被要求提供協助。

(B) To keep away from some bad things, like robberies.

為了避開像是搶劫這樣的壞事。

(C) To get some information about the unfamiliar city.

為了取到有關陌生城市的資訊。

(D) To buy some cameras in a shop with big discounts.

為了能在商店中以超低折扣價購買相機。

Short Talk 2

Help Lines

Topic	Counselor	Phone Number
Child rearing	Benjamin	2564-8952
Money Management	Jessica	2658-5142
Time arrangement	Monica	2569-5875
Relationship problem	Peggy	2425-3619

My four-year-old boy has begun to throw temper tantrums. When he doesn't get what he wants, he lies on the floor and cries and screams until he gets his way. A few days ago, when I was in a supermarket, he saw some candy that he wanted. However, it was already 6:00 PM, and I didn't want him to eat it. But he started to scream so loudly that I was too embarrassed and bought him the candy in the end. Please tell me what I should do.

中文翻譯

協助熱線

主題	諮詢顧問	電話號碼
孩童教養	Benjamin	2564-8952
金錢財富管理	Jessica	2658-5142
時間管理	Monica	2569-5875
男女感情問題	Peggy	2425-3619

我四歲的兒子已經開始會亂發脾氣了。當他得不到他想要的東西時，他就會躺在地板上又哭又叫，直到他得到他的目的為止。幾天前，我在超市時，他看到了一些他想要的糖果。但那時已經晚上六點，我不希望他吃糖。他開始尖叫，叫得非常大聲，讓我感到非常尷尬，只好買糖果給他。請告訴我該怎麼辦。

Q2 __A__ **Which help line needs to be contacted according to this talk?**

根據這段談話，應該要聯繫哪一支協助熱線？

(A) 2564-8952.
(B) 2658-5142.
(C) 2569-5875.
(D) 2425-3619.

單字解釋 ▶ child rearing 孩童教養
arrangement **n** 安排
relationship problem 男女感情問題
throw a temper tantrum 亂發脾氣
get one's way 得到某人的目的

試題分析 ▶ 本題問：根據這段談話，說話者應該要打哪一支協助熱線。從談話中的 My four-year-old boy has begun to throw temper tantrums. When he doesn't get what he wants, he lies on the floor and cries and screams... 可以得知，說話者明顯是遇到了孩童教養上的問題，故答案要選 (A)。

情境解析

可能情境包括：買郵票、寄信、與郵差的對話、排隊寄包裹等。

1 I need some stamps.
我需要一些郵票。

2 Is there a post office nearby?
這附近有郵局嗎？

3 Did you go to the post office yesterday? 你昨天去郵局了嗎？

4 Please send it by express.
請用限時專送寄。

5 Do you know where the nearest post office is? 你知道最近的郵局在哪裡嗎？

6 I'm going to the post office to mail a package. 我要去郵局寄包裹。

7 It takes a month by sea, 5 days by air.
海運需要 1 個月，空運只需要 5 天。

模擬試題

 015.mp3

情境
主題
15
Post Office（郵局）

模擬
試題

第一部分　看圖辨義

作答說明

試題冊上有數幅圖畫，每一圖畫有 1~3 個描述該圖的題目，每題
請聽光碟放音機播出題目以及四個英語敘述之後，選出與所看到
的圖畫最相符的答案，每題只播出一遍。

Picture A　Q1 ～ Q2

答案欄

Picture B　Q3 ～ Q4

答案欄

每題請聽光碟放音機播出一英語問句或直述句後，從試題冊上 A、B、C、D 四個回答或回應中，選出一個最適合者作答。每題只播出一遍。

(A) Yes, sir. May I help you?

(B) Just around the corner. You can't miss it.

(C) Let's go for some stamps.

(D) Who needs to go there?

(A) Yes, I am going to pass it.

(B) No, I went there 2 hours ago.

(C) Let's go to the police station.

(D) Do you have change for a dollar?

(A) Why not go to the park?

(B) Yes, I will go there immediately.

(C) Don't you need some chips?

(D) Who needs to go there?

第三部分 簡短對話

每題請聽光碟放音機播出一段對話及一個相關的問題之後，從試題冊上 A、B、C、D 四個選項中選出一個最適合者作答。每段對話及問題只播出一遍。

Conversation 1

Q 1

答案欄

(A) She has to save money in a bank.

(B) She has to shop.

(C) Because she will get some stamps.

(D) Because she wants to send a parcel.

Conversation 2 新題型

Q 2

Taipei Post Office
Open Five Days a week (Mon-Fri)
Opening Time: 9:00 AM
Closing Time:17:00 PM

答案欄

(A) 9:15 AM.

(B) 17:00 PM.

(C) 16:45 PM.

(D) 16:00 PM.

每題請聽光碟放音機播出一段談話及一個相關的問題後，從試題冊上 A、B、C、D 四個選項中選出一個最適合者作答。每段談話及問題只播出一遍。

Short Talk 1

Q 1

(A) At the period of Chinese New Year vacation, all post offices are busy.
(B) People who work in the post office deliver packages of food and gifts all over Taiwan.
(C) People who work in the post office should be a good truck driver.
(D) They wear beautiful green uniforms that never change.

答案欄

Short Talk 2

Q 2

Mail & Postage		
Mail	**fee**	**Mailing day(s)**
Regular	$7	3 days
Express	$20	1 day
Registered Regular	$25	3 days
Registered Express	$40	1 day

答案欄

(A) $7.
(B) $20.
(C) $25.
(D) $40.

答案解析

第一部分 看圖辨義

 For questions number 1 and 2, please look at picture A.
問題 1 跟問題 2 請看圖片 A。

Q1 ___D___ **Where is it?**

這裡是哪裡？
(A) Internet café. 網咖。
(B) Office building. 辦公大樓。
(C) Apartment. 公寓。
(D) Post office. 郵局。

Q2 ___B___ **Which description matches the picture A?**

哪一敘述符合圖 A。
(A) Nobody is waiting for line C.
沒有人在 C 道等待。
(B) You can buy some stamps in this place.
你可以在這個地方買些郵票。
(C) The person in line A is probably the 64th.
排在 A 道的這個人可能是第 64 位。
(D) The place is for students to study in.
這個地方是給學生唸書的。

For questions number 3 and 4, please look at picture B.
問題 3 跟問題 4 請看圖片 B。

Q3 ___B___ **What does the man want to do?**

男子想要做什麼？
(A) He wants to write a letter.
他想要寫信。
(B) He mails someone a letter.
他寄信給某人。

(C) He reads the letter carefully.

他小心地讀信。

(D) He throws away the letter.

他把信丟掉。

Q4　　**C**　**What is the man wearing?**

男子正穿戴著什麼？

(A) Shorts with an umbrella.

短褲，並帶著雨傘。

(B) Pants with a T-shirt.

長褲與 T 恤。

(C) Sandals and an umbrella.

涼鞋，並帶著雨傘。

(D) Glasses and a scarf.

眼鏡與圍巾。

第二部分 問答

Q1　　**B**　**Where is the nearest post office?**

最近的郵局在哪裡？

(A) Yes, sir. May I help you?

是的，先生。我可以幫你嗎？

(B) Just around the corner. You can't miss it.

就在轉角附近，你不會找不到的。

(C) Let's go for some stamps.

我們去買一些郵票吧。

(D) Who needs to go there?

誰需要去那裡？

單字解釋 ▶ the nearest 最近的　　　　　　stamp **n** 郵票

around the corner 在轉角附近

試題分析 ▶ 本題問：最近的郵局在哪裡。可知答案為選項 (B)：就在轉角附近，你不會找不到的。

Q2 **B** **Are you going to the post office?**

你正要去郵局嗎？

(A) Yes, I am going to pass it.
是的，我會經過。

(B) No, I went there 2 hours ago.
不，我兩小時前去過了。

(C) Let's go to the police station.
我們去警察局吧。

(D) Do you have change for a dollar?
你有零錢可換嗎？

單字解釋 ▶ post office 郵局　　　　　police station 警察局

試題分析 ▶ 本題問：你是否正要去郵局。可知答案為選項 (B)：不，我兩小時前去過了。

Q3 **B** **Could you do me a favor? Go to the post office and buy some envelopes.**

你能幫我一個忙嗎？去郵局幫我買一些信封袋。

(A) Why not go to the park?
為何不去公園呢？

(B) Yes, I will go there immediately
沒問題，我馬上去。

(C) Don't you need some chips?
你不需要一些薯片嗎？

(D) Who needs to go there?
誰需要去那裡？

單字解釋 ▶ do me a favor 幫我一個忙　　　envelope **n** 信封
immediately **adv** 立即地

試題分析 ▶ 本題問：請對方幫自己一個忙，去郵局買一些信封袋，問對方是否可以。答案為選項 (B)：沒問題，我馬上去。

Conversation 1

W: Robert, are you going downtown now?

M: Yes, why?

W: Could you give me a ride to the post office? I need to mail a package.

中文翻譯

女： Robert，你現在要去市區嗎？

男：是的，怎樣？

女：你可以載我去郵局嗎？我需要郵寄包裹。

Q1 ___D___ **Why does the woman need a ride?**

這女子為何需要搭便車？

(A) She has to save money in a bank.

她必須在銀行存錢。

(B) She has to shop. 她必須去購物。

(C) Because she will get some stamps.

因為她將買一些郵票。

(D) Because she wants to send a parcel.

因為她要寄一個包裹。

單字解釋 ▶ post office 郵局

試題分析 ▶ 本題問：女子為何要搭便車。從對話最後的 I need to mail a package 可知答案為選項 (D)：因為她要寄包裹。

Conversation 2

```
               Taipei Post Office

Open Five Days a week (Mon-Fri)

Opening Time: 9:00 AM

Closing Time: 17:00 PM
```

M: Oh, boy, I forgot to mail an important parcel to my daughter in California.

W: I've noticed you are easy to forget things these days.

M: These days I am burning the candle at both ends. I have too many things to do both at work and at home. That's the reason why I forgot the parcel I should have sent.

W: I can take it to the post office for you.

M: I appreciate it. But you had better hurry. Only fifteen minutes left before it closes.

中文翻譯

```
               台北郵局

一週開放五日（週一至週五）

開始營業時間：早上 9 點

結束營業時間：下午 5 點
```

男：天啊！我忘了去寄重要包裹給我在加州的女兒。

女：我發現你最近很容易忘東忘西的。

男：最近我真是蠟燭兩頭燒。我在工作上與家裡同時有太多事情要做。這就是為何我會忘記我該寄包裹這件事。

女：我可以幫你把包裹帶到郵局去。

男：太感謝了。但是你最好要快點。離結束營業時間只剩下十五分鐘了。

Q2 __C__ **When does the conversation take place?**

對話發生在何時？

(A) 9:15 AM.

早上 9 點 15 分。

(B) 17:00 PM.

下午 5 點整。

(C) 16:45 PM.

下午 4 點 45 分。

(D) 16:00 PM.

下午 4 點整。

單字解釋 ▶ parcel **n** 包裹

burn the candle at both ends 蠟燭兩頭燒（慣用語）

試題分析 ▶ 本題問：對話所發生的時間點是在何時。在對話中可聽到 But you had better hurry. Only fifteen minutes left before it closed., 表示建議對方快點前往郵局，離結束營業只剩十五分鐘。再參照圖表說明，結束營業時間是下午 5 點整，所以現在時間為下午 4 點 45 分，故答案要選 (C)。

第四部分 簡短談話

Short Talk 1

It's February, and Chinese New Year is upcoming. At the period of time, all post offices are busy. They are getting ready for busy holiday season. They deliver packages of food and gifts all over Taiwan. Almost all packages are delivered on the ground by truck. People who work in the post office should be a good truck driver. They wear beautiful green uniforms that change according to the seasons.

中文翻譯

現在是二月，農曆新年即將到來。在這段期間，所有的郵局都很忙。他們正在為這個忙碌的假期時節做準備。他們在全台配送著食物或是禮品的包裹。現在幾乎所有的包裹都正由貨車配送中。在郵局服務的工作者都應該是優良的貨車司機。他們穿著隨著季節替換的美麗綠色制服。

Q1 **D** **Which statement is NOT true from this talk?** 根據這段談話，下列敘述何者不正確？

(A) At the period of Chinese New Year vacation, all post offices are busy.
在農曆新年期間，所有的郵局都很忙碌。

(B) People who work in the post office deliver packages of food and gifts all over Taiwan.
在郵局服務的工作者，都在全台配送著裝滿食物的包裹或是禮品。

(C) People who work in the post office should be a good truck driver.
在郵局服務的工作者，都應該是優良的貨車司機。

(D) They wear beautiful green uniforms that never change. 他們穿著從來都不會改變的美麗綠色制服。

單字解釋 ▶ upcoming **adj** 即將到來的　　　　truck driver 貨車駕駛員
green uniform 綠色制服

試題分析 ▶ 本題問：根據談話，何者不正確。在談話中聽到 They wear beautiful green uniforms that change according to the seasons.，可知他們會穿著隨季節做變更的美麗綠色制服，選項(D)明顯與內容不符。故答案要選 (D)。

Short Talk 2

Mail & Postage		
Mail	**fee**	**Mailing day(s)**
Regular	$7	3 days
Express	$20	1 day
Registered Regular	$25	3 days
Registered Express	$40	1 day

Lisa, I am calling to tell you I forgot to take that envelope with me this morning. Therefore, I couldn't mail it on my way to work. Enclosed the envelope is a contract that I need my client to sign for me. My client needs it tomorrow or the day after tomorrow, so it's a bit urgent. Would you mind going to the post office and mailing it for me? Oh, please have it registered because it's really important. Oh, take some small cash with you. You need to pay postage.

 中文翻譯

郵寄與郵資		
郵寄	費用	需郵寄天數
平信	7 元	三天
快捷	20 元	一天
平信掛號	25 元	三天
快捷掛號	40 元	一天

Lisa，我來電是要告訴你今早我忘了把那封信封帶在身邊。因此我在上班途中無法把它寄出。信封內有一份我要請我客戶簽名的合約。我的客戶明天或後天就需要它，所以有些緊急。你介意替我到郵局一趟去把它寄出嗎？對了，請用掛號寄出，因為它十分重要。然後帶些零錢在身邊，你需要付郵資的。

Q2 __D__ **How much will Lisa pay for the postage?**

Lisa 要付多少郵資？

(A) $7. 7元。
(B) $20. 20元。
(C) $25. 25元。
(D) $40. 40元。

單字解釋 ▶ regular mail 平信　　　　　express mail 快捷
　　　　　registered mail **n** 掛號　　　postage **n** 郵資

試題分析 ▶ 本題問：Lisa 要付多少郵資。在談話中可以得知 My client needs it tomorrow or the day after tomorrow, so it's a bit urgent.，表示客戶明天或後天需要這份合約，言下之意必須在兩天之內就要寄到，從圖表的 Mailing day(s) 可知，要以 Express（快捷）寄出。談話中又聽到 Oh, please have it registered because it's really important.，表示要用掛號寄出。所以要用快捷掛號信（Registered Express），從圖表可知需要 40 元，故答案要選 (D)。

情境
主題 **16** **Business**
（商務接洽）

Hint
常
考
句
子

 可能情境包括：公事、與同事談公事、公差、與老
闆或上司的對話等。

1 The business in cram schools are going down. 補習班的生意愈來愈糟了。

2 How many business trips do you have per year? 你一年有多少次出差？

3 I am going to have a meeting with our president. 我將與我們的總裁開會。

模擬試題　 **016.mp3**

第一部分　**看圖辨義**

 試題冊上有數幅圖畫，每一圖畫有 1~3 個描述該圖的題目，每題
請聽光碟放音機播出題目以及四個英語敘述之後，選出與所看到
的圖畫最相符的答案，每題只播出一遍。

Picture A　Q1 ～ Q2

第二部分 問答

作答說明　每題請聽光碟放音機播出一英語問句或直述句後，從試題冊上 A、B、C、D 四個回答或回應中，選出一個最適合者作答。每題只播出一遍。

Q1
(A) He did a great work.
(B) He lives with his family.
(C) He's a businessman. He needs to travel a lot.
(D) He is living for his mother.

Q2
(A) How do you do?
(B) I'm in the living room.
(C) I'm an English teacher.
(D) I am watching TV.

(A) No, he can't go there.

(B) What a wonderful and easy vacation trip he has.

(C) Good luck to him.

(D) Hong Kong is a good place for shopping.

第三部分 簡短對話

作答說明 每題請聽光碟放音機播出一段對話及一個相關的問題之後,從試題冊上 A、B、C、D 四個選項中選出一個最適合者作答。每段對話及問題只播出一遍。

Conversation 1

(A) They are talking about Joe's occupation.

(B) They are talking about Joe's life.

(C) They think Joe should find a job as an engineer.

(D) They think Joe should quit his present job.

Conversation 2

HDD Business Center
Floor Directory

Level 4	CEO's Office & IT Dept.
Level 3	Personnel Dept. & Finance Dept.
Level 2	Law affairs & Accounting Dept.
Level 1	Marketing Dept. & Ad Dept.

(A) Level one.

(B) Level two.

(C) Level three.

(D) Level four.

第四部分 簡短談話 新題型

作答說明 每題請聽光碟放音機播出一段談話及一個相關的問題後,從試題冊上 A、B、C、D 四個選項中選出一個最適合者作答。每段談話及問題只播出一遍。

Short Talk 1

(A) Someone who is interested in high technology.

(B) Someone who seeks for some job offers.

(C) Someone who is interested in architecture.

(D) Someone who wants to improve their communication skill.

Short Talk 2

Prohibited in the company	
Item 1	Have personal phone calls
Item 2	Browse websites
Item 3	Copy personal papers
Item 4	Play online games

(A) Item 1.

(B) Item 2.

(C) Item 3.

(D) Item 4.

答案解析

第一部分 看圖辨義

 提示

For questions number 1 and 2, please look at picture A.
問題 1 跟問題 2 請看圖片 A。

Q1 __D__ **What is Mr. Wade going to do at 1:00?**

Wade 先生將在 1 點時做什麼？

(A) He's going to have a class. 他將去上課。

(B) He's going to discuss a new project.
他將討論一個新提案。

(C) He's going to have a meeting. 他將去開會。

(D) He's going to type something. 他將打一些的東西。

Q2 __C__ **Which description is correct?**

哪一項描述是正確的？

(A) Mr. Wade makes a call after having a meeting.
Wade 先生在開完會後要打一通電話。

(B) Mr. Wade makes a call after playing with the
computer. Wade 先生在打完電腦後打電話。

(C) Mr. Wade has a meeting before playing with the
computer. Wade 先生在用電腦前有一個會議。

(D) Mr. Wade plays with the computer before he has a
meeting. Wade 先生在開會前打電腦。

第二部分 問答

Q1 __C__ **What does Joe do for a living?**

Joe 做什麼維生（Joe 的工作是什麼）？

(A) He did a great work. 他做得很棒。

(B) He lives with his family. 他與他的家人同住。

(C) He's a businessman. He needs to travel a lot.
他是一個商人，他需要經常旅遊。

(D) He is living for his mother. 他為了母親而活。

do for a living 以…維生

本題問：Joe 做什麼維生（工作是什麼）。可知答案為選項 (C)：他是商人，他需要經常旅遊。

Q2　　C　　What do you do, Michelle?

Michelle，你做什麼工作？
(A) How do you do? 你好嗎？
(B) I'm in the living room. 我在客廳裡。
(C) I'm an English teacher. 我是英文老師。
(D) I am watching TV. 我正在看電視。

單字解釋 ▶ What do you do?（義同 What is your job?）你的工作是什麼？

試題分析 ▶ 本題問：你的工作是什麼。可知答案為選項 (C)：我是英文老師。

Q3　　C　　Jack is going to stay in Hong Kong for 3 years because his company decides to have a branch there.

Jack 將要待在香港三年，因為他的公司決定要在那裡設立分公司。
(A) No, he can't go there. 不，他不能去那裡。
(B) What a wonderful and easy vacation trip he has.
　　他有多麼棒且愜意的度假旅行啊。
(C) Good luck to him. 祝他好運。
(D) Hong Kong is a good place for shopping.
　　香港是一個購物天堂。

單字解釋 ▶ decide to 決定…
branch n 分支機構

試題分析 ▶ 本題說：Jack 將要待在香港三年，因為他的公司將在香港設分公司。可知答案為選項 (C)：祝他好運。(B) 的選項是一句感嘆句，但其中提到的度假旅遊與原意不符。

第三部分 簡短對話

Conversation 1

W: What does Joe do for a living?
M: I am not sure. Probably he is an engineer.
W: Really? He looks like a rich man.
M: You can say that again.

中文翻譯

女：Joe 做什麼工作維生？
男：我不確定。也許他是位工程師。
女：真的嗎？他看起來像是位有錢人。
男：妳說的對極了。

Q1　__A__　**What are they talking about?** 他們在談什麼？
(A) They are talking about Joe's occupation.
　　他們在談 Joe 的工作。
(B) They are talking about Joe's life.
　　他們正在談論 Joe 的人生。
(C) They think Joe should find a job as an engineer.
　　他們認為 Joe 應該找一份工程師的工作。
(D) They think Joe should quit his present job.
　　他們認為 Joe 應該辭去他的現有工作。

單字解釋 ▶ do for a living 以⋯維生
試題分析 ▶ 本題問：他們在談什麼。從第一句的 What does Joe do for a living? 可知，答案為選項 (A)：談 Joe 的工作。

Conversation 2

HDD Business Center Floor Directory	
Level 4	CEO's Office & IT Dept.
Level 3	Personnel Dept. & Finance Dept.
Level 2	Law affairs & Accounting Dept.
Level 1	Marketing Dept. & Ad Dept.

M: Sally, can you do me a favor?

W: What is it?

M: Mind giving this document to Lisa on your way to J&D Company? This case should be done ASAP. When you see Lisa, ask her to make it top priority.

W: Got it. Tell me her department in HDD business center again?

M: Human Resources Department.

HDD商業中心 樓層說明	
4 樓	執行長辦公室與資訊部門
3 樓	人事部門與財務部門
2 樓	法務部門與會計部門
1 樓	行銷部門與廣告部門

男：Sally，可以幫我個忙嗎？

女：什麼事呢？

男：介意在妳去 J&D 公司的途中，把這文件交給 Lisa 嗎？這個案子需要盡快被完成。你看到 Lisa 時，請她優先處理這件事。

女：了解。可以再告訴我她在 HDD 商業中心的哪個部門嗎？

男：人力資源部。

Q2　__C__　**Which floor will Sally probably go to?**

Sally 可能會去幾樓？

(A) Level one.

1 樓。

(B) Level two.

2 樓。

(C) Level three.

3 樓。

(D) Level four.

4 樓。

單字解釋 ▶ ASAP（as soon as possible 的縮寫） 盡快

top priority 優先處理事項

試題分析 ▶ 本題問：Sally 可能會去的樓層。在對話的一開始知道 Sally 是對話中的女子。在對話的最後 Sally 提到 Tell me her [Lisa] department in HDD business center again，表示請男子告訴 Sally 說，Lisa 在 HDD 商業中心的哪個部門，男子回人力資源部（Human Resources Department）。從圖表可知，人事部門在三樓，故答案要選 (C)。

Short Talk 1

Ladies and gentlemen: it is my honor to welcome such an outstanding group of foreign buyers to the opening of our computer fair. As you all know, this is the largest trade exhibition in the nation, and I am sure your presence at this trade event will be crucial to its success. And now, let's have a look at this advanced new model.

中文翻譯

各位女士先生，我很榮幸歡迎一群傑出的國外買家來到我們的電腦展開幕式。如同各位所知，這是本國最大的貿易展，而我相信各位的出席，對於這場展覽的成功將至關重要。現在請先來看看這台先進的新機型。

Q1 ___A___ **Who might be attending this event?**

誰可能會參與這活動？

(A) Someone who is interested in high technology.
對高科技有興趣的人。

(B) Someone who seeks for some job offers.
想找工作的人。

(C) Someone who is interested in architecture.
對建築有興趣的人。

(D) Someone who wants to improve their communication skill. 想要改善溝通技巧的人。

單字解釋 ▶ outstanding **adj** 傑出的　　　　buyer **n** 買家

試題分析 ▶ 在談話中提到 it is my honor to welcome ~ foreign buyers to ~ computer fair.，可知談話中的活動是指電腦展，而來此電腦展的人為一些買家。後面又提到 let's have a look at this advanced new model.，可知現場有最先進的新機型。故答案要選 (A)。

Short Talk 2

Prohibited in the company	
Item 1	Have personal phone calls
Item 2	Browse websites
Item 3	Copy personal papers
Item 4	Play online games

May I have your attention, please? Some staff members have been using the company photocopier for personal documents. This is absolutely not acceptable. From now on, the policy must change. Staff can only use the equipment and supplies for company work. That is to say, when you finish your copy, I will check your documents page by page. I apologize if you find this unpleasant. Thank you for your cooperation regarding this matter.

中文翻譯

公司內部禁止事項	
第 1 項	打私人電話
第 2 項	瀏覽網頁
第 3 項	印個人文件
第 4 項	玩線上遊戲

請大家注意一下。有一些公司員工，一直使用公司影印機印個人文件。這是絕對不能接受的。從現在開始，政策必須改變。公司設備與物品，員工們只能使用於公司的事務上。換言之，當各位印完之後，我會一頁一頁地檢查各位的文件。如果這讓各位覺得不愉快，我在此向您道歉。感謝各位在這件事情上的配合。

Q2 ___C___ **Which item on the list should be prohibited according to the speaker?**

根據說話者所言，表格中哪一項應被禁止？

(A) Item 1. 事項一。
(B) Item 2. 事項二。
(C) Item 3. 事項三。
(D) Item 4. 事項四。

單字解釋 ▶ prohibited adj 被禁止的
browse v 瀏覽
photocopier n 影印機
acceptable adj 可接受的
cooperation n 合作

試題分析 ▶ 本題問：表格中哪一項應被禁止。從談話中的 Some staff members have been using the company photocopier for personal documents. This is absolutely not acceptable. 可以得知，使用公司影印機印個人文件是不能接受的，言下之意禁止印個人文件，故答案要選(C)。

Hint
常
考
句
子

可能情境包括：買家具、讚美家具、住宅環境好壞、如何到某人家等。

1 What a nice armchair.
好棒的一張扶手椅。

2 How can I get to your place?
我要如何去你家？

3 How much is the vase?
這個花瓶多少錢？

4 I live in an apartment.
我住在一間公寓裡。

5 There is a supermarket and a post office in the neighborhood.
附近有一家超市及一間郵局。

6 I will place a television in front of the sofa.
我將在沙發前面放置一台電視。

7 The house is well furnished.
這棟房子被裝潢得很好。

模擬試題

第一部分　看圖辨義

作答說明 試題冊上有數幅圖畫，每一圖畫有 1~3 個描述該圖的題目，每題請聽光碟放音機播出題目以及四個英語敘述之後，選出與所看到的圖畫最相符的答案，每題只播出一遍。

Picture A　Q1 ～ Q2

Picture B　Q3 ～ Q4

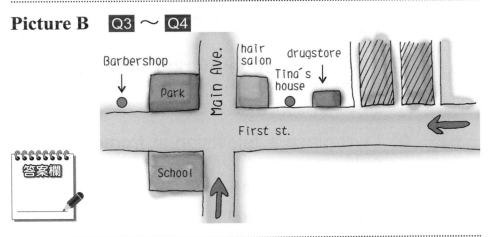

每題請聽光碟放音機播出一英語問句或直述句後，從試題冊上 A、B、C、D 四個回答或回應中，選出一個最適合者作答。每題只播出一遍。

Q 1

(A) You bet. It's great.

(B) Nice to talk to you again.

(C) Yes, my arm is so hurt.

(D) Yes, this is mine.

答案欄

Q 2

(A) They get along with each other.

(B) No. They study in different schools.

(C) Yes. They live in the same apartment building.

(D) My neighborhood is quiet.

答案欄

Q 3

(A) Just turn right at next corner.

(B) I got to your home yesterday.

(C) I always take a bus.

(D) Can you give me a ride?

答案欄

第三部分 簡短對話

每題請聽光碟放音機播出一段對話及一個相關的問題之後，從試題冊上 A、B、C、D 四個選項中選出一個最適合者作答。每段對話及問題只播出一遍。

Conversation 1

(A) It's too expensive.

(B) The location is not good enough.

(C) The living room is too small.

(D) It's hard to believe there's a good apartment.

Conversation 2

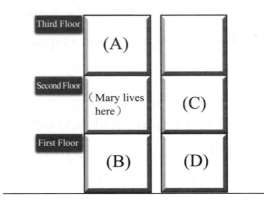

(A) Apartment A.

(B) Apartment B.

(C) Apartment C.

(D) Apartment D.

第四部分 簡短談話 新題型

作答說明
每題請聽光碟放音機播出一段談話及一個相關的問題後，從試題冊上 A、B、C、D 四個選項中選出一個最適合者作答。每段談話及問題只播出一遍。

Short Talk 1

Q 1

答案欄

(A) It's more expensive, but it's worth it.
(B) It's not as convenient as before.
(C) It's difficult to afford the mortgage.
(D) Many artists and professors prefer not to live in this neighborhood.

Short Talk 2

Q 2

Property Auction Catalog		
Item/Location	Description	Asking Price
item 1 Xinyi District	2 beds, 1.5 baths	30 million
item 2 Zhongshan District	4 beds, 2 baths	40 million
item 3 Neihu District	3 beds, 1 bath	30 million
item 4 Zhonghe District	1 bed, 1 bath	10 million

答案欄

(A) Item 1.
(B) Item 2.
(C) Item 3.
(D) Item 4.

答案解析

第一部分 看圖辨義

For questions number 1 and 2, please look at picture A.
問題 1 跟問題 2 請看圖片 A。

Q1   C   **What kind of store is it?**

這是什麼樣的店？

(A) Drugstore. 藥局。

(B) Barbershop. 理髮廳。

(C) Furniture shop. 家具行。

(D) Fortune teller stand. 算命攤。

Q2   C   **What description is correct?**

哪一項敘述是正確的？

(A) The bedside table costs $1,350.
    床頭櫃要花 1,350 元。

(B) It costs $2,600 to buy a couch.
    買沙發要花 2,600 元。

(C) The desk is more expensive than the lamp.
    書桌比檯燈貴。

(D) The couch is the cheapest item in the store.
    沙發是這家店裡最便宜的品項。

....

For questions number 3 and 4, please look at picture B.
問題 3 跟問題 4 請看圖片 B。

Q3   D   **How can I get to Tina's house?**

我要怎麼去 Tina 的家？

(A) Walk up the First Street and turn right on Main Ave.
    走 First 街，於 Main 大道右轉。

(B) Walk along the Main Ave. and turn left on First
    Street. Tina's house is on the right between the hair
    salon and the drugstore. 沿著 Main 大道走，在 First 街左
    轉。Tina 的家在右手邊，位在髮廊與藥局之間。

(C) Walk up the First Street for 2 blocks, and Tina's house is on your left.
走 First 街，過兩個街區後，Tina 的家就在你的左手邊。

(D) Walk along the Main Ave. and turn right on First Street. Tina's house is on the left between the hair salon and the drugstore. 沿著 Main 大道走，在 First 街右轉，Tina 的家在左手邊，位在髮廊與藥局之間。

Q4 __C__ **Which description is correct?**
哪一項敘述是正確的？

(A) Tina's house is opposite the barbershop.
Tina 的家在理髮廳的對面。

(B) The barbershop is just across from the park.
理髮廳在公園的對面。

(C) Tina's house is next to the drugstore.
Tina 的家在藥局旁邊。

(D) Tina's house is between the school and the drugstore. Tina 的家位在學校與藥局之間。

第二部分 問答

Q1 __A__ **What a nice armchair!**
好棒的扶手椅！

(A) You bet. It's great.
你說的對，它棒極了。

(B) Nice to talk to you again.
很高興再次與你談話。

(C) Yes, my arm is so hurt.
是的，我的手臂好痛。

(D) Yes, this is mine.
是的，這是我的。

單字解釋 ▶ you bet 你說的對　　　　　armchair **n** 扶手椅

試題分析 ▶ 本題說：好棒的扶手椅，可知答案為選項 (A)：你說的對，它棒極了。

Q2 ___C___ **Are Li and Robert neighbors?**

Li 與 Robert 是鄰居嗎？

(A) They get along with each other.

他們彼此相處得好。

(B) No. They study in different schools.

不是。他們在不同的學校讀書。

(C) Yes. They live in the same apartment building.

是呀。他們住在同一棟公寓大樓。

(D) My neighborhood is quiet.

我居住的社區很安靜。

單字解釋 ▶ neighbors **n** 鄰居　　　　　neighborhood **n** 鄰近的地區

get along with 與…相處得好

試題分析 ▶ 本題問：Li 與 Robert 是鄰居。可知最適合的回應是選項 (C)：
是呀。他們住在同一棟公寓大樓。

Q3 ___A___ **Kimberley, how can I get to your home?**

Kimberley，我要如何才能到你家？

(A) Just turn right at next corner.

在下一個街角右轉就可以了。

(B) I got to your home yesterday.

我昨天去了你家。

(C) I always take a bus.

我總是搭公車。

(D) Can you give me a ride?

你可以載我嗎？

單字解釋 ▶ corner **n** 轉角，角落

give a ride 接送一程（義同 give a lift）

試題分析 ▶ 本題問：Kimberley，我要如何才能到你家。可知說話者在問
Kimberley 的家的所在位置。因此答案為選項 (A)：在下一個
街角右轉就可以了。

第三部分 簡短對話

Conversation 1

W: I just saw a good apartment for rent in the newspaper.

M: Really? What does it say?

W: It has two bedrooms, a kitchen, a bathroom and a small living room.

M: Sounds great. Where is it located?

W: Just near our office.

M: That sounds too good to be true.

中文翻譯

女：我剛在報紙上看見一個出租的好公寓。

男：真的嗎？它怎麼說？

女：有兩房、一個廚房、一個浴室與一個小客廳。

男：聽起來不錯。它位在哪裡？

女：就在我們的辦公室附近。

男：好得難以相信是真的。

Q1 ___D___ **What does the man think about the house?**

男子認為這間房子如何？

(A) It's too expensive. 太貴了。

(B) The location is not good enough. 位置不夠好。

(C) The living room is too small. 客廳太小了。

(D) It's hard to believe there's a good apartment.

很難想像有一個這麼好的公寓。

單字解釋 ▶ locate Ⅴ 使⋯座落於

試題分析 ▶ 本題問：男子對這房子有什麼想法。從男子最後的 That sounds too good to be true. 可知答案為選項 (D)：很難想像有一個這麼好的公寓。

Conversation 2

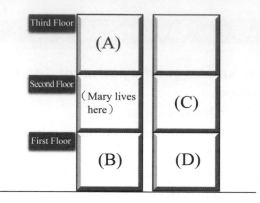

M: Guess what I have decided to do.

W: What?

M: I have decided to move.

W: That's a surprise! How long have you been thinking about moving?

M: For a long time actually. I considered moving a few years ago, but never did.

W: So, we won't be neighbors anymore. So sad that I will lose a nice neighbor living above me.

M: All good things must come to an end. I'll miss you, Mary.

中文翻譯

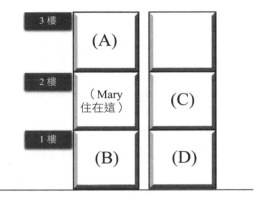

3樓 (A)

2樓 （Mary 住在這） (C)

1樓 (B) (D)

男：猜猜我決定要做什麼？
女：什麼？
男：我決定要搬家了。
女：那真是令人驚訝！你考慮搬家多久了？
男：事實上已經很久了。幾年前我就考慮要搬家，但都沒去做。
女：所以我們將不再是鄰居了。真難過我要失去一位住在我樓上的好鄰居了。
男：天底下沒有不散的宴席。我會想念你的，Mary。

Q2 ___A___ **Look at the building. Where is the man living now?** 請看這張大樓圖示。男子目前住在哪裡？
(A) Apartment A. 公寓 A。
(B) Apartment B. 公寓 B。
(C) Apartment C. 公寓 C。
(D) Apartment D. 公寓 D。

單字解釋 ▶ landlord **n** 房東   neighbor **n** 鄰居

試題分析 ▶ 本題問：男子目前住在圖表中的哪裡。在對話中可知男子要搬家。接著女子提到 So sad that I will lose a nice neighbor living above me.，表示自己要失去了一位住在自己樓上的一位鄰居，可以得知男子住在女子樓上。從對話最後男子說的 I'll miss you, Mary. 可知女子是Mary，而圖表中女子（Mary）住在左棟大樓的二樓，所以男子住在同一棟的三樓。故答案要選 (A)。

Short Talk 1

Hi, Daisy, I am calling to tell you I've moved to a new apartment. It's better than my old one. It's much bigger and it's in a safer neighborhood. People tell me that lots of artists, musicians and professors are living in this area. Of course, it's more expensive, but I am doing pretty well on my job now; therefore, paying the mortgage won't be a problem for me. Come to visit me!

中文翻譯

嗨！黛西！我來電是要告訴你我搬到新公寓裡，這比我舊的那間要好。它大多了，而且是在一個更為安全的地區。人們都告訴我說，很多藝術家、音樂家以及教授都住在這附近。當然也比較貴，但我現在工作順利，因此付房貸對我來說將不是問題。要過來看看我喔！

Q1 __A__ **How does the speaker feel about the new place he's living in?** 說話者覺得他現在新住的地方如何？
(A) It's more expensive, but it's worth it.
   比較昂貴，但值得。
(B) It's not as convenient as before. 沒有以前來得方便。
(C) It's difficult to afford the mortgage. 負擔房貸很困難。
(D) Many artists and professors prefer not to live in this neighborhood. 很多藝術家及教授都比較不想要住這區。

單字解釋 ▶ neighborhood **n** 鄰近地區   mortgage **n** 房貸

試題分析 ▶ 本題問：說話者覺得自己新住的地方如何。在談話中有聽到 I've moved to a new apartment ~ better than my old one ~ much bigger and it's in a safer neighborhood.，後面也提到 it's more expensive，可知 (A) 正確。此外談話中也提到 artists, musicians and professors are living in this area. 可知藝術家、音樂家以及教授都住在這附近，所以(D) 不正確。說話者也有提到 but I am doing pretty well on my job now ~ paying the mortgage won't be a problem for me. 可知付房貸對說話者來說不是問題，所以(C) 也不正確。(B)在談話中沒提到。故答案要選 (A)。

Short Talk 2

Property Auction Catalog

Item/Location	Description	Asking Price
item 1 Xinyi District	2 beds, 1.5 baths	30 million
item 2 Zhongshan District	4 beds, 2 baths	40 million
item 3 Neihu District	3 beds, 1 bath	30 million
item 4 Zhonghe District	1 bed, 1 bath	10 million

Next up I would like to introduce you to an ideal apartment for a nuclear family. This one is in a very good neighborhood, with the additional benefit of being close to the MRT system. The asking price of this apartment is reasonable, only 30 million NT dollars. It has a big living room, a nice kitchen, two bedrooms, more than one bathroom and a balcony with magnificent view.

不動產拍賣型錄

標的／地點	內容描述	開價
第 1 項／信義區	兩房，一套半衛浴	3 千萬
第 2 項／中山區	四房，兩套衛浴	4 千萬
第 3 項／內湖區	三房，一套衛浴	3 千萬
第 4 項／中正區	一房，一套衛浴	1 千萬

接下來我想介紹一戶適合小家庭的理想公寓給您。它位於一個非常棒的區域裡，而且還有個附加的優點，臨近捷運系統。這一戶要價合理，只需 3 千萬台幣。它有一個大的客廳、很棒的廚房、兩房、超過一套的衛浴設備，以及能看到美景的陽台。

Q2 ___A___ **Which item of the properties is the speaker talking about?** 說話者在談論的是哪一項不動產標的？
(A) Item 1. 第 1 項。
(B) Item 2. 第 2 項。
(C) Item 3. 第 3 項。
(D) Item 4. 第 4 項。

單字解釋 ▶ property **n** 不動產　　　　　　　auction **n** 拍賣
nuclear family 核心家庭、小家庭
neighborhood **n** 鄰近地區，整個街坊
benefit **n** 好處、優勢　　　　　reasonable **adj** 合理的
magnificent **adj** 美好的，壯觀的

試題分析 ▶ 本題問：說話者在談論哪一個不動產標的。在談話中可以得知，The asking price of this apartment is ~ 30 million NT dollars，可知房價是 3 千萬台幣。接著又說 a big living room, a nice kitchen, two bedrooms, more than one bathroom and a balcony，可知有客廳、一個廚房、兩房、超過一套的衛浴設備及陽台。從圖表中可知，價格是 3 千萬，又是兩房與超過一套以上的衛浴設備，答案是 (A)。

Hint
常考句子

可能情境包括：搭乘交通工具、計程車資、火車時刻表、班機時刻表、加油與油資等。

1 How much does it cost from Taipei to Kenting if taking a bus?
從台北到墾丁搭巴士要花多少錢？

2 I want to take a cab, but I am afraid I don't have enough money.
我想要坐計程車，但是我恐怕沒有足夠的錢。

3 I seldom go to work on foot.
我很少走路上班。

模擬試題  **018.mp3**

第一部分 看圖辨義

試題冊上有數幅圖畫，每一圖畫有 1~3 個描述該圖的題目，每題請聽光碟放音機播出題目以及四個英語敘述之後，選出與所看到的圖畫最相符的答案，每題只播出一遍。

243

Picture A Q1 ～ Q2

第二部分 **問答**

每題請聽光碟放音機播出一英語問句或直述句後,從試題冊上 A、B、C、D 四個回答或回應中,選出一個最適合者作答。每題 只播出一遍。

Q 1
(A) 5 times.

(B) Around 150 dollars.

(C) About 5 miles.

(D) I guess this is the second time.

Q 2
(A) Yes, sir. May I help you?

(B) I think you run out of your money.

(C) More guests will run in the park.

(D) Yes, you are totally right.

(A) Yes, sir. May I help you?

(B) I can lift it myself.

(C) Do you have a driver's license?

(D) Sure, where are you going to?

簡短對話

每題請聽光碟放音機播出一段對話及一個相關的問題之後,從試題冊上 A、B、C、D 四個選項中選出一個最適合者作答。每段對話及問題只播出一遍。

Conversation 1

(A) Maybe 140 in case of taking a taxi.

(B) Taking a taxi is more expensive than taking a bus.

(C) Taking a taxi is slower than taking a bus.

(D) The woman will take a cab.

Flight Schedule

Fight Number	Departure Time	Status
#173	3:00 PM	Available
#128	4:00 PM	Fully booked
#176	5:00 PM	Available
#188	6:00 PM	Canceled

(A) #173.

(B) #128.

(C) #176.

(D) #188.

每題請聽光碟放音機播出一段談話及一個相關的問題後，從試題冊上 A、B、C、D 四個選項中選出一個最適合者作答。每段談話及問題只播出一遍。

 Short Talk 1

Q 1

(A) Stand in line.

(B) Upright their seats.

(C) Fasten their seat belts.

(D) Serve the beverages.

 答案欄

 Short Talk 2

Q 2

Flight Schedule		
Fight Number	Destination	Baggage Claim Area
FA266	New York	Terminal 2 / Section 2
BA305	Taipei	Terminal 2 / Section 1
KA910	Taipei	Terminal 1 / Section 4
UA235	London	Terminal 4 / Section 2

(A) FA266

(B) BA305

(C) KA910

(D) UA235

 答案欄

答案解析

For questions number 1 and 2, please look at picture A.
問題 1 跟問題 2 請看圖片 A。

Q1 ___A___ **What kind of transportation is it?**

這是什麼交通工具？

(A) Subway. 地鐵。
(B) Highway. 高速公路。
(C) Wagon 馬車。
(D) Spacecraft. 太空梭。

Q2 ___C___ **Which description is right?** 哪一個敘述是對的？

(A) One woman is getting off the train.
一位女子正要下火車。

(B) This is a MRT station. 這是一個捷運站。
(C) One man is getting off the train.
一位男子正要下火車。
(D) Two kids are playing in the train.
兩個小孩正在火車上玩。

Q1 ___B___ **How much does it cost from here to Taipei if I take a cab?**

如果我搭計程車從這裡到台北要花多少錢？

(A) 5 times. 5 次。
(B) Around 150 dollars. 大概 150 元。
(C) About 5 miles. 大約 5 英哩。
(D) I guess this is the second time.
我猜這是第 2 次。

單字解釋 ▶ cost **v** 花費　　　　　　　cab **n** 計程車

試題分析 ▶ 本題問：從這裡到台北搭計程車要多少錢。從 How much 和 cost 可知是問金額，因此答案為選項 (B)：大概 150 元。

Q2 ___D___ **Look, we are running out of gas. We'd better get to the service station now.**

看，我們快用完汽油了，我們最好現在去加油站。

(A) Yes, sir. May I help you? 是的，先生。我可以幫你嗎？

(B) I think you run out of your money.

我想你快用完你的錢了。

(C) More guests will run in the park.

更多的客人將在公園裡跑。

(D) Yes, you are totally right. 是的，你完全正確。

單字解釋 ▶ run out of 用完…　　　　　service station 加油站
guest **n** 客人

試題分析 ▶ 本題說：快用完汽油了，最好快去加油站。可知答案為選項
(D)：是的，你完全正確。

Q3 ___D___ **John, I am in a terrible hurry. Can you give me a lift?**

John，我很趕時間，你可否載我一程？

(A) Yes, sir. May I help you? 是的，先生。我可以幫你嗎？

(B) I can lift it myself. 我可以自己抬。

(C) Do you have a driver's license? 你有駕照嗎？

(D) Sure, where are you going to? 沒問題，你要去哪裡？

單字解釋 ▶ in a terrible hurry 十分匆忙　　give me a lift 載我一程
lift **v** 舉；**n** 順道搭載

試題分析 ▶ 本題問：我很趕時間，你可否載我一程。可知答案為選項
(D)：沒問題，你要去哪裡？

Conversation 1

W: How much does it cost from here to Taipei if I take a cab?

M: I am not sure. Maybe 150.

W: How about taking a bus?

M: It's cheaper. You only need to pay 30 dollars, but it's slower.

中文翻譯

女：假如我搭計程車從這裡到台北要花多少錢？

男：我不確定。大概 150 元。

女：那搭公車呢？

男：更便宜。妳只需花 30 元，但會比較慢。

Q1 ___B___ **Which statement is true?** 哪一個敘述為真？

(A) Maybe 140 in case of taking a taxi.
若搭計程車可能要 140 元。

(B) Taking a taxi is more expensive than taking a bus.
搭計程車比搭公車貴。

(C) Taking a taxi is slower than taking a bus.
搭計程車比搭公車慢。

(D) The woman will take a cab. 女子將搭計程車。

單字解釋 ▶ cost **v** 花費 　　　　　 cab **n** 計程車

試題分析 ▶ 本題問：哪一項敘述是真的。從對話中可知，搭計程車大概 150 元，且當女子問到搭公車的價格時，男子提到搭公車會比搭計程車慢，所以(A)、(C)不正確。選項 (D) 在對話中沒有提到。可知答案為選項 (B)：搭計程車比搭公車貴。

Conversation 2

Flight Schedule

Fight Number	Departure Time	Status
#173	3:00 PM	Available
#128	4:00 PM	Fully booked
#176	5:00 PM	Available
#188	6:00 PM	Canceled

W: United Airline. May I help you?

M: Hello, this is Charles Chen calling. I'd like to change my flight.

W: When do you want it to be?

M: I'd like to reschedule the flight at 4:00 PM.

W: I am sorry, Mr. Chen, the 4:00 PM flight is completely booked. I can put you on the waiting list.

M: Do you have another flight after that? I hope you have one before 7:00 PM.

 中文翻譯

班機行程表

班機號碼	出發時間	狀態
#173	下午 3:00	有機位
#128	下午 4:00	客滿
#176	下午 5:00	有機位
#188	傍晚 6:00	已取消

女：美國航空你好，有什麼是我可以效勞嗎？

男：你好，我是 Charles Chen，我想要變更我的班機。

女：你想要改到什麼時候呢？

男：我想改成下午 4 點的班機。

女：抱歉，Chen 先生。下午 4 點的班機已完全客滿。我可以將你放到候補名單上。

男：你們有沒有在該航班之後的其他航班呢？我希望你們有傍晚 7 點前的班機。

Q2   C   **Which flight may the woman arrange for the man?** 女子可能會安排哪一班機給男子？

(A) #173. 173 號班機。

(B) #128. 128 號班機。

(C) #176. 176 號班機。

(D) #188. 188 號班機。

單字解釋 ▶ reschedule **V** 重新安排

completely booked= fully booked 客滿

試題分析 ▶ 本題問：女子可能會安排哪一班機給男子。在對話中男子一開始提到 I'd like to reschedule the flight at 4:00 PM，表示想改成下午 4 點的班機。從表格中與對話中可知，這個時間的班機已客滿。接著男子問 Do you have another flight after that? I hope you have one before 7:00 PM.，表示男子想要下午 4 點這一班之後、7 點之前的其他班機。在 4 點後與 7 點之前只有 176 號的班機可以搭，因此答案要選(C)。

第四部分 簡短談話

Short Talk 1

This is your captain speaking. The control tower has advised us that there will be some turbulence within the next 15 to 30 minutes. Please fasten your seat belts and be seated all the time. Also, please turn off your cellular phones and recording devices on the flight. If you need extra assistance, ask our flight attendants for help. Thank you for your cooperation, and enjoy your flight.

中文翻譯

這是機長廣播。塔台傳來了通知，提醒接下來的十五到三十分鐘內會有亂流出現。請各位繫好安全帶，並持續坐在座位上。此外，在機上請關閉你的手機以及錄音設備。若您需要額外的協助，請向空服員提出請求。謝謝您的配合，並享受這趟飛行。

Q1 __C__ **What should passengers do?** 乘客應該要做什麼？
(A) Stand in line. 排隊。
(B) Upright their seats. 將椅背弄直。
(C) Fasten their seat belts. 繫上他們的安全帶。
(D) Serve the beverages. 送上飲料。

單字解釋 ▶
captain n 機長　　　　　　control tower 塔台
turbulence n 亂流　　　　　cellular phone 手機
recording device 錄音設備　flight attendant 空服員

試題分析 ▶ 本題問：乘客應該要做的事情為何。在談話中提到 there will be some turbulence... Please fasten your seat belts and be seated all the time.，表示會有亂流出現，請乘客繫好安全帶，並持續坐在座位上。故答案要選 (C)。

Short Talk 2

Fight Number	Destination	Baggage Claim Area
	Flight Schedule	
FA266	New York	Terminal 2 / Section 2
BA305	Taipei	Terminal 2 / Section 1
KA910	Taipei	Terminal 1 / Section 4
UA235	London	Terminal 4 / Section 2

Can I have your attention? We'll be arriving soon at Taoyuan Airport. The fasten seat belt light is on. Please remain seated until the plane has come to a complete stop. You can claim your luggage at section four in the baggage claim area. We hope you had a pleasant flight and that you enjoy your stay in Taipei.

班機號碼	目的地	行李領取處
	班機時刻表	
FA266	紐約	第二航廈／第二區
BA305	台北	第二航廈／第一區
KA910	台北	第一航廈／第四區
UA235	倫敦	第四航廈／第二區

請各位注意。我們即將抵達桃園機場。繫上安全帶的指示燈號已亮起。請持續坐在座位上，直到班機完全停止。各位可以在行李領取處第四區取回行李。我們希望各位有一趟愉快的飛行，也希望各位待在台北時有個愉快的時光。

Q2 ___C___ **On which flight is this announcement taking place?** 這個機上廣播是在哪一班班機上廣播的？
(A) FA266 FA266 號航班
(B) BA305 BA305 號航班
(C) KA910 KA910 號航班
(D) UA235 UA235 號航班

單字解釋▶ terminal **n** 航廈　　　　　baggage claim area 行李認領處

試題分析▶ 本題問：這段談話是在哪一班班機上廣播的。在談話中提到 You can claim your luggage at section four in the baggage claim area.，從 section four in the baggage claim area 可知是指行李領取處的第四區。接著又說 We hope ～ that you enjoy your stay in Taipei.，表示祝福聽者在台北有個愉快的時光。根據關鍵字「行李領取處的第四區」以及「台北」，可知班機號碼是 KA910，故答案選 (C)。

常
考
句
子

可能情境包括：點餐、訂位、選餐廳、請服務生介
紹餐點等。

---

1 I want a table by window.
我要一個靠窗的座位。

2 I have made a reservation for 2.
我有訂兩人的座位。

3 May I have your order?
我可以幫你點餐了嗎？

4 How would you like your steak?
你的牛排要幾分熟？

5 Would you bring me another fork, please?
請另外拿一支叉子給我好嗎？

6 May I have the check, please?
可以給我帳單嗎？

7 What's today's special?
今日特餐是什麼？

模擬試題

019.mp3

第一部分　看圖辨義

作答說明　試題冊上有數幅圖畫，每一圖畫有 1~3 個描述該圖的題目，每題請聽光碟放音機播出題目以及四個英語敘述之後，選出與所看到的圖畫最相符的答案，每題只播出一遍。

Picture A　Q1 ～ Q2

答案欄

Picture B　Q3 ～ Q4

答案欄

第二部分 問答

 作答說明 每題請聽光碟放音機播出一英語問句或直述句後，從試題冊上 A、B、C、D 四個回答或回應中，選出一個最適合者作答。每題 只播出一遍。

 Q 1

(A) Yes, sir. May I help you?

(B) I'd like to make a reservation, too.

(C) No sweat. How many people will come?

(D) Yes, we should reserve wild animals.

 答案欄

 Q 2

(A) Sure, please follow me.

(B) There is a window in the restaurant.

(C) The seat near the window is broken.

(D) I'm available.

 答案欄

 Q 3

(A) Yes, what's today's special?

(B) Yes, my cell phone is out of order.

(C) No, you don't have to do it, but if you want, that's OK.

(D) Take it easy.

第三部分 **簡短對話**

 每題請聽光碟放音機播出一段對話及一個相關的問題之後，從試
題冊上 A、B、C、D 四個選項中選出一個最適合者作答。每段對
話及問題只播出一遍。

Conversation 1

 Q 1

(A) In the market.

(B) In the coffee shop.

(C) In the movie theater.

(D) In the barbershop.

Conversation 2

Q 2

Appetizer Menu	
Options:	
Salad with dressing and peanuts	$350
French fries and onion rings	$280
Pea Soup	$300
Potato and beef Soup	$380

(A) $280.

(B) $300.

(C) $350.

(D) $380.

259

第四部分 簡短談話 新題型

 每題請聽光碟放音機播出一段談話及一個相關的問題後，從試題
冊上 A、B、C、D 四個選項中選出一個最適合者作答。每段談話
及問題只播出一遍。

Short Talk 1

Q 1

(A) Because you have to wait even if you have made a reservation before.
(B) Because it takes a long time to eat many dumplings.
(C) Because they only sell fried rice and steamed dumplings.
(D) Because people have to learn some cooking skills.

Short Talk 2

Q 2

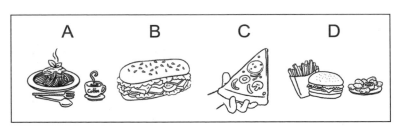

(A) A.
(B) B.
(C) C.
(D) D.

答案解析

第一部分 看圖辨義

 For questions number 1and 2, please look at picture A.
問題 1 跟問題 2 請看圖片 A。

Q1 ___A___ **What kind of restaurant is it?**
這是什麼樣的餐廳？

(A) It's a Chinese food restaurant. 是中式料理餐廳。
(B) It's a French food restaurant. 是法式料理餐廳。
(C) It's an American food restaurant. 是美式料理餐廳。
(D) It's a Greek food restaurant. 是希臘料理餐廳。

Q2 ___D___ **Which one is right?** 哪一項是對的？
(A) A bowl of beef noodles costs $210.
一碗牛肉麵要花 210 元。

(B) To come to this restaurant, we don't need to make a reservation. 來這間店不需要事先預約訂位。
(C) The sour & spicy soup is $190.
酸辣湯是 190 元。
(D) We can have chicken soup in this restaurant.
我們可以在這家餐廳喝到雞湯。

 For questions number 3 and 4, please look at picture B.
問題 3 跟問題 4 請看圖片 B。

Q3 ___A___ **What kind of restaurant is Boris in?**
Boris 在什麼樣的餐廳裡？

(A) He is in a steakhouse. 他在牛排館。
(B) He is in a fast food store. 他在速食店。
(C) He is in the pizza house. 他在披薩店。
(D) He is in a Chinese food restaurant.
他在中式料理餐廳。

Q4 ___C___ **Where does Boris want to go?**

Boris 想要去哪裡？
(A) A dining room. 飯廳。
(B) A fitting room. 更衣室。
(C) A rest room. 廁所。
(D) A study room. 書房。

第二部分 問答

Q1 ___C___ **Hello, I'd like to make a reservation for dinner.** 你好，我想要預訂晚餐的座位。

(A) Yes, sir. May I help you?
   是的，先生。我可以幫你嗎？
(B) I'd like to make a reservation, too.
   我也想訂位。
(C) No sweat. How many people will come?
   沒問題，有幾位會來？
(D) Yes, we should reserve wild animals.
   是的，我們應該保育野生動物。

單字解釋▶ make a reservation 預約訂位（reservation 的動詞是 reserve，有保留的意思）

試題分析▶ 本題說：我想要預訂晚餐的座位。答案為選項 (C)：沒問題，你們有幾位。本題考的是以「直述句」說明目的，回答應與其相關。make a reservation 是本句的關鍵詞。此外，考生必須了解 no sweat 是 no problem 的意思。同時，不可把 make a reservation 與 reserve 的意思弄錯而誤選(D)。

Q2 ___A___ **Is there a window seat available?**
   有靠窗的位子嗎？
(A) Sure, please follow me. 有，請跟我來。
(B) There is a window in the restaurant.
   餐廳裡有一扇窗戶。

(C) The seat near the window is broken.
窗戶旁的座位壞了。

(D) I'm available. 我有空。

單字解釋 ▶ window seat 靠近窗邊的座位
available **adj** 空出來的，有空的

試題分析 ▶ 本題問：有靠窗的位子嗎。可知答案為選項 (A)：有，請跟我來。本題考的是以常考的「Yes-No 問句」來提問，回答應與「是」或「不是」相關。(A) 句中的 Sure 即是本句的關鍵字。此外，考生必須了解 I'm available. 的意思是「我有空」，而這與問題無關，不可誤選成(D)。

Q3 ___A___ **Welcome to our steakhouse. May I take your order?**
歡迎來到我們的牛排館，我可以為你點餐嗎？

(A)Yes, what's today's special?
好的，今日特餐是什麼呢？

(B) Yes, my cell phone is out of order.
是的，我的手機壞了。

(C) No, you don't have to do it, but if you want, that's OK. 不，你不必這麼做，但若你要這麼做也無妨。

(D) Take it easy. 放輕鬆。

單字解釋 ▶ steakhouse **n** 牛排館　　　take your order 為你點餐
today's special 今日特餐

試題分析 ▶ 本題問：歡迎來到我們的牛排館，我可以為你點餐嗎。可知答案為選項 (A)：好的，今日的特餐是什麼。本題考的是以 May I ...? 開頭的「Yes-No 問句」來提問，很明顯是服務生的問話，回答應與「是」或「不是」相關。(A) 句中的 Yes 即是本句的關鍵字。此外，考生必須了解 out of order 的意思是「壞了」，而這與問題無關，不可誤選成(B)。而 take it easy 的意思是「放輕鬆」。

第三部分 簡短對話

Conversation 1

W: May I take your order, please?
M: Yes, I'd like a cup of hot coffee.
W: Any desserts?
M: Yes, an apple pie, please.

中文翻譯

女：請問我可以為你點餐嗎？
男：好的，我想要一杯熱咖啡。
女：需要任何甜點嗎？
男：好，一個蘋果派。

Q1 __B__ **Where probably are the man and the woman?** 男子與女子可能在哪裡？
(A) In the market. 在超市。
(B) In the coffee shop. 在咖啡廳。
(C) In the movie theater. 在電影院。
(D) In the barbershop. 在理髮廳。

單字解釋 ▶ take an order 點餐

試題分析 ▶ 本題問：男子與女子所在的場所。從點餐的行為可知，答案為選項 (B)：在咖啡店。

Conversation 2

Appetizer Menu

Options:

Salad with dressing and peanuts	$350
French fries and onion rings	$280
Pea Soup	$300
Potato and beef Soup	$380

W: Look at this menu. There are four choices for starters.

M: Yeah, but I am not sure what to get. I am a vegetarian.

W: How about some fries and onion rings?

M: No, they are too greasy for me.

W: How about some salads?

M: Fresh vegetables are good, but I am allergic to nuts.

W: Okay, I know what to order for you now.

 中 文 翻 譯

開胃菜菜單

選擇：	
加配料與花生的沙拉	$350
薯條與洋蔥圈	$280
豆子湯	$300
馬鈴薯與牛肉湯	$380

女：看看這菜單。有四種開胃菜可以選擇。

男：是呀，但是我不確定要吃什麼。我是素食者。

女：來些薯條與洋蔥圈如何？

男：不要，它們對我而言太油了。

女：來些沙拉如何？

男：新鮮蔬菜是很好，但是我對堅果過敏。

女：好，那我現在知道要替你點什麼了。

Q2　__B__　**How much is the appetizer they are going to order?**

他們要點的開胃菜是多少錢？

(A) $280.

　　280 元。

(B) $300.

　　300 元。

(C) $350.

　　350 元。

(D) $380.

　　380 元。

單字解釋 ▶ dressing **n**（拌沙拉等用的）調味料，佐料

appetizer（義同 starter）**n** 開胃菜　　　vegetarian **n** 素食者

greasy **adj** 油膩的　　　　　　　　　　allergic **adj** 過敏的

試題分析 ▶ 本題問：說話者要點的那道開胃菜是多少錢。在對話中男子提到自己是素食者，表示不會選牛肉湯。又提到對堅果過敏，以及覺得薯條與洋蔥圈太油膩，只剩豆子湯（pea soup）的選項，因此答案選 (B)。

第四部分 簡短談話

Short Talk 1

Last night, we dined at a new restaurant, Din Fung Tai. We reserved a table at 8:00 PM. We travelled a long way to eat there. We arrived at 8:00 PM, but we waited for our table until 8:30 PM. Finally, we ordered our food. My wife wanted fried rice with a pork chop, and I tried some steamed dumplings. The food there was really delicious. In short, I recommend Din Fung Tai to anyone who loves yummy food and is always patient.

中文翻譯

昨天晚上我們在一家叫鼎豐泰的新餐廳用餐。我們有預約晚上 8 點的座位。我們走了一大段路到了那兒。我們是八點到的，但我們等到 8 點半才能入座。終於我們點餐了。我太太想吃排骨炒飯，而我嘗試了一些蒸餃。那裡的食物真的很好吃。總之，我推薦任何喜歡美食且總是有耐心等待的人到鼎豐泰。

Q1 __A__ **Why does the speaker say "I recommend Din Fung Tai to anyone who is always patient"?**
為什麼說話者說「我推薦任何有耐心等待的人到鼎豐泰」？

(A) Because you have to wait even if you have made a reservation before.
因為即使你已事先預訂座位，你仍需等待。

(B) Because it takes a long time to eat many dumplings.
因為要吃很多蒸餃，會很費時。

(C) Because they only sell fried rice and steamed dumplings. 因為他們只賣炒飯與蒸餃。

(D) Because people have to learn some cooking skills.
因為人們必須學習一些煮飯的技巧。

單字解釋 ▶ fried rice 炒飯   pork chop 排骨
                 steamed dumpling 蒸餃   yummy food 美味食物
                 patient adj 有耐心的

試題分析 ▶ 本題問：說話者說「我推薦任何有耐心等待的人到鼎豐泰」這
                句話的理由。在談話中提到 We reserved a table at 8:00 PM.
                ~ We arrived at 8:00 PM, but we waited for our table until
                8:30 PM.，表示雖然預約了八點的座位，且也準時八點到，但
                仍得等到八點半才能入座，言下之意，要來這間餐廳吃美食的
                人都得要有耐心。故答案要選 (A)。

Short Talk 2

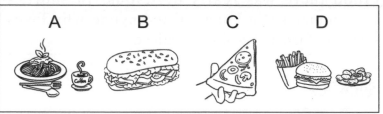

Hi, there! I am your waitress, Judy. What can I get you today? Let me introduce our today's special. Our special today is New York style pizza. It has a thin crust, a thin layer of tomato sauce, and a layer of mozzarella cheese. You can have sausage or pepperoni on your pizza if you want. New York style pizza is not a heavy dish. It's so thin that you can fold it in half and eat it with one hand.

中文翻譯

嗨！我是你們的服務生 Judy。今天我可以為您帶來什麼餐點呢？容我來為您介紹我們的今日特餐。我們的今日特餐是紐約式披薩。它有薄的餅皮，一層薄的番茄醬，以及一層莫扎瑞拉起司。若你要的話，也可以在上面加上香腸或義式辣香腸。紐約式披薩不是一道很容易讓你飽的食物。它很薄，以至於你可以把它折成一半，用一隻手拿著吃。

Q2 ___C___ **What is the special dish in the restaurant where Judy works?**

在 Judy 所服務的餐廳裡提供什麼特餐？

(A) A. 特餐 A。

(B) B. 特餐 B。

(C) C. 特餐 C。

(D) D. 特餐 D。

單字解釋▶ today's special 今日特餐　　thin crust 薄的餅皮

layer **n** （一）層　　mozzarella cheese 莫扎瑞拉起司

sausage **n** 香腸　　pepperoni **n** 義式辣香腸

試題分析▶ 本題問：根據談話內容，在 Judy 所服務的餐廳裡提供什麼樣的特餐。在談話中 Our special today is New York style pizza 可以得知，特餐是披薩。之後又提到 It has a thin crust，從薄的餅皮可知，答案要選(C)。

常考句子

情境解析 可能情境包括：地震、政治事件、新措施、疫情等。

1 Coronavirus killed millions of people in the world. 新冠肺炎害死全球數百萬計的人。

2 Everybody likes to talk about star signs. 每個人都喜歡討論星座。

3 The earthquake took place in Turkey.
地震發生在土耳其。

4 A commuter train derailed and crashed into an apartment building.
一輛通勤的火車出軌，撞進了一棟公寓。

5 The typhoon was located at 490 km southeast of Taiwan at 8 pm.
颱風 8 點的時候位於台灣東南方 490 公里的地方。

6 More than 300,000 people died in the tsunami and over 1.2 million are homeless across 13 countries.
30 萬以上的人死於這次的海嘯中，而且在 13 個國家內超過 120 萬的人無家可歸。

模擬試題

020.mp3

第一部分　看圖辨義

試題冊上有數幅圖畫，每一圖畫有 1~3 個描述該圖的題目，每題
請聽光碟放音機播出題目以及四個英語敘述之後，選出與所看到
的圖畫最相符的答案，每題只播出一遍。

Picture A Q1 ～ Q2

答案欄

Picture B Q3 ～ Q4

答案欄

第二部分 問答

Q 1

(A) That's why everyone in the world still remembers her.

(B) That's the reason why I need a prize.

 答案欄

(C) She likes prizes so much.

(D) Give me a chance to win the big prize.

Q 2

(A) According to the report, tomorrow we will have a sunny day.

(B) Did you go to the hospital last time?

 答案欄

(C) Yes, he caught a cold.

(D) You can say that again.

Q 3

(A) Yes, I heard about it.

(B) That's the reason why Turkey is a popular place.

 答案欄

(C) Americans always have turkey on Thanksgiving Day.

(D) Is that your turkey?

第三部分　簡短對話

 每題請聽光碟放音機播出一段對話及一個相關的問題之後，從試題冊上 A、B、C、D 四個選項中選出一個最適合者作答。每段對話及問題只播出一遍。

Conversation 1

 Q 1

(A) Mother Teresa is a great person.

(B) Mother Teresa wins a prize often.

(C) Mother Teresa likes to be a poor person.

(D) Mother Teresa has been dead for years.

 答案欄

Conversation 2

Q 2

Pharmacy Notice	
Time for selling masks	
Saturday	9:00AM-12:00PM
Sunday	9:00AM-12:00PM
Thursday	9:00AM-12:00PM

(A) Tuesday.

(B) Wednesday.

(C) Saturday.

(D) Sunday.

 答案欄

第四部分 簡短談話 新題型

作答說明 每題請聽光碟放音機播出一段談話及一個相關的問題後，從試題冊上 A、B、C、D 四個選項中選出一個最適合者作答。每段談話及問題只播出一遍。

Short Talk 1

(A) Education.

(B) Tariff.

(C) Commerce.

(D) Health.

Short Talk 2

How to use vouchers? Dos & Don'ts!
√ Shop in any shopping malls and stores
√ Eat at the restaurant or night market
√ Pay tuition
✕ Pay bills
✕ Deposit in the bank account
✕ Use after January first, 2021

(A) In 2019.

(B) In 2020.

(C) In 2021.

(D) In 2022.

答案解析

 For questions number 1 and 2, please look at picture A.
問題 1 跟問題 2 請看圖片 A。

Q1 _____A_____ **Where is it?** 這是哪裡？

 (A) It's a hospital. 醫院。
(B) It's a dentist. 牙醫診所。
(C) It's a barbershop. 理髮廳。
(D) It's a bookstore. 書店。

Q2 _____B_____ **Which description is right?** 哪一項敘述是對的？

 (A) Many people are in the hospital because they broke their legs.
很多人因為摔斷腿而在醫院。
(B) Many people cough and have a flu.
很多人咳嗽與感冒。
(C) Doctors are busy working in the office.
醫生正在辦公室忙。
(D) Few people are dying. 少數幾個人瀕臨病危。

 For questions number 3 and 4, please look at picture B.
問題 3 跟問題 4 請看圖片 B。

Q3 _____C_____ **What happened here?** 這裡發生什麼事？

(A) A big typhoon. 有大颱風。
(B) A big air crash. 有慘烈墜機。
(C) A big quake. 有大地震。
(D) A big fire. 有大火。

Q4 _____C_____ **Which description is correct?**
哪一項敘述是正確的？

(A) Two people in the picture are shaving.
圖片中的兩個人正在刮鬍子。

(B) Two people in the picture are shaking hands.
　　圖片中的兩個人正在握手。

(C) Two people in the picture are hugging tightly.
　　圖片中的兩個人正在緊緊相擁。

(D) Two people in the picture are taking a shower.
　　圖片中的兩個人正在洗澡。

第二部分 問答

Q1 ___A___ **Mother Teresa won the Nobel Prize due to her great work on helping poor people.**

泰瑞莎修女因為幫助窮人的偉大功勞，而獲得了諾貝爾獎。

(A) That's why everyone in the world still remembers her. 這就是為什麼全世界的人仍然記得她。

(B) That's the reason why I need a prize.
　　這就是為何我需要得獎的原因。

(C) She likes prizes so much. 她非常喜歡得獎。

(D) Give me a chance to win the big prize.
　　給我一個機會贏得大獎。

單字解釋 ▶ Noble Prize 諾貝爾獎　　　　　due to 由於…

work on 從事…

試題分析 ▶ 本題說：泰瑞莎修女因為幫助窮人，而獲得了諾貝爾獎。從選項中可知，最適合的答案為選項 (A)：這就是為什麼全世界的人仍然記得她。

Q2 ___D___ **Coronavirus killed millions of people in the world. That's really terrible.**

新冠肺炎害死全球數百萬計的人。真是太可怕了。

(A) According to the report, tomorrow we will have a sunny day. 根據報導，明天有太陽。

(B) Did you go to the hospital last time?
　　你上次有去醫院嗎？

(C) Yes, he caught a cold. 是的，他感冒了。

(D) You can say that again. 你說的對極了。

millions of 數百萬計的
You can say that again. 你說的對極了。

試題分析 ▶ 本題說：新冠肺炎害死全球數百萬計的人。從選項中可知，最
適合的答案為選項 (D)：你說的對極了。本題考的是以「直述
句」說明目的，回答應與其相關。

Q3 __A__ **The big earthquake in Turkey killed thousands of people.**
在土耳其的大地震害死了數以千計的人。
(A)Yes, I heard about it. 是的，我聽說了。
(B) That's the reason why Turkey is a popular place.
那就是為何土耳其是個受歡迎的地方。
(C) Americans always have turkeys on Thanksgiving
Day. 美國人在感恩節總是吃火雞。
(D) Is that your turkey? 那是你的火雞嗎？

單字解釋 ▶ earthquake 地震   thousands of 數以千計的
Turkey 土耳其   Thanksgiving Day 感恩節
試題分析 ▶ 本題說：在土耳其的大地震害死了數以千計的人。答案為選項
(A)：是的，我聽說了。

Conversation 1

W: Mother Teresa won the Nobel Prize duc to her great work on helping poor people.

M: That's why everyone in the world still remembers her.

....

中文翻譯

女：泰瑞莎修女因為幫助窮人的偉大功績而獲得了諾貝爾獎。

男：那就是為什麼全世界的人仍然記得她。

Q1 __A__ **What does the man imply?**

男子暗示什麼？

(A) Mother Teresa is a great person.

泰瑞莎修女是個偉人。

(B) Mother Teresa wins a prize often.

泰瑞莎修女常常得獎。

(C) Mother Teresa likes to be a poor person.

泰瑞莎修女喜歡成為窮人。

(D) Mother Teresa has been dead for years.

泰瑞莎修女已去世多年。

單字解釋 ▶ work on 從事…

試題分析 ▶ 本題問：男子暗示什麼。可知答案為選項 (A)：泰瑞莎修女是位偉人。

Conversation 2

Pharmacy Notice
Time for selling masks

Saturday	*9:00AM-12:00PM*
Sunday	*9:00AM-12:00PM*
Thursday	*9:00AM-12:00PM*

W: Did you get the masks we need at the pharmacy?

M: You won't believe it. When I got there, they told me that all masks were sold out, and I came on a wrong day. They only sell them three days a week.

W: When will they sell masks again?

M: They asked me to come back on the weekend.

W: But we both need to go to work on the weekends, and we will have no time to line up for masks.

M: Don't worry, they also sell them tomorrow. I will get them then.

 中文翻譯

藥局公告
口罩販售時間

週六	早上 9:00-	中午 12:00
週日	早上 9:00-	中午 12:00
週四	早上 9:00-	中午 12:00

女：你在藥局有買到口罩嗎？

男：你不會相信的。當我到那裡時，他們告訴我所有的口罩都賣完了。而且我來錯天了。他們一週僅賣三天。

女：他們何時會再賣口罩呢？

男：他們要我週末再過來。

女：但我們兩位週末都要上班，而且我們沒時間排隊買口罩。

男：別擔心，他們明天也有賣。到時我會去買。

Q2 __B__ **What day does this conversation happen?**

這段對話是發生在哪一天?

(A) Tuesday. 週四。
(B) Wednesday. 週三。
(C) Saturday. 週六。
(D) Sunday. 週日。

單字解釋 ▶ pharmacy **n** 藥局　　　　　　　mask **n** 口罩
line up 排隊

試題分析 ▶ 本題問:這段對話是發生在哪一天。在對話中可以知道兩人週末都要上班(we both need to go to work on the weekends),所以沒辦法在週六日買口罩。從圖表可知,藥局賣口罩的時間只剩下週四。接著男子又說 Don't worry, they also sell them tomorrow 及 I will get them,表示明天也有賣,也就是在說禮拜四也有賣,言下之意對話的時間是週三,因此答案選(B)。

第四部分 簡短談話

Short Talk 1

The USA Vice Minister of Trade paid an unannounced visit to Taiwan last Tuesday for talks with that country's president. The two officials discussed the improvement in trade relations between the two countries. Commercial affairs are the purpose of this visit. It is believed that the two parties discussed a new trade pact, including selling pork to Taiwan, although the exact details of their talks have not been officially released.

 中文翻譯

美國的貿易副部長在上週二突訪台灣，並與該國總統會談。雙方官員會談如何改善兩國間的貿易關係。商業事務是這趟訪問的目的。據説兩方討論了一個新的貿易協定，包括販售豬肉到台灣，雖然實際會談內容尚未正式由官方公布。

Q1 __C__ **What is the purpose of this visit?**

這趟訪問的目的是什麼？
(A) Education. 教育。
(B) Tariff. 關稅。
(C) Commerce. 商業。
(D) Health. 健康。

Vice Minister of Trade 貿易副部長
pay an unannounced visit 未經宣布的訪問，突然的訪問
It is believed that 據說 　　　　　trade pact 貿易協定
be officially released 官方公布

試題分析 ▶ 本題問：這趟訪問的目的。在談話中提到 The two officials discussed the improvement in trade relations between the two countries. 以及 Commercial affairs are the purpose of this visit.，表示雙方官員會談如何改善兩國間的貿易關係。商業事務是訪問的目的。從 Commercial 可知答案要選 (C)。

Short Talk 2

How to use vouchers? Dos & Don'ts!

√ Shop in any shopping malls and stores
√ Eat at the restaurant or night market
√ Pay tuition
✕ Pay bills
✕ Deposit in the bank account
✕ Use after January first, 2021

On behalf of Angel City government, I'd like to explain some policies on how to use vouchers issued by Angel City government. You can use these vouchers at any kinds of stores, including shopping malls, department stores, supermarkets and grocery stores. You can use them to pay your school fee. However, you can't deposit them in the bank or post office. You can't use them to pay bills, including your credit card bills or utility bills. Most important of all, you have to use them within one year. That is to say, please use them before the end of this year. Thank you in advance for your understanding and cooperation. Angel City government always cares about what its citizens need.

中文翻譯

> **如何使用禮券？適用與不適用的事！**
> √ 可用在任何購物商城或商店購物
> √ 可用在餐廳或夜市飲食花費
> √ 可用來支付學費
> × 不可用來付帳單
> × 不可存入銀行帳戶
> × 不可在 2021 年 1 月 1 日後使用

代表天使市政府，我要來解釋由天使市政府所發行的禮券的使用辦法。您可以在各種商店使用這禮券，包含購物商城、百貨公司、超市及雜貨店。您可以使用此禮券來支付學校的費用。然而，不能將它們存入銀行或郵局，不能用它們來支付帳單，包括信用卡帳單或水電瓦斯費帳單。更重要的是，您必須在一年內使用完，也就是說，要在今年年底前使用完畢。在此先感謝各位的理解與配合。天使市政府總是在乎各位市民所需。

Q2 __B__ **When is this talk happening?**

這段談話是在何時進行的？
(A) 2019. 2019年。
(B) 2020. 2020年。
(C) 2021. 2021年。
(D) 2022. 2022年。

單字解釋▶ voucher n 票券，禮券　　tuition n 學費
issue v 發放，發行　　deposit v 存入
utility bill 水電瓦斯費帳單

試題分析▶ 本題問：這段談話進行的時間。在談話中提到 you have to use them within one year ~ please use them before the end of this year.，可知聽者必須在一年內用掉禮券，且要在今年年底前使用完畢。在圖表中註明 2021 年 1 日 1 日後不能再使用。言下之意，現在是 2020 年，故答案要選(B)。

情境解析　可能情境包括：計畫郊遊、與朋友或家人去郊遊、討論要帶的食物、討論野餐地點等。

1 I want to have a picnic next weekend.
下週末我想去野餐。

2 What do you have for a picnic?
你野餐吃什麼？

3 I enjoyed the picnic.
我很喜歡這個野餐。

4 But for the rain, we would go on a picnic.
要不是這場雨，我們會去野餐。

5 I hope the weather tomorrow will be fine.
我希望明天是好天氣。

6 What time should we meet?
我們應該幾點見面？

7 They are going on a picnic.
他們正要去野餐。

模擬試題

🔘 **021.mp3**

第一部分　看圖辨義

試題冊上有數幅圖畫，每一圖畫有 1~3 個描述該圖的題目，每題請聽光碟放音機播出題目以及四個英語敘述之後，選出與所看到的圖畫最相符的答案，每題只播出一遍。

Picture A　Q1 ～ Q2

答案欄

Picture B　Q3 ～ Q4

Lilian　Will

答案欄

情境主題 ㉑ Picnics（郊遊野餐）

模擬試題

285

第二部分 問答

每題請聽光碟放音機播出一英語問句或直述句後，從試題冊上 A、B、C、D 四個回答或回應中，選出一個最適合者作答。每題只播出一遍。

 Q 1

(A) Sure, let's go for sandwich immediately.

(B) So am I.

(C) Whom do you want to go with?

(D) What's for tomorrow's picnic?

 Q 2

(A) Yes, that's a bad idea.

(B) Can you pick it up for me?

(C) How many people will come here?

(D) No, that's really boring.

 Q 3

(A) Yes, the picnic basket was very heavy.

(B) What a shame. Did you go on a picnic finally?

(C) How many people will come here?

(D) Do you like rainy days?

第三部分 簡短對話

 作 答 說 明 每題請聽光碟放音機播出一段對話及一個相關的問題之後，從試題冊上 A、B、C、D 四個選項中選出一個最適合者作答。每段對話及問題只播出一遍。

Conversation 1

Q 1

(A) Sure, and they also bring some salad.
(B) No, but they will take them next time.
(C) No.The man will go to the traditional market to buy other things.
(D) They want to have something different.

Conversation 2 新題型

Q 2

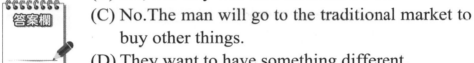

Weather Forecast	
Friday	
Saturday	
Sunday	
Monday	

 答案欄

(A) On Friday.
(B) On Saturday.
(C) On Sunday.
(D) On Monday.

每題請聽光碟放音機播出一段談話及一個相關的問題後，從試題冊上 A、B、C、D 四個選項中選出一個最適合者作答。每段談話及問題只播出一遍。

Short Talk 1

Q 1

(A) Sheep and donkeys.

(B) Swans and geese.

(C) Pet dogs and cats.

(D) Deers and fish.

Short Talk 2

Q 2

	The San Diego Zoo	The National Zoo
Hours	Every day 9:00AM-16:00PM	Every day (except Monday) 6:00AM-20:00PM
Number of animals	4000	3600
Size	100 acres	163 acres
Admission fee **For adult**	$20	$30
Admission fee **For child** （under 12）	$10	$20

(A) $ 50.　　　　　(C) $ 70.

(B) $ 60.　　　　　(D) $ 80.

答案解析

第一部分 看圖辨義

提示
For questions number 1 and 2, please look at picture A.
問題 1 跟問題 2 請看圖片 A。

Q1 __C__ **What are they doing?** 他們正在做什麼？

(A) They are having a vacation. 他們正在度假。
(B) They are playing cards. 他們正在玩牌。
(C) They are having lots of fun. 他們正玩得很愉快。
(D) They are standing in the grass. 他們正站在草地上。

Q2 __A__ **Why do they have to leave the place?**
他們為何必須離開這地方？

(A) Because it rains cats and dogs. 因為下大雨。
(B) Because they had better go home now.
因為他們最好現在回家。
(C) Because it's snowy and cold.
因為下雪且很冷。
(D) Because it's too hot. 因為太熱了。

提示
For questions number 3 and 4, please look at picture B.
問題 3 跟問題 4 請看圖片 B。

Q3 __B__ **What do Will and Lilian probably say?**
Will 跟 Lilian 兩人可能在說什麼？

(A) Let's go to school.
我們去上學吧。
(B) For the picnic, what do we have in the bag?
我們要去野餐的袋子裡裝有什麼？
(C) Tomorrow they will get your books.
明天他們將拿到你的書。
(D) What are you talking about?
你在說什麼？

Q4 __D__ **What are they doing?** 他們正在做什麼？

(A) They are talking about a party. 他們正在討論一個派對。

(B) They are talking about money. 他們正在討論金錢。

(C) They are having a discussion about education.
他們正在討論教育。

(D) They are talking about a trip. 他們正在討論一次出遊。

第二部分 問答

Q1 __B__ **What are we having for the picnic, Bill? I am definitely tired of sandwiches again.**

Bill，我們野餐要吃什麼？我已經厭倦又要吃三明治。

(A) Sure, let's go for sandwich immediately.
好，我們馬上去吃三明治吧。

(B) So am I. 我也是。

(C) Whom do you want to go with? 你想跟誰去？

(D) What's for tomorrow's picnic? 明天的野餐吃什麼？

單字解釋 ▶ definitely 絕對地　　　　　　　　tired of 厭倦…

immediately adv 立即地

試題分析 ▶ 本題問：野餐要吃什麼？我已經厭倦又要吃三明治。可知答案
為選項 (B)：我也是。(A) 句中的「我們馬上去吃三明治吧」，
雖然有提及 sandwich 一詞，但與原句意完全相反。此外，考
生必須了解 So am I 是表達「我也是」的倒裝句。

Q2 __D__ **Why not go for a picnic next time?**

下次去野餐如何？

(A)Yes, that's a bad idea.
是的，那是個糟糕的主意。

(B) Can you pick it up for me?
你可以幫我把它撿起來嗎？

(C) How many people will come here?
有幾個人會來這裡？

(D) No, that's really boring.
不要，那真的很無聊。

單字解釋▶ picnic **n** 野餐

試題分析▶ 本題問：下次去野餐如何。從選項中可知，最適合的答案為選
項 (D)：不要，那很無聊。

Q3 ____B____ **It was raining heavily when I left for a picnic yesterday.**

昨天當我出發去野餐時，雨下得很大。

(A)Yes, the picnic basket was very heavy.

　是的，野餐籃很重。

(B) What a shame. Did you go on a picnic finally?

　好可惜，你們最後有去野餐嗎？

(C) How many people will come here? 有幾個人會來這裡？

(D) Do you like rainy days? 你喜歡雨天嗎？

單字解釋▶ leave for 出發前往…　　　　　　　　shame 可惜

試題分析▶ 本題說：昨天當我出發去野餐時，雨下得很大。可知答案為反
問對方的選項 (B)：好可惜，你們最後有去野餐嗎。

第三部分 簡短對話

Conversation 1

W: What's for the picnic, Bill? I am definitely tired of having sandwiches again.

M: Let's have salad instead.

W: I think that's not enough. We have 5 people total.

M: OK, OK. I think I'll go around the supermarket, and try to find something we can eat for the picnic.

中文 翻 譯

女：Bill，野餐吃什麼？我真的厭倦又要吃三明治了。

男：我們改吃沙拉吧。

女：我想那不夠吃。我們一共有 5 個人。

男：好吧。我想我會去一趟超市，試著找一些我們野餐可以吃的東西。

Q1 ___D___ **Do the speakers have sandwiches for picnic in the end?** 說話者們最後野餐會吃三明治嗎？

(A) Sure, and they also bring some salad.

當然，他們也會帶一些沙拉。

(B) No, but they will take them next time.

不，但是他們下次會帶。

(C) No. The man will go to the traditional market to buy other things.

不，男子會去傳統市場買一些其他的東西。

(D) They want to have something different.

他們想換不一樣的東西。

單字解釋 ▶ definitely adv 絕對地　　　　　　tired of 厭倦…

試題分析 ▶ 本題問：說話者們野餐是否會吃三明治。從男子提到的「我們改吃沙拉吧」以及「我會去一趟超市，找一些野餐可以吃的東西」可知答案為選項 (D)：他們想換不一樣的東西。

Conversation 2

Weather Forecast	
Friday	
Saturday	
Sunday	
Monday	

M: Katie, I am planning a picnic next week. Wanna join us?

W: Oh, Danny, you are a real peach! Sure, I like picnicking.

M: But I usually play it by ear what day we should go. I don't always decide the date in advance.

W: That's not good. At least, we should consider the weather. It looks like we will have a sunny day on Sunday. Let's go on Sunday.

M: It's too hot to have a picnic. We will all get sunburns.

W: So, maybe we should pick up a cloudy day with no rain or snow.

M: Okay.

天氣預報		
週五		
週六		
週日		
週一		

男：Katie，我計畫下週安排一個野餐。你想加入嗎？

女：喔，Danny，你人真是好！當然，我愛野餐。

男：但是我通常是臨時決定哪天要去。我總是不會事先訂好日期。

女：那不太好吧。至少，我們應該考慮一下天氣狀況。看起來週日會有太陽。我們週日去吧。

男：太熱了，沒辦法野餐。我們都會曬傷的。

女：所以，也許我們應該選擇不會下雨、不會下雪的多雲日子。

男：好的。

Q2 ___D___ **What day will Dan and Katie most likely have a picnic?** Dan 與 Katie 最有可能哪天去野餐？

(A) On Friday. 週五。

(B) On Saturday. 週六。

(C) On Sunday. 週日。

(D) On Monday. 週一。

單字解釋 ▶ picnic n 野餐　　　　　　　in advance 預先，事先

You are a real peach! 你人真是好！（慣用語，用 peach [桃子] 形容人很好）

play it by ear 事前無準備臨時做決定（慣用語）

試題分析 ▶ 本題問：Danny 與 Katie 最有可能去野餐的時間。在對話中，女子原本提到 It looks like we will have a sunny day on Sunday. Let's go on Sunday.，建議週日去野餐，但男子回應 It's too hot to have a picnic. We will all get sunburns.，表示週日的天氣太熱，不適合野餐。女子之後提到 maybe we should pick up a cloudy day with no rain or snow.，表示建議選擇不會下雨、不會下雪的多雲日子。從圖表中可知答案要選(D)。

第四部分 簡短談話

Short Talk 1

Have you heard about petting zoo? We are here at the City Petting Zoo. People can touch and feed animals as they like in this zoo. Children always love to feed deers and donkeys. I like to feed sheep, but their sharp teeth sometimes scare me. There are a lot of geese and swans. They are my favorite because I like their big feet. Going to the petting zoo is really an ideal excursion for all families.

....

中文翻譯

你有聽過動物農場嗎？我們現在的所在位置就在市立動物農場。人們可以隨自己喜好觸碰與餵食動物農場內的動物。孩子們總是喜歡餵食鹿與驢子。我喜歡餵食綿羊，但是他們尖銳的牙齒有時會嚇到我。這裡有很多鵝與天鵝，他們是我的最愛，因為我喜歡它們的大腳。到動物農場對於所有家庭來說，真是個理想的出遊經驗。

Q1 __B__ **What kind of animals does the speaker like the most?** 說話者最喜歡哪種動物？
(A) Sheep and donkeys. 綿羊與驢子。
(B) Swans and geese. 天鵝與鵝。
(C) Pet dogs and cats. 寵物狗與貓。
(D) Deers and fish. 鹿與魚。

單字解釋 ▶ petting zoo（裡面有養溫和小動物、供兒童撫摸、餵食的）愛畜動物園，動物農場
swan **n** 天鵝 　　　　　excursion **n** 出遊旅行

試題分析 ▶ 本題問：說話者最喜歡的動物。在談話中提到 There are a lot of geese and swans. They are my favorite because I like their big feet.，表示這裡的鵝與天鵝是說話者的最愛。故答案要選 (B)。

	The San Diego Zoo	The National Zoo
Hours	Every day 9:00AM-16:00PM	Every day (except Monday) 6:00AM-20:00PM
Number of animals	4000	3600
Size	100 acres	163 acres
Admission fee For adult	$20	$30
Admission fee For child （under 12）	$10	$20

When I was in the USA, I'd like to have an excursion to some zoos. There are two famous zoos. One is the San Diego Zoo, and the other is the National Zoo. I often went to one of them. I liked the one better than the other because it had more animals to see. It opens every day. Although the size is smaller, the admission fee is much cheaper. That is the reason why all my family members, including my husband and my two sons who are both 10 years old, like to go there.

中文 翻 譯

	聖地牙哥動物園	國家動物園
開放時間	每天 早上 9 點到下午 4 點	每天（除了週一） 早上 6 點到晚上 8 點
動物數量	4 千種	3 千 6 百種
面積	1 百公畝	1 百 63 公畝
成人入場費	20 元	30 元
兒童入場費（12歲以下）	10 元	20 元

當我在美國時，我喜歡到一些動物園去遠足。有兩個有名的動物園。一個是聖地牙哥動物園，另一個是國家動物園。我經常去這兩間的其中一間。我喜歡其中一間勝於另一間的理由是，因為那間有較多的動物可以看，且它每天都開放。雖然那間的面積較小，但門票費用卻便宜許多。這也就是為何我的家人，包括我先生與我兩個讀小學的兒子，都喜歡去那一間的緣故。

Q2 ___B___ **If the speaker and the speaker's family go to the zoo they like most, how much admission fee will they pay?**

若說話者以及其家人去他們最愛的動物園，他們將付多少錢的入場費？

(A) $ 50. 五十元。
(B) $ 60. 六十元。
(C) $ 70. 七十元。
(D) $ 80. 八十元。

單字解釋▶ admission fee 入場費

試題分析▶ 本題問：如果說話者及其家人要去他們最愛的動物園，他們要付的入場費總額是多少。在談話中提到 I liked the one ~ because it had more animals to see.，可知說話者喜歡的那一間動物園裡面的動物數量比較多，之後又提到 It opens every day. Although the size is smaller, the admission fee is much cheaper.，表示這一間是每天都開放，且面積比較小，但門票費用便宜。透過圖表可知，聖地牙哥動物園每天開放、動物數量比國家動物園多，面積比國家動物園小。由此可知，說話者會去聖地牙哥動物園。門票部分，說話者與其先生要算成人價（即兩張 $20 的票），兩位小孩因為不到 12 歲，要算孩童價（即兩張 $10 的票），故答案要選(B)。

常考句子

可能情境包括：預約掛號、眼睛痛、牙痛、背痛等。

1 I need to see a dentist.
我需要去看牙醫。

2 God, my back is killing me.
天啊，我的背痛死了。

3 I got the flu. That's why I stayed home today.
我感冒了。那就是我今天待在家裡的原因。

4 Do you have eye drops?
你有眼藥水嗎？

5 I think I broke my bone.
我想我骨折了。

6 Are you allergic to anything?
你會對什麼東西過敏嗎？

7 Take the medicine 3 times a day.
一天服用這個藥 3 次。

模擬試題

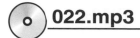 022.mp3

第一部分 看圖辨義

 作答說明

試題冊上有數幅圖畫，每一圖畫有 1~3 個描述該圖的題目，每題
請聽光碟放音機播出題目以及四個英語敘述之後，選出與所看到
的圖畫最相符的答案，每題只播出一遍。

Picture A Q1 ～ Q2

Picture B Q3 ～ Q4

每題請聽光碟放音機播出一英語問句或直述句後，從試題冊上 A、B、C、D 四個回答或回應中，選出一個最適合者作答。每題只播出一遍。

(A) Yes, sir. May I help you?

(B) It's really an eyesore.

(C) No sweat. Let me have a check.

(D) Yes, we should wear glasses.

(A) No, please follow me.

(B) Yes, there is one on the corner.

(C) Yes, I need some pills.

(D) No, but there is a fire station.

(A) Yes, I shut it down.

(B) Don't shout at me.

(C) Yes, you need a shirt.

(D) No, but I'll give you some medicine.

第三部分 簡短對話

 每題請聽光碟放音機播出一段對話及一個相關的問題之後，從試題冊上 A、B、C、D 四個選項中選出一個最適合者作答。每段對話及問題只播出一遍。

Conversation 1

Q 1

(A) In the concert.

(B) In a market.

 答案欄

(C) In a doctor's office.

(D) In the hall.

Conversation 2

Q 2

Dr. Wu's Schedule (Updated already)			
Time	**Mon.**	**Tue.**	**Wed.**
13:00-14:00 PM	Mrs. Davis	Break	Mr. Kim
14:00-15:00 PM	Break	Break	Break
15:00-16:00 PM	Break	Mr. Wilson	Mr. Brown
16:00-17:00 PM	Ms. Smith	Break	Ms. Lee

(A) Davis.

 答案欄

(B) Brown.

(C) Kim.

(D) Wilson.

作答說明 每題請聽光碟放音機播出一段談話及一個相關的問題後，從試題冊上 A、B、C、D 四個選項中選出一個最適合者作答。每段談話及問題只播出一遍。

Short Talk 1

 Q1

(A) Press one.
(B) Press two.
(C) Stay on line.
(D) Wait for a beep.

 答案欄

....

Short Talk 2

Q2

Family Medical Clinic	
Patient (In order to protect privacy, we show last name only)	**Symptom**
*** Wang	Cough / Sneeze / Running nose / Dizzy
*** Chung	Have red spots all over body
*** Parker	Vomit
*** Anderson	Sore throat

 答案欄

(A) Wang
(B) Chung
(C) Parker
(D) Anderson

答案解析

第一部分 看圖辨義

提示

For questions number 1 and 2, please look at picture A.
問題 1 跟問題 2 請看圖片 A。

Q1 __D__ **Where is the drugstore?** 藥局在哪裡？

(A) It's between the hair salon and the bookstore.
它在髮廊與書店之間。
(B) It's across from the park. 它在公園對面。
(C) It's next to the bookstore. 它在書店旁邊。
(D) It's opposite the barbershop. 它在髮廊對面。

Q2 __B__ **How can you get to the drugstore?**
可以怎麼去藥局？
(A) Walk to the corner, and turn left. 走到轉角處再左轉。
(B) Walk along Main Avenue, and it's on the right.
沿著 Main 大道走，然後它就在右手邊。
(C) Walk to the corner, and turn right. Walk along First
Street. And it's on the right.
走到轉角處再右轉，沿著 First 街走。藥局在右手邊。
(D) Walk to the corner, and turn left. Walk along First
Street. And it's on the right.
走到轉角處再左轉，沿著 First 街走。藥局在右手邊。

提示

For questions number 3 and 4, please look at picture B.
問題 3 跟問題 4 請看圖片 B。

Q3 __B__ **What's the matter with William?**
William 怎麼了？

(A) He has a terrible flu. 他得了重感冒。
(B) He has a stomachache. 他有胃痛。
(C) He coughs and sneezes. 他咳嗽、打噴嚏。
(D) He has a headache. 他有頭痛。

Q4 ___A___ **Why doesn't William see the doctor?**

為何 William 不去看醫師？

(A) Because the doctor has a day off. 因為醫生休診。
(B) Because he doesn't go to the clinic. 因為他沒去診所。
(C) Because doctors are busy working in the office.
　　因為醫生正在辦公室忙。
(D) Because William has recovered.
　　　因為 William 已經康復了。

第二部分 問答

Q1 ___C___ **Doctor, I have an eyesore.**

　　　醫生，我眼睛痛。
(A)Yes, sir. May I help you? 是的，先生。我可以幫你嗎？
(B) It's really an eyesore. 這真是礙眼。
(C) No sweat. Let me have a check. 沒問題，讓我檢查一下。
(D)Yes, we should wear glasses. 是的，我們應該戴眼鏡。

單字解釋 ▶ eyesore **n** 眼睛紅腫；礙眼的東西
　　　　　　 no sweat 沒問題

試題分析 ▶ 本題說：醫生，我眼睛痛。答案為選項 (C)：沒問題，我幫你
　　　　　　 檢查。其中的 (B) It's really an eyesore　是礙眼、眼中釘的意
　　　　　　 思。

Q2 ___B___ **Is there a drugstore nearby?** 這附近有藥局嗎？

(A) No, please follow me.
　　　沒有，請跟我來。
(B) Yes, there is one on the corner.
　　　有，轉角那裡就有一間。
(C) Yes, I need some pills.
　　　是的，我需要一些藥丸。
(D) No, but there is a fire station.
　　　不，但是有一間消防局。

單字解釋 ▶ drugstore **n** 藥局　　　　　　　nearby **adv** 在附近

on the corner 在角落　　　　　　pill **n** 藥丸

fire station 消防局

試題分析 ▶ 本題問：這附近有藥局嗎。可知答案為選項 (B)：有，轉角那裡就有一間。

Q3 ___D___ **Do I need a shot?** 我需要打針嗎？

(A) Yes, I shut it down. 是的，我關掉了。

(B) Don't shout at me. 不要對我吼叫。

(C) Yes, you need a shirt. 是的，你需要一件襯衫。

(D) No, but I'll give you some medicine.

不用，但我會給你一些藥。

單字解釋 ▶ shot **V** 射擊，注射　　　　　shut down 關閉

medicine **n** 藥

試題分析 ▶ 本題問：我需要打一針嗎。可知答案為選項 (D)：不用，但我會給你一些藥。

第三部分 簡短對話

Conversation 1

W: I have an appointment with Dr. Smith at two o'clock. My son Tim has a cold.

M: Please have a seat.

中文翻譯

女：我與 Smith 醫師兩點鐘有約。我的兒子 Tim 感冒了。

男：請坐。

Q1 ___C___ **Where did this conversation take place?**

這個對話發生在哪裡？

(A) In the concert. 在音樂會。

(B) In a market. 在市場。

(C) In a doctor's office. 在診所。

(D) In the hall. 在大廳。

Conversation 2

Dr. Wu's Schedule (Updated already)

Time	Mon.	Tue.	Wed.
13:00-14:00 PM	Mrs. Davis	Break	Mr. Kim
14:00-15:00 PM	Break	Break	Break
15:00-16:00 PM	Break	Mr. Wilson	Mr. Brown
16:00-17:00 PM	Ms. Smith	Break	Ms. Lee

M: Pardon me, is this Dr. Wu's office?

W: It sure is. Do you have an appointment?

M: No, but I just live nearby. Can I make an appointment with you right now?

W: Dr. Wu has a pretty busy schedule these days. But fortunately for you, someone just had a cancellation for this Wednesday at 1:00 PM. Can you make it?

M: I will be here on time.

W: Your name and phone number please.

中文翻譯

Wu 醫師時間表（已經更新）			
時間	週一	週二	週三
下午13:00-14:00	Davis 太太	休診	Kim 先生
下午14:00-15:00	休診	休診	休診
下午15:00-16:00	休診	Wilson 先生	Brown 先生
下午16:00-17:00	Smith 小姐	休診	Lee 小姐

男：不好意思，這是 Wu 醫師的診所嗎？

女：是。你有掛號嗎？

男：沒有，但我就住在這附近。我可以現在跟你掛號嗎？

女：Wu 醫師最近相當忙碌。但你很幸運，有人剛剛取消了本週三下午一點的看診。你有辦法趕來嗎？

男：我會準時到。

女：請給我您的名字與電話號碼。

Q2 __C__ **What most likely is the man's last name?**

男子的姓氏最有可能是什麼？

(A) Davis. Davis。

(B) Brown. Brown。

(C) Kim. Kim。

(D) Wilson. Wilson。

單字解釋 ▶ make an appointment 預約　　　cancellation **n** 取消

Can you make it? 你趕得來嗎？

試題分析 ▶ 本題問：男子的姓氏。在對話中得知男子要預約門診，女子說 But fortunately for you, someone just had a cancellation for this Wednesday at 1:00 PM.，表示有人取消週三下午一點的診。男子也表示能準時來這個診（I will be here on time）。從圖表上可知，此圖表已經更新，而週三下午 13:00-14:00 該欄上註明男子的姓為 Mr. Kim，故答案要選(C)。

Short Talk 1

You have reached the voice mail of Dr. Brian Adam's office. If this is an emergency, please hang up and call my cell phone number. If you want to make an appointment, please press one to speak with my assistant. If you want to ask some questions about prescription or medical advice, please press two. Otherwise, wait for the beep and leave your message. Thank you.

中文翻譯

您已進入 Brian Adam 醫生診所的語音信箱。假如很緊急,請掛掉、重新改撥我的手機號碼。假如想要預約,請按「一」和我的助理聯繫。若想問有關於處方箋或醫藥方面的建議,請按「二」。其他事情,請在嗶聲之後留下您的訊息。謝謝。

Q1 ___A___ **How can you make an appointment with Dr. Brian Adam?** 可以怎麼跟 Brian Adam 醫生約診?

(A) Press one. 按「一」。　(C) Stay on line. 保持在線上。
(B) Press two. 按「二」。　(D) Wait for a beep. 等待嗶聲。

單字解釋▶ voice mail 語音信箱　　　　　emergency **n** 緊急事件
make an appointment 預約　　prescription **n** 處方箋
medical advice 醫藥方面的意見　beep **n** 嗶聲

試題分析▶ 本題問:跟 Brian Adam 醫生約診的方式。在談話中提到 If you want to make an appointment, please press one to speak with my assistant. 提到想要預約,請按「一」和助理聯繫。故答案要選 (A)。

Short Talk 2

Family Medical Clinic	
Patient (In order to protect privacy, we show last name only)	**Symptom**
*** Wang	Cough / Sneeze / Running nose / Dizzy
*** Chung	Have red spots all over body
*** Parker	Vomit
*** Anderson	Sore throat

It's a busy afternoon at Family Medical Clinic. Lots of people are sitting in the waiting room and thinking about the questions they are going to ask the doctor. Peggy wants to know whether she has the flu because she coughed and sneezed all the time. Patty is wondering if she has measles. Linda wants to find out whether she is pregnant or not because this morning she threw up a lot. Ruby wants to ask the doctor if she has to put some medicine on her tonsils for her sore throat.

 中文翻譯

家醫診所	
病患 （為保護隱私，名單僅顯示姓式）	症狀
*** Wang	咳嗽／打噴嚏／流鼻水／頭暈
*** Chung	全身上下長紅疹
*** Parker	嘔吐
*** Anderson	喉嚨痛

現在是家醫診所忙碌的下午時間。有很多人正坐在候診室等待，並思考著待會要問醫師的一些問題。Peggy 想要知道她是否得到流行性感冒，因為她不斷咳嗽、打噴嚏。Patty 在想她是否得到麻疹。Linda 想要知道她是否懷孕了，因為她今天早上吐了很多。Ruby 想要問醫生說她是否需要針對喉嚨痛在扁桃腺上塗藥。

Q2　__B__　**What's Patty's last name?** Patty 的姓氏是什麼？
(A) Wang. Wang。
(B) Chung. Chung。
(C) Parker. Parker。
(D) Anderson. Anderson。

單字解釋 ▶　privacy n 隱私　　　　　symptom n 症狀
　　　　　　 measles n 麻疹　　　　 pregnant adj 懷孕的
　　　　　　 tonsils n 扁桃腺　　　 vomit（義同 throw up）v 嘔吐

試題分析 ▶　本題問：Patty 的姓。從表格中可知，左欄是姓氏，右欄是這些人的症狀。在談話中提到，Peggy ~ has the flu because she coughed and sneezed all the time，症狀是咳嗽、打噴嚏、流鼻水、頭暈的人是 Peggy Wang；從 Linda ~ is pregnant ~ she threw up a lot. 可知，症狀是嘔吐的人是 Linda Parker；從 Ruby ~ put some medicine on her tonsils for her sore throat. 可知，症狀是喉嚨痛的人是 Ruby Anderson。雖然沒學過 measles，但透過刪去法可知，Patty 的姓氏是 Chung，故答案要選(B)。

Hint
常
考
句
子

可能情境包括：問時間、遲到早退、約定某一時間等。

1 Do you have the time?
現在幾點？

2 Do you have time?
你有沒有空？

3 It's time to go to bed, kids
孩子們，上床睡覺的時間到了。

模|擬|試|題

 **023.mp3**

第一部分 看圖辨義

作答說明

試題冊上有數幅圖畫，每一圖畫有 1~3 個描述該圖的題目，每題請聽光碟放音機播出題目以及四個英語敘述之後，選出與所看到的圖畫最相符的答案，每題只播出一遍。

Picture A   Q1 ～ Q2

答案欄

3:25AM · 16:35AM

Taipei · Tokyo · Los Angeles · San Francisco

Picture B   Q3 ～ Q4

答案欄

Ian

Time?

Picture C   Q5 ～ Q6

答案欄

Yvonne

Chris

Time?

?

每題請聽光碟放音機播出一英語問句或直述句後，從試題冊上 A、B、C、D 四個回答或回應中，選出一個最適合者作答。每題只播出一遍。

(A) The concert is at 7:30.

(B) The movie is on Thursday at 6:30.

(C) You mean the movie titled "Soul"?

(D) Yes, we should go for a play.

(A) Yes, I am free this afternoon.

(B) No, I am sorry I don't.

(C) I want to go to the Internet café.

(D) It's a quarter after five.

(A) Yes, I need to take the bus, too.

(B) That's a good idea. I need a break.

(C) Do you have the time?

(D) I have some pocket money.

第三部分 簡短對話

 每題請聽光碟放音機播出一段對話及一個相關的問題之後，從試題冊上 A、B、C、D 四個選項中選出一個最適合者作答。每段對話及問題只播出一遍。

Conversation 1

Q 1

答案欄

(A) It's 3:05.
(B) It's 2:55.
(C) It's 5:03.
(D) It's 3:00.

Conversation 2 新題型

Q 2

National Bank Hours
Thursday: 9:00 AM-3:30 PM **(Regular)**
Friday: Dragon Boat Festival **(Closing)**
Saturday: Weekend **(Closing)**
Sunday: Weekend **(Closing)**
Monday: 9:00 AM-3:30 PM **(Regular)**

答案欄

(A) Thursday.
(B) Friday.
(C) Saturday.
(D) Sunday.

作答說明 每題請聽光碟放音機播出一段談話及一個相關的問題後，從試題冊上 A、B、C、D 四個選項中選出一個最適合者作答。每段談話及問題只播出一遍。

Short Talk 1

 Q 1

(A) Sport highlight.
(B) News.
(C) Weather report.
(D) An interview.

 答案欄

Short Talk 2

 Q 2

TV News Regular Schedule

★ 4:00 PM (Local Weather)
★ 6:00 PM (Local News)
★ 8:00 PM (World News)
★ 10:00 PM (Jim's Talk)

 答案欄

(A) 6:00 PM.
(B) 7:00 PM.
(C) 8:00 PM.
(D) 9:00 PM.

答案解析

第一部分 看圖辨義

提示 For questions number 1 and 2, please look at picture A.
問題 1 跟問題 2 請看圖片 A。

Q1 ___D___ **What time is it in Tokyo?** 東京現在是幾點？

(A) It's 25 past 4. 4 點 25 分。
(B) It's 3:25. 3 點 25 分。
(C) It's half past 4. 4 點 30 分。
(D) It's 25 to 5. 4 點 35 分。

Q2 ___C___ **Which description doesn't match picture A?**

哪一項敘述不符合圖片 A？
(A) There are 4 clocks in the picture. 圖片裡有四個時鐘。
(B) It's 5 o'clock in L.A. 洛杉磯現在是 5 點。
(C) It's afternoon in Taipei. 台北現在是下午。
(D) It's morning in Tokyo. 東京現在是早上。

提示 For questions number 3 and 4, please look at picture B.
問題 3 跟問題 4 請看圖片 B。

Q3 ___B___ **What is Ian doing?** Ian 正在做什麼？

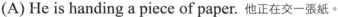

(A) He is handing a piece of paper. 他正在交一張紙。
(B) He is asking the time. 他正在問時間。
(C) He is asking for the direction. 他正在問路。
(D) He is walking and chatting with a passer-by.
他正邊走邊和路人聊天。

Q4 ___D___ **What does Ian probably say?** Ian 可能會說什麼？

(A) Excuse me, do you have time? 抱歉，請問你有空嗎？
(B) Sorry, can I have a watch? 抱歉，我可以有一支錶嗎？
(C) Do you have time? 你有空嗎？
(D) Do you know what the time is? 你知道現在幾點嗎？

提示 For questions number 5 and 6, please look at picture C.
問題 5 跟問題 6 請看圖片 C。

Q5   B   What is Chris doing?

Chris 正在做什麼？

(A) He is asking Yvonne for money. 他正在向 Yvonne 要錢。
(B) He is asking the time. 他正在問時間。
(C) He is asking if she needs a watch.
　　他正在問她是否需要手錶。
(D) He is asking if she has time later.
　　他正在問她晚點是否有空。

Q6   D   Why doesn't Yvonne tell Chris the time?

Yvonne 為什麼不告訴 Chris 時間？

(A) Because she is not Chris' friend.
　　因為她不是 Chris 的朋友。
(B) Because she is not available. 因為她沒空。
(C) Because she has no time. 因為她沒有時間。
(D) Because she doesn't know the time, either.
　　因為她也不知道時間。

第二部分 問答

Q1   C   There's a movie on Tuesday at 7:30.

星期二的 7 點半有一場電影。

(A) The concert is at 7:30. 音樂會是在 7 點半。
(B) The movie is on Thursday at 6:30.
　　電影是在星期四的 6 點半。
(C) You mean the movie titled "Soul"?
　　你是說《靈魂急轉彎》這部電影嗎？
(D) Yes, we should go for a play. 是的，我們應該去看戲。

單字解釋 ▶ concert n 音樂會

試題分析 ▶ 本題說：星期二的 7 點半有一場電影。可知選項中最適合的答案為選項 (C)：你是說《靈魂急轉彎》這部電影嗎。

情境主題 ㉓ Time（時間）

答案解析

317

Q2 ___D___ **Do you have the time?** 現在幾點？
(A)Yes, I am free this afternoon. 是的，我今天下午有空。
(B) No, I am sorry I don't. 不，我很抱歉我沒有。
(C) I want to go to the Internet café. 我要去網咖。
(D) It's a quarter after five. 現在是 5 點 15 分。

> **單字解釋 ▶** Internet café 網咖
>
> **試題分析 ▶** 本題問：現在幾點鐘。可知答案為選項 (D)：現在是 5 點 15
> 分。

Q3 ___B___ **We still have some time. Let's take a rest.**
我們還有一些時間，休息一下吧。
(A)Yes, I need to take the bus, too. 是的，我也需要搭公車。
(B) That's a good idea. I need a break.
好主意，我需要休息了。
(C) Do you have the time? 現在幾點？
(D) I have some pocket money. 我有一些零用錢。

> **單字解釋 ▶** take a rest 休息　　　　　　break **n** 休息
> pocket money 零用錢
>
> **試題分析 ▶** 本題說：我們還有一些時間，休息一下吧。答案為選項 (B)：
> 好主意，我需要休息了。

第三部分 簡短對話

Conversation 1

W: Do you have the time?
M: Sure. It's five to three.
W: OK. Let's go out for dinner in 5 minutes.

中文翻譯

女：你知道現在幾點嗎？
男：當然，差 5 分 3 點。
女：好的，那麼我們五分鐘之後出門吃晚餐。

Q1 ___B___ **What time is it?** 現在是幾點？
(A) It's 3:05. 3 點 5 分。　　(C) It's 5:03. 5 點 3 分。
(B) It's 2:55. 2 點 55 分。　　(D) It's 3:00. 3 點。

單字解釋 ▶ (minutes) to (hours) 差幾分是幾點
試題分析 ▶ 本題問：現在幾點。從 five to three（差五分鐘就要三點）可知答案為選項 (B)：2 點 55 分。

Conversation 2

National Bank Hours

Thursday: 9:00 AM-3:30 PM **(Regular)**
Friday: Dragon Boat Festival **(Closing)**
Saturday: Weekend **(Closing)**
Sunday: Weekend **(Closing)**
Monday: 9:00 AM-3:30 PM **(Regular)**

W: What is wrong? You left your wallet at the office? Again?

M: Oh, I am so embarrassed. Can you lend me $2000?

W: Okay, Okay, but when will you pay me back?

M: Let's see…It's 4:00 PM now. Tomorrow is a national holiday, so the bank won't be open. Then we have the weekend. How about Monday?

W: Don't you know there is a kind of machine called ATM in the world?

國家銀行營業時間

國家銀行營業時間
週四：早上 9 點到下午 3 點半（正常營業）
週五：端午節（不營業）
週六：週末（不營業）
週日：週末（不營業）
週一：早上 9 點到下午 3 點半（正常營業）

女：怎麼了？你又把皮夾放在辦公室了嗎？

男：啊，真是糗。你可以借我兩千元嗎？

女：好啦好啦，但你何時還我？

男：我想想…現在下午 4 點了。明天是國定假日所以銀行不開，接著就是週末了。週一還你如何？

女：難道你不知道世界上有一種機器叫做自動提款機嗎？

Q2 ___A___ **What day does the conversation take place?** 對話發生在星期幾？

(A) Thursday. 週四。　　(C) Saturday. 週六。

(B) Friday. 週五。　　(D) Sunday. 週日。

單字解釋 ▶ wallet n 皮夾　　　　　　embarrassed adj 尷尬的
ATM（即 Automated Teller Machine）n 自動提款機

試題分析 ▶ 本題問：對話發生的時間。在對話中提到 Tomorrow is a national holiday, so the bank won't open. Then we have the weekend.，表示隔天是國定假日，銀行不開，且接著是週末。從表格可知，週五是端午節，即對話中提到的國定假日，之後兩天是週末，故可推測對話的時間是週四，答案要選 (A)。

第四部分 簡短談話

Short Talk 1

Coming up after the news is our sport highlight. Then, our reporter Carol Urban will interview Brian Abrams about his new book, the best seller in the bookstores, *How to manage your finances and save big money before 30*. Mr. Abrams is a known professional on finance management. This is an educational and informative show, and you cannot miss it. Now, here's Martin Cook with today's news.

中文翻譯

新聞之後將為您帶來體壇焦點新聞。接著，我們的記者 Carol Urban 將訪問 Brian Abrams 有關於他的新書，即各大書店暢銷書「如何在三十歲前管理你的財務並存下大錢」。Abrams 先生是一位有名的財務管理專家。這是一場具有教育性與知識性的節目，你絕不可以錯過。現在，時間交給 Martin Cook，帶來今日新聞。

Q1 __B__ **Which show will be first?** 哪一個節目會先進行？
(A) Sport highlight. 體壇焦點新聞。
(B) News. 新聞。
(C) Weather report. 氣象報導。
(D) An interview. 訪談。

單字解釋 ▶ sport highlight 體壇焦點新聞　　reporter n 記者
finance n 財務　　educational adj 教育性的
informative adj 知識性的

試題分析 ▶ 本題問：會先進行的節目是什麼。在談話中一開始提到 Coming up after the news is our sport highlight. 可知會先進行新聞，之後會進行體壇焦點新聞。最後提到 Now, here's Martin Cook with today's news.，表示現在要進行的是新聞。故答案要選 (B)。

Short Talk 2

TV News Regular Schedule

★ 4:00 PM (Local Weather)
★ 6:00 PM (Local News)
★ 8:00 PM (World News)
★ 10:00 PM (Jim's Talk)

An update to our TV news for today, Tuesday, May 2nd. Due to the President's press conference today, we will have a special breaking news program. Instead of local news at 6:00 PM, we will be broadcasting the President's speech. Therefore, local news, world news and Jim's Talk will be one hour later than their regular time. Please stay tuned for all latest news.

電視新聞常態時刻表

★下午 4 點（當地氣象）
★晚上 6 點（當地新聞）
★晚上 8 點（世界新聞）
★晚上 10 點（Jim 脫口秀）

為您帶來，今日五月二日星期二，本台新聞最新消息。由於今日的總統記者會，我們將會為各位插播特別新聞節目。原定 6 點的「當地新聞報導」節目，我們將會改播總統演説。因此，「當地新聞」、「世界新聞」以及「Jim 脫口秀」都會比原定時間晚一小時播出。請持續收看本頻道所有最新新聞消息。

Q2 __D__ **What time will "World News" be shown today?** 「世界新聞」今日將於何時播出？
(A) 6:00 PM. 晚上 6 點。
(B) 7:00 PM. 晚上 7 點。
(C) 8:00 PM. 晚上 8 點。
(D) 9:00 PM. 晚上 9 點。

單字解釋 ▶ press conference 記者會　　　broadcast **v** 播放

試題分析 ▶ 本題問：「世界新聞」今天播出的時間。在談話中提到 Due to the President's press conference today, we will have a special breaking news program.，表示由於今日的總統記者會，將會插播特別新聞節目。最後又提到 local news, world news and Jim's Talk will be one hour later than their regular time.，可知「當地新聞」、「世界新聞」以及「Jim 脫口秀」都會比原定時間晚一小時播出。

從圖表可知，「世界新聞」原本是晚上 8 點播，晚一小時的話是晚上 9 點。故答案為(D)。

常考句子

可能情境包括：抱怨商品品質、寫申訴信、客訴服務態度等。

1 The radio I bought here doesn't work.
我在這裡買的收音機不能用。

2 The book is dirty. Can you find me a new one?
這書很髒，你能找一本新的給我嗎？

3 I need a cheeseburger, not a beefburger. 我要起司堡，不是牛肉漢堡。

4 I think you gave me the wrong change.
我想你找錯錢了。

5 I just want to get my money back.
我只想要拿回我的錢。

6 I don't think I ordered this.
我不認為我點了這個。

7 I'd like to talk to your manager.
我想找你們經理談談。

模擬試題

 024.mp3

第一部分 看圖辨義

 作答說明

試題冊上有數幅圖畫，每一圖畫有 1~3 個描述該圖的題目，每題請聽光碟放音機播出題目以及四個英語敘述之後，選出與所看到的圖畫最相符的答案，每題只播出一遍。

Picture A   Q1 ～ Q2

Picture B   Q3 ～ Q4

325

第二部分　問答

每題請聽光碟放音機播出一英語問句或直述句後，從試題冊上 A、B、C、D 四個回答或回應中，選出一個最適合者作答。每題只播出一遍。

(A) Say, you should come here tomorrow.

(B) OK, let's turn down the loud music.

(C) It's not so bad as you said.

(D) I wish I could go with you.

(A) You can buy a TV set.

(B) I'm in the living room.

(C) No sweat. I will change a whole new one for you.

(D) Yes, but that is yours.

(A) Why not complain about it?

(B) I don't like writing a letter.

(C) What happened? Anything wrong?

(D) Yes, I will certainly write to you.

第三部分　**簡短對話**

 每題請聽光碟放音機播出一段對話及一個相關的問題之後，從試題冊上 A、B、C、D 四個選項中選出一個最適合者作答。每段對話及問題只播出一遍。

Conversation 1

Q 1

(A) The woman bought a coat in a store yesterday.

(B) The shop manager doesn't want to give back the money.

(C) The clerk doesn't have the woman's money back.

(D) The woman doesn't want the coat anymore.

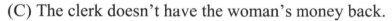

Conversation 2

Q 2

> ABC department Store
> # Kevin Shu
> Customer Service Manager
> Mob: 0936-569-859
> Tel: (02)2659-8956
> Line ID: @@655
> Email: Kevin@abc.com.tw

(A) By telephone.

(B) By Line.

(C) By email.

(D) By Facebook.

每題請聽光碟放音機播出一段談話及一個相關的問題後，從試題冊上 A、B、C、D 四個選項中選出一個最適合者作答。每段談話及問題只播出一遍。

Short Talk 1

(A) His schedule is always different.

(B) His manager is a difficult person to work with.

(C) He doesn't have good medical benefits, and only have two sick days in a year.

(D) He gets too much work.

Short Talk 2

> ### NOTICE
>
> Starting today, the 6th floor washrooms are now reserved for:
>
> ### Managers, Lawyers, and Accountants
>
> Other people can use the washrooms on the 5th floor.
>
> Thank you for your cooperation on this matter.

(A) She is a manager in marketing division.

(B) She thinks the decision is fair.

(C) She is probably an engineer.

(D) She read the notice about how to deal with discrimination.

答案解析

第一部分 看圖辨義

 For questions number 1 and 2, please look at picture A.
問題 1 跟問題 2 請看圖片 A。

Q1 __B__ **What may Simon complain about?**
Simon 可能會抱怨什麼？

(A) He may complain about the price of the tape
recorder. 他可能會抱怨那台錄音機的價格。

(B) He may complain about the quality of the tape
recorder. 他可能會抱怨那台錄音機的品質。

(C) He may complain about the size of the tape
recorder. 他可能會抱怨那台錄音機的尺寸。

(D) He may complain about the appearance of the tape
recorder. 他可能會抱怨那台錄音機的外觀。

Q2 __D__ **Does Simon exchange a new tape
recorder?** Simon 換到一台新的錄音機嗎？

(A) Yes, and the sales person apologizes for her mistake.
有，而且銷售人員為她的錯誤道歉。

(B) Yes, and Simon feels happy after talking with the
sales person. 有，而且 Simon 在和銷售人員談過後很開心。

(C) No, but the manager says sorry to him.
沒有，但經理向他說聲抱歉。

(D) We have no ideas according to the picture.
根據圖片我們無法得知。

 For questions number 3 and 4, please look at picture B.
問題 3 跟問題 4 請看圖片 B。

Q3 __B__ **What's the name of the store?**
這間店的店名是什麼？

(A) Taipei Railway Station Branch. 台北火車站分店。

(B) KKK store. KKK 商店。

(C) Tape Recorder store. 錄音機店。

(D) We can't say from the picture. 我們無法從圖片中知道。

Q4 ___C___ **What's wrong with Miss Wang's tape recorder?** Wang 小姐的錄音機有什麼問題？

(A) It's broken down. 它壞掉了。

(B) Its backward button is out of order. 它的倒轉鍵故障了。

(C) Its forward button is dead. 它的快轉鍵壞了。

(D) Its pause button doesn't work at all. 它的暫停鍵毫無作用。

第二部分 問答

Q1 ___C___ **The party is so lousy. I wish I didn't come here.** 這個派對太糟了。我真希望我沒有來這裡。

(A) Say, you should come here tomorrow.

看吧，你明天應該來這裡。

(B) OK, let's turn down the loud music.

好的，我們把吵鬧的音樂關小聲點。

(C) It's not so bad as you said. 它沒像你說的那麼糟啦。

(D) I wish I could go with you. 我希望能和你一起去。

單字解釋 ▶ lousy **adj** 糟的　　　　　　　　　turn down 關小聲，調低

試題分析 ▶ 本題說：這個派對太糟了，真希望我沒有來這裡。選項中最適合的回應為選項 (C)：它沒像你說的這麼糟。

Q2 ___C___ **I am sorry, I bought a radio here yesterday but it doesn't work.**

抱歉，我昨天在這裡買了一台收音機，但它沒有作用。

(A) You can buy a TV set. 你可以買台電視。

(B) I'm in the living room. 我在客廳裡。

(C) No sweat. I will change a whole new one for you.

沒問題。我會換一台全新的給您。

(D) Yes, but that is yours. 是的，但那是你的。

whole new 全新的

試題分析 ▶ 本題說：我昨天在這裡買了一台收音機，但它沒有作用。可知
最適合的答案為選項 (C)：沒問題，我會換一台全新的給您。

Q3 ___C___ **I wrote a complaint letter to the shop's manager.** 我寫了一封客訴信給這家店的經理。

(A) Why not complain about it? 何不抱怨一下？
(B) I don't like writing a letter. 我不喜歡寫信。
(C) What happened? Anything wrong?
發生什麼事了？有什麼不對嗎？
(D) Yes, I will certainly write to you.
是的，我一定會寫信給你的。

單字解釋 ▶ complaint letter 客訴信   Anything wrong? 有什麼不對嗎？
certainly adv 當然

試題分析 ▶ 本題說：我寫了一封客訴信給這家店的經理。可知答案為選項
(C)：發生什麼事了？有什麼不對嗎。

Conversation 1

W: Yesterday I bought a coat in your store. But the zipper is broken.

M: OK, I will have a new one for you.

W: In fact, I want my money back.

M: I'm sorry we can't have your money back.

W: But I don't want your coat. And ...

M: Maybe you should talk to our manager.

中文翻譯

女：昨天我在你們店裡買了一件外套，但是拉鍊壞掉了。

男：好的，我會換一件新的給妳。

女：其實，我想要把錢退回來。

男：很抱歉，我們不能退錢給妳。

女：可是我不想要你們的外套，而且…

男：也許妳應該跟我們經理談。

Q1 ___B___ **Which one is not true?** 哪一項不是真的？

(A) The woman bought a coat in a store yesterday.
女子昨天從一間店買了一件外套。

(B) The shop manager doesn't want to give back the money. 這間店的經理不想要退錢。

(C) The clerk doesn't have the woman's money back.
店員沒退錢給女子。

(D) The woman doesn't want the coat anymore.
女子不再想要這件外套了。

單字解釋 ▶ zipper n 拉鍊

試題分析 ▶ 本題問：哪一項不符合對話內容。可知答案為選項 (B)：店經理不想要退錢。對話中並未提及經理是否會退錢給女子。

Conversation 2

ABC department Store

Kevin Shu
Customer Service Manager

Mob: 0936-569-859
Tel: (02)2659-8956
Line ID: @@655
Email: Kevin@abc.com.tw

W: Did you have fun shopping in the department store? Did you use the membership card I lent to you to have some more discounts?

M: As a matter of fact, no, I had a bad time.

W: How come?

M: After my purchase, I found a mistake on the receipt. When I asked a desk lady, she even gave me a look. I just felt as if I had owed a million dollars to the desk lady.

W: Sounds like you had a bad shopping experience. Here, this is the name card of a customer service manager in ABC department store. I know the guy. He is my neighbor.

M: Thank you. I will contact him and express my dissatisfaction right away.

 中文翻譯

ABC 百貨公司

Kevin Shu
客服經理

手機：0936-569-859
電話：(02)2659-8956
Line ID：@@655
電子郵件：Kevin@abc.com.tw

女：你在百貨公司購物，開心嗎？你有使用我借你的會員卡來享有更多折扣嗎？

男：事實上沒有，我不開心。

女：怎麼會？

男：在買完東西後，我發現收據有誤。當我問櫃台小姐時，她竟然給我臉色。我感覺好像欠了這位櫃台小姐一百萬。

女：聽起來你遇到了個糟糕的購物經驗。來，這是 ABC 百貨公司客服經理的名片。我認識這個人。他是我鄰居。

男：謝謝你。我會立刻聯絡他，來表達我的不滿。

Q2 ___D___ **What is NOT the way for the man to contact Kevin?** 以下哪一種方式，男子是無法聯絡 Kevin 的？

(A) By telephone. 透過電話。

(B) By Line. 透過 Line。

(C) By email. 透過電子郵件。

(D) By Facebook. 透過臉書。

單字解釋▶ membership card 會員卡　　　as a matter of fact 事實上
give me a look 給我一個臉色（慣用語）
dissatisfaction **n** 不滿

試題分析▶ 本題問：男子無法用哪種方式聯絡 Kevin。從對話與圖表可知，Kevin 是百貨公司客服經理。在對話中得知女子給了男子一張 Kevin 的名片，而在名片上可以找到 Kevin 的聯絡方式，其中沒看到臉書的聯絡方式，故答案要選(D)。

第四部分 簡短談話

Short Talk 1

My name is Nelson. I am a security screener at the airport. I sit at the scanner. I check people when they walk through the gate. I work full time. My schedule is always different, which is really annoying. I don't have good medical benefits, and only have two sick days in a year. That is indeed not enough. What's worse, my manager is a difficult person to work with. Getting a promotion in the future is never easy to me.

中文 翻譯

我的名字是 Nelson。我是一位在機場操作掃描儀的安檢人員。我會坐在掃描儀前。當人們走過安檢門時，我會檢查。我是全職工作者。我的工作時間總是不固定，這樣的狀況真的很煩人。我沒有好的醫療福利，而且一年只有兩天的病假。這真的不夠。更糟的是，我的經理是個在工作上難相處的人。要在未來升遷，對我而言，更是不容易的事。

Q1　　D　**What is Not Nelson's complaint about his job?** 下列何者不是 Nelson 對他工作抱怨的項目？

(A) His schedule is always different.
　　他的工作時間總是不固定。

(B) His manager is a difficult person to work with.
　　他的經理是個難相處的人。

(C) He doesn't have good medical benefits, and only have two sick days in a year.
　　他沒有好的醫療福利，而且一年僅有兩天的病假。

(D) He gets too much work. 他有太多的工作量。

335

單字解釋 ▶ security screener 安檢掃描人員   scanner **n** 掃描儀

annoying **adj** 煩人的   medical benefit 醫療福利

試題分析 ▶ 本題問：何者不是 Nelson 對他工作抱怨的項目。在談話中提
到 My schedule is always different, which is really
annoying.、I don't have good medical benefits, and only have
two sick days in a year. ，以及 my manager is a difficult
person to work with，可知(A)、(B)、(C)都有提到。但並未提
及他的工作量太多，故答案要選 (D)。

Short Talk 2

NOTICE

Starting today, the 6th floor washrooms are now
reserved for:

Managers, Lawyers, and Accountants

Other people can use the washrooms on the 5th floor.
Thank you for your cooperation on this matter.

I am Angela. I have to make a complaint. This morning
I read a sign on the washrooms. I can't use the 6th floor
washrooms anymore. I have to go to the 5th floor. In
my opinion, this decision is not only inconvenient but
also rude to us. Only some certain people can use
certain washrooms. Isn't that discrimination? I can't
believe this is happening in this modern 21st century. Is
it true that staff working in IT, HR, and Marketing will
be inferior to some other people in this company? That
is really ridiculous.

中文翻譯

公告

從今日起，六樓的洗手間僅開放給以下人士：

經理、律師與會計師

其他人士可使用五樓的洗手間。
感謝您在此事上的配合。

我是 Angela。我必須要申訴。今天早上我看到各個洗手間的一項告示。我再也不能使用六樓的洗手間了。我必須要去五樓。就我的觀點來看，這項決定對我們來說不僅不方便，也非常無禮。只有部分人士可以使用部分的洗手間。那就不就是歧視嗎？我真不敢相信這件事會發生在現代這二十一世紀。資訊部門、人事部門和行銷部門的員工，會比公司的其他人來的劣等嗎，這不會是真的吧？實在是太荒謬了。

Q2 ___C___ What can be inferred from Angela?

從 Angela 的言論，可以推測出什麼？

(A) She is a manager in marketing division.
她是行銷部的經理。

(B) She thinks the decision is fair. 她認為這項決定是公平的。

(C) She is probably an engineer. 她可能是工程師。

(D) She read the notice about how to deal with discrimination. 她讀了有關於如何處理歧視的公告。

單字解釋 ▶ make a complaint 抱怨   discrimination n 歧視
ridiculous adj 荒謬的   be inferior to 劣於

試題分析 ▶ 本題問：從 Angela 的言論，可以推測出的細節內容為何。在談話的一開始可以得知，Angela 在對一項決定抱怨（I have to make a complaint 以及 I can't use the 6th floor washrooms anymore. I have to go to the 5th floor ~ this decision is not only inconvenient but also rude to us.），可知 Angela 無法使用六樓廁所。從圖表的 the 6th floor washrooms are now reserved for: Managers, Lawyers, and Accountants 可知，只有經理、律師與會計師能用六樓廁所。言下之意，(A)和(B)都不正確。(D)在本談話中並未提到，僅提到此決定帶有歧視意味，所以(D)也不正確。由於 Angela 不是經理、律師與會計師，所以有可能是其他部門的人士，因此(C)是有可能的。因此要選(C)。

情境主題 ㉕ Sports （運動）

常考句子 Hint

情境解析 可能情境包括：討論運動、在健身中心、最喜歡的球類、相約看球賽等。

1 **What kind of sports do you dislike?**
你不喜歡何種運動？

2 **I do exercises in the gym every day.**
我每天在健身房做運動。

3 **Let's go and watch the football game!**
我們去看美式足球賽吧！

4 **I like swimming the most.**
我最喜歡游泳。

5 **He is really my hero.**
他真是我心目中的英雄。

6 **May I join you?**
我可以加入你們嗎？

7 **Have you ever watched a rugby game?**
你曾經觀賞過橄欖球比賽嗎？

模擬試題

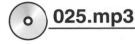 **025.mp3**

第一部分 看圖辨義

作答說明 試題冊上有數幅圖畫，每一圖畫有 1~3 個描述該圖的題目，每題請聽光碟放音機播出題目以及四個英語敘述之後，選出與所看到的圖畫最相符的答案，每題只播出一遍。

Picture A Q1 ～ Q2

答案欄

Picture B Q3 ～ Q5

答案欄

第二部分 **問答**

Q 1

(A) These products are on sale.

(B) I love sailing and watching movies.

(C) But I am ready to go sailing!

(D) Do you want to go with me?

Q 2

(A) Could you help me setting the table?

(B) OK! Why not?

(C) My father was a tennis player.

(D) Do you want to go with me?

Q 3

(A) I hate golf.

(B) I'd like to play baseball.

(C) I like playing bowling as well.

(D) Do you like tennis?

第三部分 簡短對話

 每題請聽光碟放音機播出一段對話及一個相關的問題之後，從試題冊上 A、B、C、D 四個選項中選出一個最適合者作答。每段對話及問題只播出一遍。

Conversation 1

Q 1

答案欄

(A) Shopping.

(B) Studying nature.

(C) Exercise and activity.

(D) How to go on a diet.

Conversation 2 新題型

Q 2

Survey Results	
Popular Individual Sports in New Taipei City	
Yoga	50%
Weight Training	30%
Jogging	60%
Cycling	30%

答案欄

(A) Yoga.

(B) Weight training.

(C) Jogging.

(D) Cycling.

第四部分 簡短談話 新題型

作答說明 每題請聽光碟放音機播出一段談話及一個相關的問題後，從試題冊上 A、B、C、D 四個選項中選出一個最適合者作答。每段談話及問題只播出一遍。

Short Talk 1

(A) Because the competition is international.

(B) Because the crowd is out of control.

(C) Because the skaters will have a wonderful show on the ice.

(D) Because Peggy is having a great time.

Short Talk 2

Olympics in history		
year	season	city
2016	Summer	**Rio** (Brazil)
2014	Winter	**Sochi** (Russia)
2012	Summer	**London** (UK)
2010	Winter	**Vancouver** (Canada)

(A) 2010.

(B) 2012.

(C) 2014.

(D) 2016.

答案解析

第一部分 看圖辨義

提示

For questions number 1 and 2, please look at picture A.
問題 1 跟問題 2 請看圖片 A。

Q1 ___B___ **What is the woman doing?** 女子正在做什麼？

(A) She is running in the park. 她正在公園裡跑步。
(B) She is running on the running machine.
她正在跑步機上跑步。
(C) She is lifting weights. 她正在舉重。
(D) She is riding a bike. 她正在騎腳踏車。.

Q2 ___D___ **Which description is right?** 哪一項敘述是對的？

(A) She is slim. 她很苗條。
(B) She is going jogging. 她正要去慢跑。
(C) She is having lunch. 她正在吃午餐。
(D) She is doing exercises. 她在做運動。

提示

For questions number 3 and 4, please look at picture B.
問題 3 跟問題 4 請看圖片 B。

Q3 ___D___ **What are the three people doing now?**

這三個人正在做什麼？

(A) They are playing cards. 他們正在玩牌。
(B) They are playing volleyball. 他們正在打排球。
(C) They are playing golf. 他們正在打高爾夫球。
(D) They are playing basketball. 他們正在打籃球。

Q4 ___B___ **Which description is correct?**

哪一項敘述是正確的？

(A) One of the people is wearing sandals. 其中一人穿著涼鞋。
(B) One of the people is bald. 其中一人是光頭。
(C) One of the people is holding a ball. 其中一人正拿著球。
(D) One of the people is wearing a coat.
其中一人正穿著外套。

第二部分 問答

Q1 __C__ **Let's not go sailing. Let's watch a video instead.** 我們別去划船了,不如來看影片吧。
(A) These products are on sale. 這些商品拍賣中。
(B) I love sailing and watching movies.
　　我喜歡划船和看電影。
(C) But I am ready to go sailing! 但我已準備好要去划船了!
(D) Do you want to go with me? 你要和我一起去嗎?

單字解釋▶ go sailing 去划船　　　　　　　　instead **adv** 取而代之
試題分析▶ 本題說:我們別去划船了,不如來看影片吧。從選項中可知最適合作為回應的是選項 (C):但我已準備好要去划船了。

Q2 __B__ **Let's play table tennis.** 我們來打桌球吧。
(A) Could you help me setting the table?
　　您可否幫我擺碗筷?
(B) OK! Why not? 好呀!有何不可。
(C) My father was a tennis player. 我父親曾是網球員。
(D) Do you want to go with me? 你要和我一起去嗎?

單字解釋▶ table tennis(義同 ping-pong)乒乓球
set the table 擺放碗筷,準備好餐桌
試題分析▶ 本題說:我們來打桌球吧。從選項中可知最適合作為回應的是選項 (B):好呀!有何不可。

Q3 __A__ **What sports do you dislike?** 你不喜歡什麼運動?
(A) I hate golf. 我討厭高爾夫球。
(B) I'd like to play baseball. 我想要打棒球。
(C) I like playing bowling as well. 我也喜歡打保齡球。
(D) Do you like tennis? 你喜歡網球嗎?

單字解釋▶ dislike **v** 不喜歡　　　　　　　play bowling 打保齡球
試題分析▶ 本題問:你不喜歡什麼運動。可知答案為選項 (A):我討厭高爾夫球。

第三部分 簡短對話

Conversation 1

W: Look at this one, Jenny and I are on the top of the mountain.

M: Mountain climbing! You two like to climb mountains?

W: Yes, I think it's good for our health.

M: Can I go with you two next time?

中文翻譯

女：看看這個，Jenny 和我在山頂上。

男：爬山！妳們兩位喜歡爬山？

女：是呀，我覺得這對我們的健康有益。

男：我下次可以和妳們一起去嗎？

Q1 __C__ **What are they talking about?** 他們正在討論什麼？

(A) Shopping. 購物。

(B) Studying nature. 研究自然。

(C) Exercise and activity. 運動和活動。

(D) How to go on a diet. 如何節食。

單字解釋 ▶ mountain climbing 爬山

試題分析 ▶ 本題問：他們在討論什麼。可知答案為選項 (C)：運動與活動。

Conversation 2

Survey Results	
Popular Individual Sports in New Taipei City	
Yoga	50%
Weight Training	30%
Jogging	60%
Cycling	30%

W: What's so much fun? You have been looking at that magazine for thirty minutes.

M: I am reading an interesting article about some popular individual sports. They aimed at the New Taipei City citizens.

W: And? Can I know the results?

M: Jogging is the number one. About 60% of people in New Taipei City love jogging.

W: Not me, especially in this hot weather.

M: I am a little surprised that only 30% of people like cycling.

W: What about my favorite sport?

M: The same as cycling.

調查結果	
新北市受歡迎的個人運動	
瑜珈	50%
重量訓練	30%
慢跑	60%
騎單車	30%

女：什麼事情這麼有趣？你一直在看那本雜誌三十分鐘了。
男：我正在讀一篇有關於一些受歡迎的個人運動的文章，主要是針對新北市的市民。
女：然後呢？結果是？
男：慢跑是第一名，約有百分之 60 的新北市市民喜歡慢跑。
女：不是我喔，尤其是在這麼熱的天氣裡。
男：我有些吃驚的是，只有百分之 30 的人喜歡騎單車。
女：那我最愛的運動呢？
男：跟騎單車一樣。

Q2 __B__ **What sport does the woman like the best?**
女子最喜歡什麼運動？
(A) Yoga. 瑜珈。
(B) Weight training. 重量訓練。
(C) Jogging. 慢跑。
(D) Cycling. 騎單車。

單字解釋 ▶ individual sport 個人的運動（非團體運動）
aim at 以…為目標
weight training 重量訓練

試題分析 ▶ 本題問：女子最喜歡的運動。在圖表與對話中可知，男子提到 only 30% of people like cycling，即只有百分之 30 的人喜歡騎單車。接著女子問到自己最愛的運動的受歡迎比例是多少，男子回說跟騎單車一樣（The same as cycling）。從圖表可知，百分比跟騎單車一樣的項目是 weight Training（重量訓練），同樣都是 30%，因此答案要選(B)。

第四部分 簡短談話

Short Talk 1

Hello, Peggy. I am calling in the stadium. My wife and I are having a great time here. Right now, we are watching the figure skating competition. Two skaters from Byelorussia are coming onto the ice. They are waving at the crowd. People are clapping and cheering. I believe that their performance will be out of this world. Talk to you soon!

中文翻譯

哈囉，Peggy。我現在在體育館打這通電話給你。我和我太太正在這裡享受愉快的時光。現在我們正在看花式溜冰比賽。兩位來自白俄羅斯的溜冰者來到了冰上。他們正向群眾揮手著。大家都拍手歡呼著。我相信他們的表演將會是世界級無與倫比的。再聊囉！

Q1 ___C___ **Why does the speaker say "out of this world"?** 為何說話者說「世界級無與倫比的」?

(A) Because the competition is international.
因為比賽是國際性的。

(B) Because the crowd is out of control. 因為群眾失控。

(C) Because the skaters will have a wonderful show on the ice. 因為溜冰者將在冰上有絕佳的演出。

(D) Because Peggy is having a great time.
因為 Peggy 玩得很盡興。

單字解釋 ▶

stadium **n** 體育館	competition **n** 比賽
figure skating 花式溜冰	crowd **n** 群眾
clap **v** 拍手	out of this world 無與倫比的

試題分析 ▶ 本題問:說話者說「世界級無與倫比的」的原因。在談話中提到 figure skating competition 以及 Two skaters from Byelorussia are coming onto the ice,可知有一場溜冰的比賽,然後有兩位溜冰者站在冰上,可知準備會有冰上的表演。接著又說 People are clapping and cheering. I believe that their performance will be out of this world.,表示大家都拍手歡呼著,並相信他們的表演會是世界級無與倫比的。故答案要選 (C)。

Olympics in history		
year	season	city
2016	Summer	**Rio** (Brazil)
2014	Winter	**Sochi** (Russia)
2012	Summer	**London** (UK)
2010	Winter	**Vancouver** (Canada)

Every two years, the Winter and the Summer Olympic Games take place. It is a great honor for a country to have the Olympics, so it is very competitive to get the Games. When a city decides that it wants to host the Olympic Games, it makes a committee of local residents. For many cities, it is very expensive to have the Olympics. For instance, if a city has an old stadium, it is probably going to build a big and new stadium. This year, our city will be a host. I am looking forward to some games, like marathons and swimming. Welcome you to come to the South America!

歷史上的奧林匹克運動會		
年份	季節	舉辦城市
2016	夏季	里約（巴西）
2014	冬季	索契（俄羅斯）
2012	夏季	倫敦（英國）
2010	冬季	溫哥華（加拿大）

冬季與夏季的奧林匹克運動會，每隔兩年就會舉辦。舉辦奧林匹克運動會對一個國家來説，是一大榮耀，所以要取得主辦權是競爭激烈的。當一個城市決定要來舉辦奧林匹克運動會時，該城市的當地市民會組成一的委員會。對很多城市而言，舉辦這樣的奧林匹克運動會是相當昂貴的。舉例來説，假如某個城市原本是有一間舊的體育館，那麼它就有可能要蓋一間又大又新的體育館。今年，我們的城市將會是主辦市，我很期待某些特定的賽程，像是馬拉松與游泳。歡迎大家來到南美洲！

Q2 ___D___ **When is the talk taking place?**

這段談話發生的時間是何時？

(A) 2010. 2010 年。

(B) 2012. 2012 年。

(C) 2014. 2014 年。

(D) 2016. 2016 年。

單字解釋 ▶ Olympic Games 奧林匹克運動會
competitive **adj** 競爭的
committee **n** 委員會

試題分析 ▶ 本題問：這段談話發生的時間。在談話中提到，This year, our city will be a host. I am looking forward to some games ~ Welcome you to come to the South America，可知今年的主辦市位在南美洲。從表格中可知，位於南美洲的城市只有巴西的里約，故答案要選(D)。

全民英檢中級聽力模擬試題

本測驗分四部分，全為四選一之選擇題，共 35 題，作答時間約 30 分鐘。

第一部分　看圖辨義　　 **026_TEST_PART1.mp3**

　　共 5 題，試題冊上有數幅圖畫，每一圖畫有 1~3 個描述該圖的題目，每題請聽光碟放音機播出題目以及四個英語敘述之後，選出與所看到的圖畫最相符的答案，每題只播出一遍。

例題：（看）

（聽）Look at the picture.
What does the woman want the boy to do?
A. Pick up the rubbish.
B. Tie his shoelaces.
C. Carry her luggage.
D. Hail a cab.

正確答案為 A。

聽力測驗第一部分自本頁開始。

A:　Questions 1 and 2

Steven

B: Questions 3 and 4

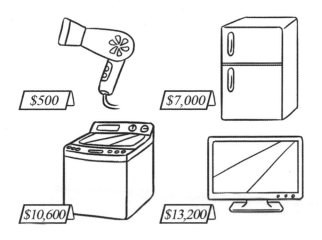

C: Question 5

共 10 題，每題請聽光碟放音機播出一英語問句或直述句後，從試題冊上A、B、C、D四個回答或回應中，選出一個最適合者作答。每題只播出一遍。

例：（聽）What happened to your feet?

（看）A.　They were too hungry.

B.　I got a new pair.

C.　My new shoes are too small.

D.　These are not mine.

正確答案為 C。

6.　A.　Let's get takeout.
　　B.　Why are you so angry at me?
　　C.　There used to be a supermarket nearby.
　　D.　We should not start working, should we?

7.　A.　I like this movie very much.
　　B.　I don't see a movie with my family.
　　C.　I think any thrillers will do.
　　D.　That's because my friends don't like science fiction movies.

8.　A.　How do you do?
　　B.　I'm in the garage.
　　C.　I'm an English teacher.
　　D.　I am sitting in the living room and watching TV.

9.　A.　I am full, thank you.
　　B.　I'm good at picking up apples.
　　C.　You are right. It's not as simple as I expected.
　　D.　Yes, we have not picnicked for a long, long time.

10.　A.　I can't find your passport.
　　B.　Are you studying in a boarding school?
　　C.　Didn't you put it in your pocket?
　　D.　I'm afraid it is not in the board meeting.

11. A. If I were he, I wouldn't tell parents what I want to do in the future.
    B. There is no smoke without fire.
    C. I am glad to be a fire fighter.
    D. Is it dangerous to be a policeman, too?

12. A. I can't find the garage you are talking about.
    B. Be patient and respectful.
    C. I wasn't attentive just now. I must have been daydreaming.
    D. Some pages in this book are missing.

13. A. I like steak with potato chips very much.
    B. Let me call a waiter for you.
    C. You can say that again. Look how burnt it is.
    D. That's because my friends like this restaurant.

14. A. Yes, I'd like the number of Jason Wang.
    B. Yes, is that 0933-539-857?
    C. I don't need any assistance.
    D. Sorry, the director isn't in his cubicle right now.

15. A. There were many seats available in the meeting.
    B. In the corner, I guess.
    C. Please have a seat and make yourself at home.
    D. He comes from the middle area in Taiwan.

共 10 題，每題請聽光碟放音機播出一段對話及一個相關的問題之後，從試題冊上 A、B、C、D 四個選項中選出一個最適合者作答。每段對話及問題只播出一遍。

例：(聽)　(Man)　　　Did you happen to see my earphones?
　　　　　　　　　　　I remember leaving them in the drawer.
　　　　　(Woman)　Did you search your briefcase?
　　　　　(Man)　　　I did but they are not there. Wait a second. Oh.
　　　　　　　　　　　They are right here in my pocket.

　　　　　Question:　Where are the man's earphones?

　　(看)　A.　The woman's pocket.
　　　　　B.　Briefcase.
　　　　　C.　The man's pocket.
　　　　　D.　Drawer.

正確答案為 C。

16. A.　She had so many rivals in her company.
　　B.　She got a better position in her company.
　　C.　She hardly ever works in her company.
　　D.　She found her lost keys in her company.

17. A.　The mail room.
　　B.　The sales department.
　　C.　The marketing department.
　　D.　The personnel office.

18. A.　Go to the musical on Saturday instead of Sunday.
　　B.　Leave his car home.
　　C.　Leave home after 6:30.
　　D.　Park their car in the park.

19. A.　Turn off the air conditioning.
　　B.　Write a business report.
　　C.　Buy some potatoes.
　　D.　Shut the door.

20. A. The man's insurance company will repair the car.
 B. The woman was shocked by what she saw.
 C. The girl was hurt badly.
 D. The girl had to pay six hundred dollars to the woman.

21.

Flyer		
TIME	EVENT	WHERE TO MEET
Saturday morning	Have a clean-up drive	Bus Station
Saturday afternoon	Plant a new garden	City Park
Sunday morning	Visit the nursing house	Nursing House
Sunday afternoon	Donate used books	City Library

 A. On Saturday morning.
 B. On Saturday afternoon.
 C. On Sunday morning.
 D. On Sunday afternoon.

22.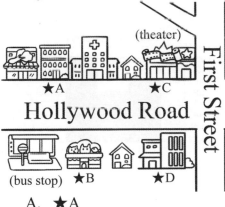

 A. ★A
 B. ★B
 C. ★C
 D. ★D

23.

House for Rent

Where : In Min-Song Community
Condition: Three Bedrooms
　　　　　 Two Bathrooms
　　　　　 A living room
　　　　　 A balcony with a
　　　　　 wonderful view
Payment: NT$ 20,000 /month
　　　　　 (NOT including utility
　　　　　 bills)
Preference: A family with
　　　　　 children
Contact: Call 0937-528-999 for
　　　　　 more information

A. Go to the woman's house.
B. Find a house with a patio.
C. Buy a copy of today's newspapers.
D. Call 0937-528-999.

24.

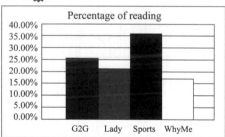

A. G2G.
B. Lady.
C. Sports.
D. WhyMe.

25.

Extension directory

Sales Dept. Ex: 001
Marketing Dept. Ex: 002
Human Resource Dept. Ex: 003
Finance Dept. Ex: 004
Law affairs Dept. Ex: 005

A. Ex 001.
B. Ex 002.
C. Ex 003.
D. Ex 004.

第四部分　簡短談話　　● 026_TEST_PART4.mp3

共 10 題，每題請聽光碟放音機播出一段談話及一個相關的問題後，從試題冊上 A、B、C、D 四個選項中選出一個最適合者作答。每段談話及問題只播出一遍。

例：（聽）

Want to have a vacation and relax a little bit? We offer some packages just like you want! Stay at a resort hotel, and enjoy our two swimming pools, two tennis courts and a private sandy beach. You will love our luxury accommodations and economical prices. Call today to book your tour, and you are ready for your beautiful vacation.

（看）　Question:　What can NOT be found in the resort hotel?
　　　　　　　　　A. A beach.
　　　　　　　　　B. A swimming pool.
　　　　　　　　　C. A log cabin.
　　　　　　　　　D. A tennis court.

正確答案為 C。

26. A. Attorneys.
    B. People who want a part-time job.
    C. People who need cancer treatment.
    D. People who have enthusiasm and two-year experience in a busy office.

27. A. Within one year.
    B. Five years.
    C. Nineteen years.
    D. Forty-five years.

28. A. Copy machines.
    B. Water fountains.
    C. Vending machines.
    D. Technology devices.

29. A. He is reviewing some contracts.
    B. He cannot deal with tax problems.
    C. He is glad to cooperate with a company.
    D. He is an expert on gaining good reputation.

30. A. Teach students how to be a good listener.
    B. Give students some tips on talking in front of people.
    C. Describe what the audience should do during the speech time.
    D. Teach students how to write a good speech.

31.

> ## Invitation
>
> Date: Saturday, December 31st, 2020
> Time: 7:00 PM
> Place: Hayat Hotel, Room 656
> Style: Potluck
>
> LET'S CELEBRATE
> THE WONDERFUL MOMENT!
> FINAL COUNT DOWN!

   A. Make a hotel reservation.
   B. Bring their favorite pans and pots there.
   C. Show up at the party before 7:00 on the last day in 2020.
   D. Draw a crazy party and share it the moment they come to the 5-star hotel.

32.

> ## Amazing Discounts
> ### This Week Only! July 22- July 29
>
> Super U has its annual sale now! Don't miss this wonderful opportunity!
>
> We have both the highest quality and the lowest price.
>
> We are open every day from 10:00 AM to 10:00 PM except Monday.
>
> All sales are final. No return or refund.
>
> ### Come Here Now!!

   A. Super U has its discount sale once a year.
   B. Someone who needs a phone can go there every day except Monday.
   C. People who want to send back the goods they bought can go there before 10:00 PM.
   D. People cannot buy things at Super U on Mondays.

33.

Investment Performance	
Investment Items	**% Returns/ year**
Stock	30%
Foreign Currency	38%
Mutual Fund	12%
Bond	0.5%

WE CARE YOUR MONEY!
WE CAN HELP YOU MAKE MORE
MONEY!!

A. Stock.
B. Foreign currency.
C. Mutual fund.
D. Bond.

34.

WELCOME

Event	Building/ Floor	Date	Time
Speech: Future Perspectives	Building B Floor 6	10/6	11:00AM
Painting Exhibition: Still Lives	Building A Floor 5	10/5- 10/8	10:00AM- 5:00PM
Sculpture: Unforgettable Stars	Building A Floor 6	10/5- 10/8	10:00AM- 5:00PM

WE ARE WAITING FOR YOU!

A. Speech and painting exhibition take place in the same building.
B. Some unforgettable stars will show up on the fifth floor.
C. You can appreciate paintings and sculptures at 4:00 PM on October seventh.
D. All events happen at 11:00 AM.

35.

Weather Forecast for International Travelers		
Taipei		30°C – 34°C
Tokyo		8°C – 13°C
London		1°C – 10°C
New York		-10°C – 0°C

A. In Tokyo, it's sunny with a high of 10 degrees and a low of 1.
B. The marathon in London has been canceled because of snow.
C. In Taipei, it's clear with a high of 34 degrees and a low of 13.
D. Snow is expected in New York.

答案解析

 For questions number 1 and 2, please look at picture A.
問題 1 與問題 2 請看圖片 A

Q1 __D__ **What is Steven wearing?** Steven 穿戴什麼？

(A) He is wearing a raincoat and a cap.
他穿一件雨衣和戴一頂鴨舌帽。

(B) He is wearing a T-shirt and a pair of glasses.
他穿一件 T 恤，戴一副眼鏡。

(C) He is wearing a pair of sunglasses and shorts.
他戴一副太陽眼鏡，穿短褲。

(D) He is wearing a pair of sneakers and a watch.
他穿著一雙球鞋，手戴手錶。

Q2 __B__ **Which description matches the picture?**
哪一項描述符合圖片？

(A) They are practicing snowboarding.
他們正在練習滑雪板。

(B) They are having a basketball game. 他們正進行籃球賽。

(C) They are watching an exciting tennis match.
他們正在看一場刺激的網球賽。

(D) They are flying a kite in the sky. 他們正在放風箏。

 For questions number 3 and 4, please look at picture B.
問題 3 與問題 4 請看圖片 B

Q3 __B__ **In which place can you see these items?**
你會在哪個地方看到這些商品？

(A) In a shoe area. 鞋子區。

(B) In an appliance area. 家電用品區。

(C) In a furniture area. 家具區。

(D) In an apparel area. 服裝用品區。

Q4   B   **Which item is the least expensive?**

哪個品項最不貴？

(A) A TV set. 電視。

(B) A hairdryer. 吹風機。

(C) A refrigerator. 冰箱。

(D) A washing machine. 洗衣機。

提示   **For question number 5, please look at picture C.**

問題 5 請看圖片 C

Q5   B   **Which announcement will you most likely hear in this place?**

在這個地方，你最有可能聽到什麼樣的廣播？

(A) Attention patrons. We'll be closing in 10 minutes. Please bring the items you want to purchase to the cash desk now.

各位顧客請注意。 我們將在十分鐘後關門。現在，請將你想要買的商品拿到結帳櫃台來。

(B) Because of the terrible weather, today's training class has been called off. Sorry for this inconvenience we cause. Please wait for our further notice. Thank you very much.

由於天候不佳，今日的訓練課程已經取消了。對於我們所造成的不便，深感抱歉。請再等候更進一步通知。感謝。

(C) May I have your attention, please? The train number 555 bound for New York is now ready for boarding at Platform C.

請各位注意。555 號前往紐約的列車，現在可以在第 C 月台上車。

(D) Now, let's welcome our well-known speaker, Dr. Wu. Tonight he is going to share some good ideas with us on "How to cost down the train fare when commuting between your home and your office?"

現在，讓我們歡迎我們知名的講者，Wu 博士。今晚他將跟我們分享一些不錯的想法，是有關於「如何在從家裡到辦公室通勤的途中，省下各位的火車費用」的主題。

第二部分 問答

Q6 ___A___ **I am starving. What do you want to eat for supper?** 我餓死了。你晚餐想吃什麼？
(A) Let's get takeout. 我們去買外帶吧。
(B) Why are you so angry at me?
為何你對我如此生氣？
(C) There used to be a supermarket nearby.
這附近以前有間超市。
(D) We should not start working, should we?
我們不該開始工作，對吧？

單字解釋▶ starving **adj** 飢餓的　　　　supper **n** 晚餐
試題分析▶ 從關鍵字 What ~ eat for supper? 可知，本題問對方晚餐想吃什麼，從選項中的關鍵字 takeout 可知，答案選項為 A，表示建議去買外帶食物吃。

Q7 ___C___ **What kind of movies do you choose if you want to see a movie with your friend?**
如果你想與朋友一起看電影，你會選擇哪一種電影？
(A) I like this movie very much. 我非常喜歡這部片。
(B) I don't see a movie with my family.
我不和我家人看電影。
(C) I think any thrillers will do. 我想任何驚悚片皆可。
(D) That's because my friends don't like science fiction movies.
那是因為我朋友都不喜歡科幻片。

單字解釋▶ choose **v** 選擇　　　　thriller **n** 驚悚片
science fiction movie **n** 科幻片
試題分析▶ 從關鍵字 What kind of movies ~ if ~ with your friend 可知，本題問如果想與朋友一起看電影會選擇哪種電影。答案是提到電影類型 thrillers 的選項 C：我想任何驚悚片皆可。

Q8 ___C___ **What do you do for a living, Michelle?**

Michelle，你工作是做什麼的？

(A) How do you do? 你好嗎？

(B) I'm in the garage. 我在車庫。

(C) I'm an English teacher. 我是一位英文老師。

(D) I am sitting in the living room and watching TV.
我正坐在客廳看電視。

試題分析 ▶ 本題問對方以什麼為生，也就是問對方的工作。所以答案是提到職業名稱 English teacher 的選項 C，表示自己是一位英文老師。

Q9 ___C___ **The test was no picnic. Don't you think?**

這考試很不容易，你不覺得嗎？

(A) I am full, thank you. 我飽了，謝謝。

(B) I'm good at picking up apples. 我很會摘蘋果。

(C) You are right. It's not as simple as I expected.
沒錯，它沒我想像的容易。

(D) Yes, we have not picnicked for a long, long time.
是的，我們好久沒有野餐了。

單字解釋 ▶ pick up **v** 摘下，挑選　　picnic **n** / **v** 野餐
be good at 擅長於

試題分析 ▶ 本題問：這考試很不容易，你不覺得嗎。慣用語 It is no picnic 的意思是「不容易」，而相反詞 It is a piece of cake 就是「很容易」的意思。從選項可知，最適合的答案為選項 C：沒錯，它沒我想像的容易。

Q10 ___C___ **Oh, my goodness! I just can't find my boarding pass.** 糟了，我找不到我的登機證。

(A) I can't find your passport. 我找不到你的護照。

(B) Are you studying in a boarding school?
你讀寄宿學校嗎？

(C) Didn't you put it in your pocket?
你不是放在口袋裡嗎？

(D) I'm afraid it is not in the board meeting.
恐怕這不在董事會裡。

Q11 ___A___ **Kenny wants to be a bodyguard in the future, but his parents think the job is too dangerous.**

Kenny 想在未來當保鑣，但他的父母認為這項工作太危險了。

(A) If I were he, I wouldn't tell parents what I want to do in the future.

假如我是他，我是不會告訴父母我未來想做什麼。

(B) There is no smoke without fire. 無風不起浪。

(C) I am glad to be a fire fighter. 我很樂意當消防員。

(D) Is it dangerous to be a policeman, too?

當警察也很危險嗎？

Q12 ___C___ **We are not on the same page. Are you listening to me?** 我們在雞同鴨講，你有在聽我說什麼嗎？

(A) I can't find the garage you are talking about.

我找不到你說的修車廠。

(B) Be patient and respectful. 要有耐心、有禮貌。

(C) I wasn't attentive just now. I must have been daydreaming. 我剛才沒注意，我一定是在做白日夢。

(D) Some pages in this book are missing.

這書裡有幾頁不見了。

試題分析 ▶ 本題說：我們在雞同鴨講，有在聽我說話嗎。從選項可知，最適合的答案為選項 C：我剛才沒注意，我一定是在做白日夢。

Q13 ___B___ **This steak is undercooked. I want to send it back.** 這牛排沒煮熟，我要退回。

(A) I like steak with potato chips very much.
我非常喜歡牛排配馬鈴薯片。

(B) Let me call a waiter for you. 我幫你叫服務生過來。

(C) You can say that again. Look how burnt it is.
你說的對，你看它有多焦。

(D) That's because my friends like this restaurant.
那是因為我朋友都喜歡這間餐廳。

試題分析 ▶ 本題說：這牛排沒煮熟，我要退回。從選項可知，最適合的答案為選項 B：我幫你叫服務生過來。選項 C 雖然一開始提到「你說的對」，但後面的 Look how burnt it is 是指牛排煎到焦了的意思。

Q14 ___A___ **Directory assistance, may I help you?**
這裡是查號台，有什麼可以效勞的地方嗎？

(A) Yes, I'd like the number of Jason Wang.
是的，我想要 Jason Wang 的電話。

(B) Yes, is that 0933-539-857?
是的，這是 0933-539-857 嗎？

(C) I don't need any assistance. 我不需要任何協助。

(D) Sorry, the director isn't in his cubicle right now.
抱歉，主任現在不在他的辦公室裡。

Q15　B　Where will the new comer sit when he comes tomorrow morning?

那位新人明天早上來時要坐哪裡？

(A) There were many seats available in the meeting.
此會議當時有很多空位。

(B) In the corner, I guess. 我想是在那個角落吧。

(C) Please have a seat and make yourself at home.
你請坐，並把這裡當自己的家。

(D) He comes from the middle area in Taiwan.
他來自於台灣中部地區。

第三部分 簡短對話

Conversation (Question 16)

M: Congratulations! I heard that you got a promotion.

W: Yes, finally. I am so happy.

M: How did you get it? There were so many candidates who wanted to pursue this job.

W: Well, I wasn't surprised there were so many competitors. Anyway, I guess owning a hardworking attitude is the key!

中文翻譯

男：恭喜恭喜！我聽説你升遷了。

女：是呀，終於。我真是開心。

男：你是如何辦到的？有不少候補人選都想追求這份工作。

女：嗯，對於有這麼多的競爭者，我並不意外。不管怎樣，我想，抱有認真的態度才是關鍵。

Q16　__B__　**Why is the woman delighted?** 為何女子很開心？

(A) She had so many rivals in her company.
她在公司有很多對手。

(B) She got a better position in her company.
她在公司取得更好的職位。

(C) She hardly ever works in her company.
她很少在公司裡工作。

(D) She found her lost keys in her company.
她在公司裡找到她遺失的鑰匙。

單字解釋 ▶　congratulations 恭喜　　　　promotion [n] 升遷
candidate [n] 候補人選　　　pursue [v] 追求

試題分析 ▶　從 Why... woman delighted 可知，本題問：女子開心的理由。從對話關鍵字 promotion 可知，開心的原因是因為獲得升遷（got a promotion）。因此答案為選項 B：在公司取得更好的職位。

Conversation (Question 17)

M: Excuse me, I think I am lost. Could you please tell me how I can get to the sales department?

W: This is the personnel office. Just go straight and pass the marketing department. It's near the mail room.

M: Thank you so much.

中文翻譯

男：不好意思，我想我迷路了。您可以告訴我如何去銷售部門嗎？

女：這裡是人事部門。就只要直走，然後經過行銷部門。它在收發室附近。

男：感謝您。

Q17 ___B___ **What place is the man looking for?**

男子在找什麼地方？

(A) The mail room.

收發室。

(B) The sales department.

銷售部門。

(C) The marketing department.

行銷部門。

(D) The personnel office.

人事部門。

單字解釋 ▶ mail room **n** 收發室　　　　sales department **n** 銷售部門
marketing department **n** 行銷部門
personnel office **n** 人事部門　look for **v** 尋找

試題分析 ▶ 從 What place... man looking for 可知，本題問：男子在找的地方。從 Could you please tell me how I can get to the sales department 這句話可以得知，男子是在找銷售部門。從選項可知，最適合的答案為選項 B：銷售部門。

Conversation (Question 18)

W: Well, I made the call and reserved seats for Sunday evening's musical.

M: Magnificent! I'm looking forward to it. I think I will drive my car there, so we should leave home by 6:30.

W: If you ask me, I won't drive there. You know the traffic on Sunday night is always awful, and it's so difficult to find a parking space.

M: Maybe you are right!

中文翻譯

女：嗯，我有打電話預約週日晚上音樂劇的座位。

男：太棒了！我很期待。我想我會開車去，所以我們應該 6 點半前出發。

女：假如你問我的意見，我是不會開車去。你知道週日晚上的路況一直很糟。而且找停車位很困難。

男：你也許說的對。

Q18 ___B___ **What does the woman think the man should do?** 女子認為男子應該做什麼？

(A) Go to the musical on Saturday instead of Sunday. 在週六而非週日去聽音樂劇。

(B) Leave his car home. 將車子留在家裡。

(C) Leave home after 6:30. 在 6 點半之後從家裡出發。

(D) Park their car in the park. 把車子停在公園裡。

reserve v 預約　　　　　　musical n 音樂劇
magnificent adj 極好的　　　awful adj 很糟糕的

試題分析 ▶ 從 What ... woman think the man should do 可知，本題問女子認為男子應該做的事。男子一開始提到 I will drive my car there, so we should leave home by 6:30.，表示會從家裡開車去音樂劇現場，女子提到 I won't drive there. You know the traffic on Sunday night is always awful.，可知女子建議不應該開車去，因為週日晚上的路況很糟。從選項可知，最適合的答案為選項 B：將車子留在家裡。

Conversation (Question 19)

W: It's really cold in here. Why don't you turn off the air conditioner?

M: Darling, it's winter, and it's only 4 degrees centigrade. Tell me who will turn on the air conditioner on such a cold day.

W: You didn't turn on the air conditioner? Oh, I see the problem. Someone left the door open. Would you mind closing it for me now?

M: I am busy writing a business report my boss needs tomorrow. Don't be such a couch potato! Just stand up and do it!

W: Okay. Okay...

中文翻譯

女：這裡好冷，為何不關冷氣？

男：親愛的，現在是冬天，而且現在只有攝氏四度。請告訴我誰會在這麼冷的天氣開冷氣。

女：你沒開冷氣嗎？喔，我知道問題出在哪了。有人沒有關門。你介意現在幫我把門關上嗎？

男：我正忙著在寫我老闆明天需要的商業報告。別這麼懶好嗎？妳就站起來關上它嘛。

女：好啦，好啦…

Q19 ___D___ **What does the woman want the man to do?** 女子要男子做什麼？

(A) Turn off the air conditioning. 關上冷氣。
(B) Write a business report. 寫商業報告。
(C) Buy some potatoes. 買些馬鈴薯。
(D) Shut the door. 關上門。

單字解釋 ▶ air conditioner 冷氣　　　　　　centigrade **n** 攝氏
business report 商業報告
couch potato [慣用語] 沙發上的馬鈴薯（形容人很懶惰，成天坐在沙發上看電視不動，而變得肥胖，就像馬鈴薯一般）

試題分析 ▶ 從 What ... woman want the man to do 可知，本題問女子要男子做的事。從對話一開始可知，女子發現室內變冷的問題。從 Someone left the door open. Would you mind closing it for me now?得知，女子想要男子幫她關門。因此答案選項為 D：關上門。

Conversation (Question 20)

W: Oh! Boy! What happened exactly?
M: A five-year-old girl ran into the street while I was driving down the street. I slammed on the brake immediately, and then hit a lamppost.
W: Did you hurt?
M: No, but I was scared out of my skin.
W: How much do you think it's going to cost if you have it repaired?
M: I don't think it'll be more than six hundred dollars. And my insurance company will definitely take care of it.

女：老天呀，到底是發生什麼事？

男：當我開車順著街開下去時，一位五歲小女孩衝入馬路中。我立
即踩了剎車，然後就撞上了燈柱。

女：你有受傷嗎？

男：我沒有，但我嚇得魂飛魄散。

女：假如你把車拿去送修，你認為要花多少錢？

男：我想不會超過六百元，而且我的保險公司絕對會負擔的。

Q20　__B__　**According to the speakers, which statement is true?**

根據說話者，下列哪一個敘述為真？

(A) The man's insurance company will repair the car.

　　男子的保險公司將會修這輛車。

(B) The woman was shocked by what she saw.

　　女子對於她所見到的事情感到吃驚。

(C) The girl was hurt badly.

　　女孩嚴重受傷。

(D) The girl had to pay six hundred dollars to the woman.

　　女孩必須付 600 元給女子。

單字解釋▶ boy [感嘆詞] 老天呀　　　　　　　slam on the brake 急踩煞車
be scared out of the skin [慣用語] 嚇得魂飛魄散

試題分析▶ 從 which statement is true 可知，本題問選項中哪一個敘述是
對的。從對話一開始，女子用到感嘆詞 Oh! Boy! 及表示關心
的問句 What happened exactly?以及 Did you hurt?，接著男
子便描述了車禍的狀況，可知女子對於男子的狀況感到吃驚，
因此答案為選項 B：女子對於她所見到的事情感到吃驚。男子
只提到維修的費用保險公司會負擔，沒說保險公司會修車，所
以 A 不正確。

Conversation (Question 21)

	Flyer	
TIME	EVENT	WHERE TO MEET
Saturday morning	Have a clean-up drive	Bus Station
Saturday afternoon	Plant a new garden	City Park
Sunday morning	Visit the nursing house	Nursing House
Sunday afternoon	Donate used books	City Library

M: Are you doing anything special this weekend?

W: No. Why?

M: There are many community activities this weekend. Take a look at this flyer. Do you want to come?

W: Sounds nice. Let's see..., I think keeping our neighborhood from trash is always good. Moreover, it's a good occasion to be more acquainted with the neighbors in this neighborhood while cleaning up the environment together.

M: I think so too. Let's participate in one of those activities.

傳單		
時間	活動	見面地點
週六早上	清潔活動	公車站
週六下午	種植新花園	市立公園
週日早上	拜訪育幼院	育幼院
週六下午	捐出二手書	市立圖書館

男：你本週末有要做什麼特別的事嗎？
女：沒有，有什麼事情嗎？
男：本週末有很多社區活動。你看看這宣傳單。你想來嗎？
女：聽起來是不錯。我看看…，我認為讓我們的社區維持乾淨、沒有垃圾，一直都是好事。此外，透過一起打掃環境，會是一個可以讓我們更加認識這個社區一些鄰居的場合。
男：我也這麼認為。我們去參與其中一項活動吧。

Q21 ___A___ **When most likely will the speakers participate in the community activity?**
說話者最有可能於何時參加社區活動？
(A) On Saturday morning. 週六早上。
(B) On Saturday afternoon. 週六下午。
(C) On Sunday morning. 週日早上。
(D) On Sunday afternoon. 週日下午。

單字解釋 ▶ community activities 社區活動。　flyer n 傳單
occasion n 場合　　event n 活動
be acquainted with 認識…　participate in 參與…

試題分析 ▶ 從 When ... speakers participate in the community activity 可知，本題問說話者參加社區活動的時間。一開始男子提到 Take a look at this flyer. Do you want to come，表示問女子是否要參加傳單上的活動。接著女子提到 keeping our neighborhood from trash is always good 以及 cleaning up the environment，從關鍵字 keeping... from trash 和 cleaning up 可推測跟社區環境整潔相關的活動。從圖表可知，跟清潔活動對照的時間是週六早上，因此答案為選項A：週六早上。

Conversation (Question 22)

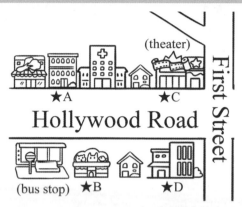

W: Excuse me, I'm trying to find Holiday Chinese Theater. Is it near here?

M: Yes, it's just at the corner of Hollywood Road and First Street.

W: Is it possible to walk there from here?

M: Well, it's possible, but it'll take around half an hour.

W: I see, so what's the best way to get there?

M: Taking the bus is a good choice. Just walk across the road and you will find the bus stop.

中文翻譯

女：不好意思，我正試著要找 Holiday 中華影城，請問是在這附近嗎？

男：是的，就在好萊塢路與第一街的交叉路口。

女：有可能從這裡走到那嗎？

男：嗯，是有可能，但要花大約半小時。

女：我懂了，那麼到那裡最佳的方式應該是什麼呢？

男：搭公車是個好選擇。就只要走到對面，你就可以找到公車站牌。

Q21   A   **Look at the map. Where are the speakers now?** 請看地圖。說話者現在在哪裡？

(A) ★A
　　★A 的位置

(B) ★B
　　★B 的位置

(C) ★C
　　★C 的位置

(D) ★D
　　★D 的位置

單字解釋 ▶ choice **n** 選擇
at the corner of 在…的交叉路口處

試題分析 ▶ 從 Where ... speakers now 可知，本題問說話者目前對話的位置在哪裡。在對話最後可知，男子建議女子搭公車，提到 Just walk across the road and you will find the bus stop.，表示只要走到對面，就可以找到公車站牌。從圖表上先找到公車站牌，而公車站牌的對面是 ★A 的位置，因此答案選項為 A。

House for Rent

Where : In Min-Song Community
Condition: Three Bedrooms
            Two Bathrooms
            A living room
            A balcony with a wonderful view
Payment: NT$ 20,000 /month (NOT including
          utility bills)
Preference: A family with children
Contact: Call 0937-528-999 for more information

W: I just saw a nice house for rent in today's newspaper.

M: Really? Tell me what it says?

W: It has three bedrooms, two bathrooms, a living room and a balcony with a wonderful view.

M: Sounds great. Where is it actually?

W: In the neighborhood where I am living.

M: That's terrific! So, what are you waiting for?

中文翻譯

房屋出租

地點：Min-Song 社區
屋況：三間臥室
       兩套衛浴
       一個客廳
       可看美景的陽台
房租：新台幣 20,000 元／月（不包含水電瓦斯費）
優先考慮：有小孩的家庭尤佳
聯絡電話：0937-528-999，來電詢問更多資訊。

全民英檢中級聽力模擬試題

答案
解析

379

女：我剛在今天的報紙上看到一間很棒的房屋要出租。
男：真的嗎？告訴我它是怎麼說的。
女：它有三間臥室、兩套衛浴、一個客廳，以及可看到美景的陽台。
男：聽起來真棒。究竟在哪呢？
女：在我現在住的區域。
男：太棒了！那妳還在等什麼？

Q23 __D__ **What does the man imply the woman should do?** 男子暗示女子應該做什麼？

(A) Go to the woman's house. 去女子的家。

(B) Find a house with a patio. 找一個有庭院的房子。

(C) Buy a copy of today's newspapers.
買一份今天的報紙。

(D) Call 0937-528-999. 撥打電話號碼 0937-528-999。

單字解釋 ▶ balcony **n** 陽台　　　　　　　preference **n** 偏好

試題分析 ▶ 從 What ~ woman should do? 可知，本題問男子暗示女子應該要做的事。圖片是關於租屋資訊。從女子的第一句話可知，有人要出租房子，在對話最後聽到男子說 That's terrific! So, what are you waiting for?，表示對於女子評估的房子也感到滿意，暗示女子可以直接連絡屋主。因此答案選 D。

Conversation (Question 24)

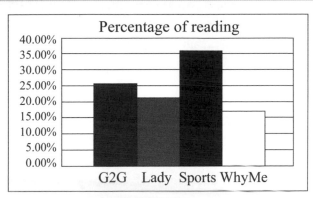

W: John, what are you reading?

M: This interesting research on which magazine is the most popular now.

W: Well, what did you find?

M: I like this magazine, which, however, isn't the most popular one. It is merely a bit less popular than *Sports*. In addition, I am wondering why people don't like *WhyMe*.

W: Sounds interesting. Can I have a look at it?

中文翻譯

女：John，你在讀什麼？

男：這篇有關於目前最受歡迎的雜誌是什麼的有趣研究報告。

女：嗯，那你有發現什麼呢？

男：我喜歡這本雜誌，但它並非最受歡迎的，其受歡迎程度僅比《Sports》雜誌稍低一點而已。而且我很好奇，為何大家不喜歡WhyMe？

女：聽起來真有趣。可以借我看一下嗎？

Q24 ___A___ **Look at the chart. Which magazine does the man like?**

看這張圖表。男子喜歡哪一個雜誌？

(A) G2G. G2G 雜誌。   (C) Sports. Sports 雜誌。

(B) Lady. Lady 雜誌。   (D) WhyMe. WhyMe 雜誌。

從 Which magazine ... man like? 可知，本題問男子喜歡的雜誌是圖表中哪一本。男子提到 I like this magazine, which... merely a bit less popular than Sports. 可知男子喜歡的雜誌的受歡迎程度僅比 Sports 雜誌稍低一點而已，在圖表上可以看到，Sports 的占比最高，占比稍微比 Sports 低的是 G2G，因此是要答案選 A。

Conversation (Question 25)

Extension directory

Sales Dept. Ex: 001
Marketing Dept. Ex: 002
Human Resource Dept. Ex: 003
Finance Dept. Ex: 004
Law affairs Dept. Ex: 005

W: Charles seems to have been pretty busy these days, doesn't he?

M: He sure does. He's been dealing with lots of resumes. Recruiting is always difficult work.

W: Arranging some interviews also takes lots of time and patience.

M: Speaking of interviews, I need some advice from him because I will meet a candidate next week. What is his extension? I need to talk to him.

W: OK, let me check the directory.

分機號碼通訊錄
銷售部門　分機：001
行銷部門　分機：002
人資部門　分機：003
財務部門　分機：004
法務部門　分機：005

女：Charles 最近似乎一直很忙，對吧？

男：他的確是。他一直在處理大量的履歷表。招募一直是很困難的工作。

女：安排面試也很花時間與耐心。

男：談到面試，我需要從他那邊得到一些建議，因為我下週要跟一位求職人選見面。他分機幾號？我需要找他談。

女：好的，我來看一下通訊錄。

Q25 ___C___ **What extension can the man reach Charles?**

男子可用幾號分機聯繫 Charles？

(A) Ex 001.

分機 001。

(B) Ex 002.

分機 002。

(C) Ex 003.

分機 003。

(D) Ex 004.

分機 004。

單字解釋 ▶ extension directory 分機號碼通訊錄　　　　resume **n** 履歷表
candidate **n** 求職者，候補人選

試題分析 ▶ 從 What extension ... reach Charles 可知，本題問可用哪一個分機聯繫 Charles。從對話一開始的一些關鍵字 Charles、dealing with lots of resumes、recruiting 可推測，Charles 應該是人資部門的職員。接著男子提到 I need some advice from him，表示需要找 Charles。透過關鍵字及圖表可推測，Charles 的分機是 003，答案為選項 C。

Short talk (Question 26)

Busy law firm requires full-time employees right away. The ideal people will be friendly, attentive and enthusiastic. They will have to deal with many lawyers and clients. Applicants must have two-year experience in a busy office. The positions are temporary. Two of our regular staff members need cancer treatments. They will be away for around half a year.

中文翻譯

忙碌的法律事務所現在需要找全職員工。友善、專注與熱忱的特質,將會是理想的人選。這些人選將必須要跟許多律師與客戶打交道。求職者必須要有兩年的豐富職場經驗。這個職位是暫時性的。我們的兩位正職員工需要進行癌症治療。他們將離開約半年的時間。

Q26   D   **Who will be interested in this ad?**

誰會對這則廣告感到興趣?

(A) Attorneys.

律師。

(B) People who want a part-time job.

想找兼職工作的人。

(C) People who need cancer treatment.

需要癌症治療的人。

(D) People who have enthusiasm and two-year experience in a busy office.

有熱忱,且有兩年豐富工作經驗的人。

ideal **adj** 理想的　　　　　　attentive **adj** 專注的
enthusiastic **adj** 有熱忱的　　temporary **adj** 臨時的
cancer treatments **n** 癌症治療

試題分析 ▶ 從 Who ... interested in this ad 可知，本題問會對這則廣告感
到興趣的對象是誰。談話中提到 Applicants must have two-
year experience in a busy office.（求職者必須要有兩年的豐富
職場經驗）以及 The ideal people will be friendly, attentive
and enthusiastic.（友善、專注與熱忱的特質，將會是理想的
人選），因此答案為選項 D。

Short talk (Question 27)

Good afternoon, ladies and gentlemen. I am your guide,
Tina. Now I would like to introduce this historic
building to all of you. This building was designed by
the famous architect, Alan Morgan. Construction was
begun in 1845 and was completed in the end of the
same year. This building has been considered one of the
finest examples of nineteenth-century French
architecture. Then five years ago, it was officially
registered as a national historic landmark.

中文翻譯

各位女士、各位先生午安。我是各位的導覽 Tina。現在，我想介紹
這個歷史性的建築物給大家。這棟建築物是由這位有名的建築師
Alan Morgan 所設計的。建築的工程自 1845 年開始，並在同年底完
工。這棟建築物被視為 19 世紀最佳法式建築代表之一。然後就在五
年前，它正式被登記為國家級歷史地標。

Q27 ___A___ **How long did it take to construct this building?** 蓋這棟建築物，花了多久時間？

(A) Within one year. 一年之內。
(B) Five years. 五年。
(C) Nineteen years. 十九年。
(D) Forty-five years. 四十五年。

單字解釋 ▶ historic **adj** 歷史的   architect **n** 建築師
architecture **n** 建築物   officially **adv** 官方地，正式地
register **v** 登記，註冊

試題分析 ▶ 從 How long... construct this building 可知，本題問蓋這棟建築物，所花的時間。談話中提到 Construction was begun in 1845 and was completed in the end of the same year.，從 completed in the end of the same year 可知建築的工程在同年底完工，言下之意是不到一年就完工，答案為選項 A。

Short talk (Question 28)

You are welcome to use any of our machines in this section. They are located on the second and fourth floor. From the elevators, they are at the far end of each hallway. Another can be found next to the drinking fountain outside the entrance on the first floor. Just insert your coins into the slot, and select what beverages you want. It's easy to use.

中文翻譯

歡迎您使用我們這一區的任何一台機器，位於二樓和四樓。從電梯走出來，它們放在走道的最底端。另外一台可以在一樓入口外的飲水機旁找到。只需將硬幣投入投幣孔，然後選擇您要的飲料即可，這很容易操作。

Q28　　C　**What is described?** 是在描述什麼？
(A) Copy machines. 影印機。
(B) Water fountains. 噴水池。
(C) Vending machines. 自動販賣機。
(D) Technology devices. 科技裝置。

單字解釋 ▶ 　section **n** 區域　　　　　　elevator **n** 電梯
　　　　　　drinking fountain 飲水機　　entrance **n** 入口
　　　　　　slot **n** 投幣孔

試題分析 ▶ 　從 What ... described 可知，本題問談話中描述的東西是什麼。談話中提到 Just insert your coins into the slot, and select what beverages you want，表示只需將硬幣投入投幣孔，然後選擇要的飲料。從投幣與飲料可推測是自動販賣機，答案為選項 C。

Short talk (Question 29)

Hello, everyone. On behalf of our company, I'm pleased to collaborate with your firm for your taxes this year. As you know, our company has had good reputation and expertise, and surely can deal with any difficult tax problems. Please review the contracts I'm handing out now. Thank you so much.

中文翻譯

大家好。我很開心代表我們公司，來和貴公司合作，處理你們今年的稅務。就如同你們所知，我們公司從過去就一直有良好的名聲與專業度，而且絕對能處理任何困難的稅務問題。請檢視一下我現在要發下去的這份合約。謝謝。

Q29   __C__   **What can be inferred about the speaker?**

關於說話者，我們可以推論出什麼？

(A) He is reviewing some contracts. 他正在檢視一些合約。

(B) He cannot deal with tax problems.
   他不會處理稅務問題。

(C) He is glad to cooperate with a company.
   他很高興能彼此合作。

(D) He is an expert on gaining good reputation.
   針對如何獲得好名聲這件事上，他是位專家。

單字解釋 ▶

on behalf of 代表⋯   collaborate with **v** 與⋯合作

reputation **n** 名聲   expertise **n** 專業度

hand out **v** 發下去，遞交

試題分析 ▶

從 What... inferred about the speaker 可知，本題問從說話者的談話中可以推論出的事實。談話中提到 On behalf of our company, I'm pleased to collaborate with your firm for your taxes this year.，表示說話者很開心代表自己公司，來和聽者的公司合作處理稅務。因此答案為選項 C。說話者在最後提到 Please review the contracts I'm handing out now.，請聽者檢視合約，而非自己在檢視合約，故選項 A 不正確。

Short talk (Question 30)

Making a speech makes a lot of students nervous. But all you need to do is just good preparation. In the first place, choose a good and interesting topic. Some people say a shocking topic always attracts audience, but actually I don't think so. Then, find related information on the topic and write out your whole speech. Next, practice saying it many times until you can say it without reading it. The time for a speech should not be too short or too long. In fact, after some practices, you will find there's nothing to worry about giving a good speech.

演講這件事會讓很多學生感到緊張。但是所有你所需要做的，就是好好地準備。第一，選擇一個好的、有趣的主題。有些人說，震撼人心的主題總是會吸引觀眾目光，但事實上我並不這麼認為。然後，找到有關於這個主題的相關資訊，接著再寫出全篇的演講稿。接下來，開口練習好幾遍，直到自己不需要看稿。演說的時間不應該太短或太長。事實上，在練習幾次之後，你就會發現根本不用擔心做一場演說。

Q30 ___B___ **What is the purpose of the talk?**

這段談話的目的是什麼？

(A) Teach students how to be a good listener.

教導學生如何成為好的傾聽者。

(B) Give students some tips on talking in front of people. 提供學生一些在人們面前說話的技巧。

(C) Describe what the audience should do during the speech time. 描述觀眾在演講期間應該做的事。

(D) Teach students how to write a good speech.

教導學生如何寫出好的演講稿。

單字解釋 ▶ preparation **n** 準備　　　　audience **n** 觀眾
related **adj** 相關的

試題分析 ▶ 從 What... purpose of the talk 可知，本題問談話的目的。談話中提到 Making a speech makes a lot of students nervous. But all you need to do is just good preparation.，表示演講總讓學生感到緊張，大家所需要做的就是好好準備。之後提到一些關於準備演講的方法，因此目的主要是提供聽者關於在觀眾面前講話的方法，故答案為選項 B。

Invitation

Date: Saturday, December 31st, 2020
Time: 7:00 PM
Place: Hayat Hotel, Room 656
Style: Potluck

**LET'S CELEBRATE
THE WONDERFUL MOMENT!
FINAL COUNT DOWN!**

My dear friends, this is Charles Chen. 2020 is drawing to a close, so I want to throw a crazy party for this wonderful moment. Let's meet at a 5-star hotel on the last day of the year. Please come to Room 656 by 7:00 P.M. And bring your favorite dish to share with us. See you then!

....

邀請函

日期：2020 年 12 月 31 日禮拜六
時間：晚上七點
地點：Hayat 飯店 656 號房
方式：百樂餐

一起慶祝這美好時刻吧！
倒數計時囉！

我親愛的朋友，我是 Charles Chen。2020 年即將結束，所以我想要為這個美好的時刻開個瘋狂的派對。我們聚聚吧，時間就在今年的最後一天，地點在一間五星級飯店。請在晚上七點前到 656 號房。並且帶一道你最喜歡的菜來跟我們分享喔！到時見！

Q31 ___C___ **What should people who want to join this party do?** 想參加這場派對的人應該做什麼？

(A) Make a hotel reservation. 預約飯店房間。

(B) Bring their favorite pans and pots there.
帶他們最愛的鍋壺去那邊。

(C) Show up at the party before 7:00 on the last day in 2020. 在 2020 年最後一天的晚上七點前到派對現場。

(D) Draw a crazy party and share it the moment they come to the 5-star hotel.
畫一個瘋狂派對，並在一到五星級飯店時分享給大家看。

單字解釋 ▶ potluck **n** 百樂餐（一人帶一道菜來分享的派對模式）

throw a crazy party 開一個瘋狂派對

draw to a close 即將結束

試題分析 ▶ 從 What should people ... join this party do 可知，本題問想參加這場派對的人應該要做的事。談話中提到 2020 is drawing to close, so I want to throw a crazy party ... Let's meet at ... on the last day of the year,以及 Please come ... by 7:00P.M.，可知說話者想在 2020 年結束前開個派對，並談到派對時間在 2020 年的最後一天，地點在一間五星級飯店，並要聽者在晚上七點前到現場，故答案為選項 C。

Amazing Discounts

This Week Only! July 22-July 29

Super U has its annual sale now! Don't miss this wonderful opportunity!

We have both the highest quality and the lowest price.

We are open every day from 10:00 AM to 10:00 PM except Monday.

All sales are final. No return or refund.

Come Here Now!!

Are you looking for a new Smartphone? Is your current phone working slowly? Look no more. Come to the most popular phone shop in town, Super U. And this week only, we offer a huge discount on any items in our store. Don't wait! Our hours are from 10:00 AM to 10:00 PM.

驚喜折扣價

僅限本週！7 月 22 日到 7 月 29 日

超級 U 目前在做年度特賣！別錯過這美好的機會！
我們的商品是最高品質，價格卻是最低。
我們每天營業，從早上十點到晚上十點，除了週一不營業。
所有銷售都是貨品既出概不退貨。不能退貨與退款。

現在就來吧！！

你在找新的智慧型手機嗎？你目前的手機跑得很慢嗎？不用再找了，來本鎮最受歡迎的電話用品店「超級 U」。僅此一週，我們店內所有品項都提供很優惠的折扣。別等了！我們的營運時間從早上十點到晚上十點。

Q32 __C__ **According to the talk, which statement is NOT correct?** 根據這段談話，哪一個敘述不正確？

(A) Super U has its discount sale once a year.
超級 U 一年辦一次特賣會。

(B) Someone who needs a phone can go there every day except Monday.
需要買電話的人，都可以在週一以外的時間到那裡買。

(C) People who want to send back the goods they bought can go there before 10:00 PM.
想要退回所購買商品的人，可以在晚上十點前到那裡。

(D) People cannot buy things at Super U on Mondays.
週一無法在超級 U 買東西。

單字解釋 ▶ annual **adj** 年度的　　　　refund **n** 退款
current **adj** 目前的

試題分析 ▶ 從 which... NOT correct 可知，本題問不正確的敘述是何者。從圖表中提到 All sales are final. No return or refund.，表示所有銷售都是貨品既出概不退貨，不能退貨與退款。因此答案為選項 C。

Investment Performance

Investment Items	% Returns / year
Stock	30%
Foreign Currency	38%
Mutual Fund	12%
Bond	0.5%

WE CARE YOUR MONEY!
WE CAN HELP YOU MAKE MORE MONEY!!

Investing in this modern century has a lot of uncertainty. Smart people, like you, all want to be intelligent investors. That's totally true and no one will deny it. This year, through our careful assistance, some of you have already known to vary your investment portfolios. According to the statistics, more people invest in the stock market than any other investment items. However, if you invest in foreign currency this year, you get better profits. Once again, I would like to remind you that higher profits mean higher risks.

中文翻譯

投資績效

投資標的	％（收益／年）
股票	30%
外匯	38%
共同基金	12%
債券	0.5%

我們在乎你的金錢！我們能幫助你賺更多錢！

在現代這個世紀做投資，有許多不確定性。如同各位一樣聰明的人，都想成為明智的投資客。這完全不用質疑，且沒有人會否認的。今年，透過我們仔細周全的協助，你們之中有些人已經知道要多樣化你們的投資組合。根據統計數據，有更多人選擇在股票市場上做投資，勝過於在其他投資標的上。然而，若你們今年投資在外匯上，你們會有更不錯的收益。重點再講一次，我想要提醒你們，越高的利潤代表有越高的風險。

Q33 ___B___ **Which investment item has more risks?**

哪一種投資標的有較高風險？

(A) Stock.

股票。

(B) Foreign currency.

外匯。

(C) Mutual fund.

共同基金。

(D) Bond.

債券。

單字解釋 ▶

uncertainty **n** 不確定性	deny **v** 否認
investment portfolio 投資組合	vary **v** 使多樣化
stock **n** 股票	foreign currency 外幣，外匯
mutual fund 共同基金	bond **n** 債券

試題分析 ▶ 從 Which investment item ... more risks 可知，本題問哪一種投資標的有較高風險。談話最後提到 I would like to remind you that higher profits mean higher risks.，表示越高的利潤就會有越高的風險，從表格中可推測，右欄的 Returns/year 下方的數值中，數值最高者為 38%，表示獲益最高，也就代表風險也高，故答案為選項 B。

WELCOME

Event	Building/Floor	Date	Time
Speech: Future Perspectives	Building B Floor 6	10/6	11:00AM
Painting Exhibition: Still Lives	Building A Floor 5	10/5-10/8	10:00AM-5:00PM
Sculpture: Unforgettable Stars	Building A Floor 6	10/5-10/8	10:00AM-5:00PM

WE ARE WAITING FOR YOU!

International School invites you and your children to join some meaningful events from October fifth to October eighth. This is a terrific opportunity to appreciate artworks and listen to a speech, as well as to meet school faculty and be familiar with our campus with different facilities. Please check the table and decide which event would interest you more.

活動	大樓／樓層	日期	時間
演說: 未來展望	B 大樓 6 樓	10 月 6 日	早上 11 點
畫展: 靜物畫	A 大樓 5 樓	10 月 5 日-10 月 8 日	早上 10 點-下午 5 點
雕塑: 難忘的巨星	A 大樓 6 樓	10 月 5 日-10 月 8 日	早上 10 點-下午 5 點

歡迎蒞臨

我們在這裡等您！

國際學校邀請您與您的孩子來參加一些有意義的活動，時間從 10 月 5 日到 10 月 8 日。這是個不錯的機會，可以欣賞藝術品、聽聽演講，同時也可見到學校教職員，並熟悉校園四周的不同設施。請看一下這張表格，並決定哪一項活動對您來說是比較有興趣的。

Q34 ___C___ **According to the talk, which statement is true?** 根據這段談話，哪一個敘述正確？

(A) Speech and painting exhibition take place in the same building. 演說與畫展在同一棟大樓裡舉行。

(B) Some unforgettable stars will show up on the fifth floor. 一些令人難忘的巨星會出現在 5 樓。

(C) You can appreciate paintings and sculptures at 4:00 PM on October seventh.
你可以在 10 月 7 日下午 4 點，欣賞到畫作與雕刻品。

(D) All events happen at 11:00 AM.
所有活動都在早上 11 點舉行。

單字解釋 ▶
perspective **n** 展望
unforgettable **adj** 讓人難忘的
school faculty 學校教職員
facility **n** 設施
still life **n** 靜物畫
meaningful **adj** 有意義的
familiar **adj** 熟悉的

試題分析 ▶
本題問選項中哪個敘述正確。從表格中的 Speech（Building B Floor 6）和 Painting Exhibition（Building A Floor 5）可知，演說和畫展的舉行地點在不同大樓，所以 A 不正確。從 Sculpture: Unforgettable Stars 以及 Building A 和 Floor 6 可知，難忘的巨星的雕刻品會出現在 6 樓，且非巨星本人，所以 B 不正確。從表格中各活動的開始時間可知，演講是在 11 點開始，另外兩活動是 10 點開始，所以 D. 不正確。對照畫展及雕塑的時間，畫展：10 月 5 日-10 月 8 日（早上 10 點-下午 5 點），雕塑：10 月 5 日-10 月 8 日（早上 10 點-下午 5 點），選項 C 的 10 月 7 日下午 4 點有在這個時間範圍內，因此 C 正確。

Short talk (Question 35)

Weather Forecast for International Travelers		
Taipei	☀	30°C – 34°C
Tokyo	☁	8°C – 13°C
London	🌧	1°C – 10°C
New York	🌨	-10°C – 0°C

Thank you for tuning in. Now it's time for the weather forecasts in some of the biggest cities in the world. It's going to be another beautiful day in Taipei. Currently, a high pressure system is covering the north of Taiwan, so we can expect a blue sky in Taipei. Tokyo is going to have a cloudy day, with the temperature from 8 degrees to 13 degrees. Because of the bad weather, the marathon held every year in London has been canceled. When you go outside, don't forget to carry your umbrella. New York is going to be snowy, with temperature from minus 10 degrees to zero.

中文 翻 譯

氣象預測 供國際旅客參考		
台北	☀	30°C – 34°C
東京	☁	8°C – 13°C
倫敦	🌧	1°C – 10°C
紐約	🌨	-10°C – 0°C

感謝您收聽本頻道。現在針對世界幾個大城市來做氣象預測。在台北，又會是個好天氣的一天。目前，一個高壓系統正籠罩在台灣的北方，所以可以預期台北天氣會有藍天白雲。東京將會是多雲的天氣，氣溫從 8 度到 13 度。每年在倫敦舉辦的馬拉松，由於天氣不佳，已被取消了，外出時別忘了攜帶雨具。紐約將會下雪，氣溫為負十度到零度。

Q35 ___D___ **According to the talk and the table, which statement is true?**

根據這則談話與表格，哪一個敘述正確？

(A) In Tokyo, it's sunny with a high of 10 degrees and a low of 1. 在東京有陽光，氣溫最高達 10 度、最低 1 度。

(B) The marathon in London has been canceled because of snow.
在倫敦舉辦的馬拉松，因為下雪已被取消了。

(C) In Taipei, it's clear with a high of 34 degrees and a low of 13. 台北是晴天，氣溫最高達 34 度、最低 13 度。

(D) Snow is expected in New York. 紐約預期會下雪。

單字解釋 ▶ tune in **v** 調入、轉入頻道　　pressure system **n** 高壓系統
temperature **n** 氣溫　　forecast **n** 預測

試題分析 ▶ 本題問選項中哪個敘述正確。從圖中可判斷，東京是最高溫 13 度、最低溫為 8 度，所以 A 不正確。談話中提到 Because of the bad weather, the marathon ... in London ... canceled.，僅提到天氣不佳所以被取消，沒提到是下雪，所以 B 不正確。從圖中可知，台北是最高溫 34 度、最低溫為 30 度，所以 C 不正確。只有選項 D 符合圖表，所以答案為選項 D。

台灣廣廈 國際出版集團
Taiwan Mansion International Group

國家圖書館出版品預行編目（CIP）資料

NEW GEPT 新制全民英檢中級聽力測驗必考題型 / 陳頎著.
-- 初版. -- 新北市：國際學村, 2021.02
　面；　公分
ISBN 978-986-454-148-5（平裝）
1.英語 2.讀本

805.1892　　　　　　　　　　　　110000233

國際學村

NEW GEPT 新制全民英檢中級聽力測驗必考題型

作　　者／陳頎
監　　修／國際語言中心委員會

編輯中心編輯長／伍峻宏・編輯／古竣元
封面設計／何偉凱・內頁排版／菩薩蠻數位文化有限公司
製版・印刷・裝訂／東豪・紘億・秉成

行企研發中心總監／陳冠蒨
媒體公關組／陳柔彣
綜合業務組／何欣穎

發 行 人／江媛珍
法律顧問／第一國際法律事務所 余淑杏律師・北辰著作權事務所 蕭雄淋律師
出　　版／國際學村
發　　行／台灣廣廈有聲圖書有限公司
　　　　　地址：新北市235中和區中山路二段359巷7號2樓
　　　　　電話：（886）2-2225-5777・傳真：（886）2-2225-8052
讀者服務信箱／cs@booknews.com.tw

代理印務・全球總經銷／知遠文化事業有限公司
　　　　　地址：新北市222深坑區北深路三段155巷25號5樓
　　　　　電話：（886）2-2664-8800・傳真：（886）2-2664-8801
郵政劃撥／劃撥帳號：18836722
　　　　　劃撥戶名：知遠文化事業有限公司（※單次購書金額未滿1000元需另付郵資70元。）

■出版日期：2021年02月
■出版日期：2023年10月2刷
ISBN：978-986-454-148-5